EXODUS

Books published by The Random House Publishing Group are available at quantity discounts on bulk purchases for premium, educational, fund-raising, and special sales use. For details, please call 1-800-733-3000.

EXODUS

THE OFFICIAL HISTORY OF THE WAR FOR CYBERTRON

ALEX IRVINE

BALLANTINE BOOKS • NEW YORK

Transformers: Exodus is a work of fiction. Names, characters, places, and incidents either are the product of the author's imagination or are used fictitiously. Any resemblance to actual persons, living or dead, events, or locales is entirely coincidental.

2011 Del Rey Mass Market Edition

Copyright © 2010 by Hasbro

Published in the United States by Del Rey, an imprint of The Random House Publishing Group, a division of Random House, Inc., New York.

DEL REY is a registered trademark and the Del Rey colophon is a trademark of Random House, Inc.

TRANSFORMERS and distinctive logo thereof are trademarks of Hasbro. Used with permission.

Originally published in hardcover in the United States by Del Rey, an imprint of The Random House Publishing Group, a division of Random House, Inc., in 2010.

ISBN 978-0-345-52252-8

Printed in the United States of America

www.delreybooks.com
www.hasbro.com

9 8 7 6 5 4 3 2

Del Rey mass market edition: July 2011

CHAPTER ONE

The Hall of Records in Iacon was closed to the public. In the archive stacks, at a workstation where he had been installed following the tradition and practice of his caste, sat a monitor named Orion Pax. He was tapped into the Communications Grid that invisibly spanned all of Cybertron, monitoring and recording every communication that passed through the Grid. Those that met certain criteria, he listened to, annotated, categorized, and saved in a different sector of the DataNet.

Like much of the rest of the great city of Iacon, the Hall was constructed of a golden-hued alloy that lent itself to the curving architectural style that predominated elsewhere in the city. The architects of Iacon had favored towering, monumental buildings topped by conical structures that looked as if they might take off. The entire city was a monument to aspirations . . . only there were no aspirations among Cybertronians anymore. They were born into a caste, a place that they would maintain for their entire lives. The civilization of Cybertron existed in a perfect stasis. It had been that way for millennia. Iacon was in some ways a memorial of a Cybertronian culture that had not existed in the memory banks of any existing Cybertronian.

Inside the Hall of Records, another kind of stasis existed. The history of Cybertron, from the mythical ages of battles among the Thirteen Primes across the billions of cycles, to the latest transmissions on the latest bands Orion Pax was charged with monitoring—all of it was here. All of it was categorized, cataloged, stored, indexed, and cross-indexed. After that, save for when the High Council or another authority got interested in a threat to civic order, the ever-growing collections in the Hall of Records were ignored.

Once—or so Orion Pax understood from reading in the older records—Cybertronian civilization had maintained links with other planets that surrounded other stars. Via a network of Space Bridges constructed with technology long abandoned, populations of Cybertronians on far-flung planets had stayed in contact with Cybertron. Gigantion, Velocitron, even the Hub, all were once part of a greater Cybertronian culture. Now the Space Bridges were all long since collapsed and degraded. The last of them, which hung in the skies between the two moons and the Asteroid Belt, had not been used since a long, long time ago. Even Orion Pax, who could ordinarily dig anything out of the records of Teletraan-1 and the DataNet, was not sure exactly how long it had been.

Now a Cybertronian like Orion Pax would not go to the stars. He would not fight nobly for the great ideals of the Primes. A Cybertronian like Orion Pax would monitor, assess, and catalog transmissions on the Grid because that is what Cybertronians of his caste did. Other castes built and engineered, governed, made laws . . . or fought in the gladiatorial pits.

From there, oddly enough, came some of the more interesting transmissions Orion Pax had heard lately. He was not a great follower of the arena, but even he knew of the most recent champion Megatronus. Quite a bold action, to assume that name—it was not just any bot who could carry the weight of one of the Thirteen Primes, whose deeds still echoed across the megacycles of history. This Megatronus had not lost a match since the early days of his career in the arena. The gladiators began with no names, and most of them ended that way as well; Megatronus had claimed not just a name, but a name that could not help but capture the attention of even those castes who pretended to pay no attention to such degraded entertainments as gladiatorial combat.

The sight of two—or more—Cybertronians tearing each other apart was something that few would admit enjoying. Yet the pits in the lower levels of Kaon were one of Cybertron's most popular tourist destinations, and the Grid was alive with broadcasts and rebroadcasts of the various tournaments that were constantly going on. The only industry in Kaon that could rival gladiatorial entertainment was recovery and reconstruction. The mechasurgical engineers of that city—and its gladiatorial rival, Slaughter City—were without peer. Arena combat was illegal across Cybertron, but the High Council in its wisdom understood that a population confined by caste needed certain outlets. So the pits in Kaon, which had begun long ago as a diversion for the workers in the great foundries there, were now entrenched, even if technically outside the law of Cybertron. In Slaughter City it was much the same.

So it was odd that from Kaon and Slaughter City, Orion Pax should be hearing and seeing arguments he could only call philosophical. And they were coming from the greatest of the illicit champions of Kaon's pits: this Megatronus.

The transmissions were fragmentary and distorted, originating as they did from deep inside the metallic bowels of Kaon. Between those lower levels and the Grid receptors, they picked up enormous interference from the industrial processes that drove Kaon . . . and, Orion Pax knew, the civilization of Cybertron. Nothing could be created without the raw materials first being refined. That happened in Kaon and the Badlands that stretched between it and the Hydrax Plateau. As long as those Badlands fueled the needs of Cybertron, the High Council would keep turning a blind optic to the gladiator pits.

Orion Pax wondered how long that would continue. He listened to the most recent of Megatronus's transmissions, fingers hovering over the interface that would determine where he cataloged it.

"Are Cybertronians not all made of the same materials? My alloys are the same as those in the frame of a High Councilor; my lubricants are the same as those that lubricated the joints of the Thirteen themselves!" Megatronus's voice scraped and rasped like one of the great machines in the factories of Kaon. Orion Pax looked up and down the row of other Cybertronians of the same caste as he. All of them would spend their careers monitoring and cataloging, feeding the vast databases of Iacon. This was the way the civilization of Cybertron had been since long before the creation of Orion Pax.

And yet they were made of the same materials as the Archivist Alpha Trion, or any member of the High Council.

Would a Councilor spend his life monitoring transmissions?

"We are individuals! Once we were free!" Megatronus's voice scraped through Orion Pax's head. What would his fellow monitors think if they could hear?

They would report this Megatronus in a nanoklik. That's what they would do, Orion Pax thought. As if in reply, Megatronus said, "The High Council, if they heard me now, would quietly render me into slag. Do not doubt it. They may be listening now. If I vanish, carry on my work. Soundwave, you and Shockwave will carry on. You are my trusted lieutenants."

A second voice came in. "Lieutenants? Are you now the general of an army, Megatronus?"

Orion Pax listened harder. He ran a check on the new voice—it was neither Shockwave nor Soundwave. He had heard them before, and had records and database entries for each.

But this new voice was not in the index he maintained to keep track of Megatronus's associates. Who was it?

It was not part of Orion Pax's job to investigate. He monitored, observed, recorded. Investigators were of another caste.

He could, however, report to Alpha Trion, the overseer. Orion Pax sampled the new voice and spent a few cycles compiling a report. It wouldn't do to present himself to Alpha Trion without a good reason, and proof of how good the reason was.

The Archivist of Iacon, Alpha Trion, was far older than Orion Pax, who had heard stories that he had existed since the great age of the Space Bridge–fueled expansion, the high point of Cybertronian civilization. What that must have been like, to be able to ride the dimensional bridges to other stars . . .

"Orion Pax," Alpha Trion said. "What brings you here to interrupt my work?"

"I seek advice." Orion activated the recording of Megatronus. Alpha Trion put down the antiquated stylus he used to make entries in the single book that sat on his desk. The Archivist of Iacon had databases and endless hard-copy records of virtually everything that had ever happened in the history of Cybertron, yet he chose stylus and book as his interface. Like many of the older Cybertronians Orion Pax knew, Alpha Trion had grown eccentric.

When the recording had played out of a wall-mounted speaker and Alpha Trion had taken his standard moment to tap his stylus on the desk and think over various potential responses, the Archivist said, "Megatronus."

"Why has he named himself after a mythical being?" Orion Pax asked.

"If the old stories are true, Megatronus believed until the end that he would be vindicated," Alpha Trion said. "He believed himself to be doing what was right even if his methods destroyed much of what he professed to believe."

"Not much of an example if you're plotting a revolution," Orion Pax said.

With a dry chuckle, Alpha Trion stood. "Indeed not. But perhaps that is not the only example to be taken from the deeds of Megatronus. Who is this upstart?"

"He has been a gladiator in Kaon. Like all of them, he began without a name, a worker who took to the arena as a way to glory. He has never lost, and his fame has grown to the point that few other gladiators will fight him one-on-one. Now it seems that he is no longer content to be the greatest gladiator in Kaon; he has grander ambitions."

"Ambition," Alpha Trion echoed. "That is not a quality encouraged on Cybertron. As you know." He fell silent, and Orion Pax thought he had detected something of a wistful tone in the Archivist's voice.

He waited, and after several cycles Alpha Trion spoke again. "Go back to your post, Orion Pax. Continue to listen. When you know what this Megatronus is planning, return to me and we will consult further."

CHAPTER TWO

After young Orion Pax had left him alone in the depths of the Hall of Records, Alpha Trion considered the situation. Unusual in one so young, he thought, to have such a sense of what has gone past, what may never return. But that was to be expected when Orion Pax spent all of his time in the Hall listening.

The High Council would have to hear of this gladiator calling himself Megatronus. But it was not clear to Alpha Trion what the best way was to present the situation.

"Covenant," he said softly. "What may we know of this Megatronus?"

The Covenant of Primus lay open on Alpha Trion's desk. He had created it in the aftermath of the War of the Primes. In the Covenant lay the entire history of the Cybertronians and the beings that gave them life, all the way back to Unicron and Primus. And the Covenant also contained the future—although that part of the Covenant remained mutable. Alpha Trion could see certain things that would happen because they became real as they appeared in the Covenant,

but he could not always know whether what he saw
would come to pass. The burden of knowing the future was Alpha Trion's, and his alone, but it was less-
ened because even what he knew of the future could
change at any moment.

And he had some power over it as well. The Quill,
that instrument young Orion Pax failed to understand, was one of the surviving artifacts of the Thirteen, and was one of the most powerful objects in the
known universe. Using it, Alpha Trion could inscribe
the future into the Covenant. This was a dangerous
power to exercise, and there was never any guarantee
that an alteration to the future would last. The
Covenant itself had the final word. It was a book of
pure destiny.

Alpha Trion flipped forward a few pages. One of
the peculiarities of the Covenant was that the
reader—who existed in a moment in time—had a difficult time understanding the book's language on its
pages dealing with the future. Even Alpha Trion
could read those pages only seldom. The further into
the future the Covenant went, the more obscure and
difficult the language became. Its first pages were
written in languages that no Cybertronian had spoken in thousands of stellar cycles. On its last pages
were words in languages that no Cybertronian had
ever yet spoken.

Alpha Trion had written it all, even the portions
written in languages that did not yet exist. Orion Pax
did not know that. Nor did any of Alpha Trion's
other underlings in the Hall of Records. None of
them would have believed it if they had been told.

And not even the most credulous of the race of Cybertronians would have taken seriously the assertion that Alpha Trion was one of the Original Thirteen—the only one, he believed, remaining on Cybertron. He had seen the history of Cybertron from its creation. He had seen allegiances form and shatter among the Primes. He had observed firsthand the murder that had destroyed the Thirteen, sending them out into the vastnesss of the universe. With the Covenant, Alpha Trion had stayed behind—to record, to observe, to exert what influence he could without giving away the truth of his identity. Most Cybertronians no longer believed in the Primes, or else considered them semihistorical myths. That was fine with Alpha Trion. It was no longer an age for mythic personalities.

Or, perhaps, it was an age for new ones.

Alpha Trion wondered what it would be like to understand the Covenant in its entirety. To assimilate all of the knowledge, the consciousness of past and future collapsing together in his mind . . .

It was the doom of the Archivist to wrestle with what he would never understand.

Hearing the name Megatronus had put Alpha Trion in a frame of thought that could almost have been called nostalgic. The days of the War of the Primes were still alive in his memory; the Golden Age that had followed, as Cybertronians had ridden the Space Bridges to the stars, was one of the great historical periods in the history of the known universe. The magnificence of it, now passed, could only be harkened back to. Alpha Trion remembered the gradual rise of the caste system. He had spent much time talking to Sentinel Prime about the direction Cybertronian civilization was going. In the end, they disagreed. Sentinel Prime defined himself by actions and thought only about near-term goals and results. Alpha Trion had no need to define himself. He was one of the Thirteen, whether any sentient being knew it or not. And he thought about more distant horizons of consequence.

After their last argument, Sentinel Prime had dismissed Alpha Trion to the Hall of Records. *Disappear into the stacks and let the dust cover you, Alpha Trion. Cybertron has no need of you anymore.* Those had been Sentinel Prime's last words.

"Megatronus," Alpha Trion whispered. Now another had arisen among the anonymous masses of downtrodden laborers claiming the name of Megatronus.

This was in the Covenant as well. Alpha Trion had not thought to see it happen in exactly this way, but since it was in the Covenant's pages, it was bound to happen. This Megatronus, this gladiator and factory worker with grandiose ambitions—how much did he even know about the Prime from whom he had chosen to borrow his name?

Alpha Trion forced himself back into the present. He began to search in recent records for any evidence of unrest in Kaon. It didn't take long before he was immersed in a story the likes of which he had not expected to find in the regimented cities of Cybertron.

He looked up and opened a Grid link between his desk and Orion Pax's. "Please return," he said.

Orion stood opposite Alpha Trion waiting for the Archivist to finish writing in the large book open on his desk. Setting down his stylus, Alpha Trion looked up at Orion Pax. "Megatronus didn't begin right away planning a revolution," he said. "Not on a planet-wide scale, in any case. He began by taking over the gangs who run the gladiator pits in Kaon and Slaughter City."

"Criminals," Orion Pax said. He started to speak, then stopped again as he realized that he had been about to say that he thought this kind of criminality was inevitable in a caste-bound society.

Alpha Trion looked at him expectantly, then went on. "Before he had a name—or took a name—he was a champion gladiator. He had some success. That meant others of his caste looked to him for his strength. He became a leader without meaning to."

Images and video flashed across a holodisplay over Alpha Trion's desk. The images were of destroyed Cybertronians, each one labeled with a name. Indexing them quickly, Orion Pax discovered that each victim had been involved in running the gladiator pits, and most of them had other criminal enterprises as well.

In the video, Megatronus—this was the first time Orion Pax had seen him—stood over the sparking and twitching body of one of the low-level crime bosses Orion Pax had already seen in a still image. "It begins here," he said directly to the camera. Behind him a number of other gladiators raised their right arms, standing silently. "You who take your pleasure from our suffering, and turn our work into your leisure . . . you have forgotten what it is to be Cybertronian. Once this was the greatest planet in the galaxy. Now we have fallen. But we rise again, because there are yet Cybertronians who can envision the restoration of our former glory. I have never had a name, but now I take the name Megatronus, naming myself for the greatest of the Thirteen, the One who refused to bow before any of the others. Only by knowing how far we have fallen will we understand what it is to rise again. Cybertron!"

"Cybertron!" roared the other gladiators in unison. The video cut out.

"You had not seen this?" Alpha Trion prompted Orion Pax, who shook his head. "Ah. This is the fruit of discouraging ambition. We train generations of Cybertronians who do not imagine what might be done."

Orion Pax, unsure what to say, remained silent. Alpha Trion smiled at him. "Never fear, Pax. I tell you simple truth. This is no game designed to entangle you in words you do not mean. All I say is that we live in a certain world. Few of us imagine what it might be like to live in another. But some of us . . . some of us remember what other worlds were like once. And some of us are foolish enough to wish that we might live in such a world again."

There was a pause in the room, broken only by the whisper of Alpha Trion's stylus on the pages of the book. "What are you writing?" Orion Pax asked at last.

"I am writing what I have learned," Alpha Trion said. "As time passes, we will all discover together whether I have understood correctly. But now you must return to your post. Think on what I have said."

"I will," promised Orion Pax.

And he did, all the way through the mazy corridors of the Hall of Records back to his station on the eighteenth floor, third from the northwest corner, where when the winds blew out of the north the cold made the lights of Iacon twinkle in the distance. He enjoyed being close to a window. Many of his colleagues were not.

Some of us are foolish enough to wish that we might live in such a world again . . .

What had Alpha Trion meant? Orion Pax turned the Archivist's words over in his mind, and could reach no conclusion. No comfortable conclusion, in any event. The only way Alpha Trion's words made sense was as an encouragement to think—was this even safe to think in one's own mind?—to think beyond caste.

To remember that Cybertron had not always been so rigidly divided.

To imagine that a future might exist in which Cybertron was restored to its former greatness.

Orion Pax listened, and cataloged, and archived, and indexed, but his mind was not on his work. The noises of the Grid were incomprehensible to him now that Alpha Trion had opened his mind to a possibility beyond Cybertron as it was.

Who was this Megatronus, this gladiator thug, killer of criminals and criminal himself, who gave voice to a longing that Orion Pax had never known he felt?

CHAPTER THREE

The pit floor was rectangular, and large enough for a regiment to hold exercises on, two hundred mechanometers on its short sides and half again that distance on the long sides. It was made of ore pebbles crushed and discarded from the foundries because their concentration of metals was too low to be useful. Spaced at irregular intervals around the floor, mechanical debris and burning heaps of trash made optics tricky and created endless opportunities for tactical ambush and blind-side attacks. Surrounding the floor, four levels of seating rose vertically to a ceiling a hundred mechanos overhead. Banks of lights in every frequency from infrared to ultraviolet drenched the floor in merciless light. The stands were jammed with workers in the factories and elemental refineries of Kaon, stomping their feet in rhythm until the entire balconies of each level bounced up and down to nearly the limits of the metal frame's tensile strength. The noise was already overwhelming, and would grow so loud in the course of the match that the gladiators would fight with no input from their audio arrays save a constant maxed-out white noise.

A hundred times and more, Megatronus had entered a pit, either this one or another much like it. Every time he had emerged victorious. The Tournament of Champions—this arena circuit's grandiose name for itself—had now changed the rules for Megatronus's opponents, allowing them to enter first and assume alt-form if they chose. Anything they could scan and assimilate might be turned into a camouflage shape. It was a cowardly way to fight, but it worked in Megatronus's favor. When he could give the opponent the first shot—the opportunity to ambush him—and survive to win a total victory despite this, he looked invincible.

Word was spreading. It was not so many stellar cycles ago that Megatronus had been merely one of the more fearsome gladiators in the Kaon pits. Now he was without question the most feared. It had not been so long ago that Megatronus still had no name. Now he had chosen a name to strike fear into the timid and inspire loyalty among those who would follow him. That it was not his name did not concern him in the least; he who was born with no name did not care where his name came from when he took one.

There, he thought. My opponent is there.

His optics had locked on a heap of discarded body parts, the kind of scrap heap seen in the aftermath of an industrial accident, when dead Cybertronians lay awaiting reclamation and reconstruction. It was obvious, but Megatronus had long since realized that few of his opponents had any tactical subtlety.

Above and around him, the crowd thundered. He looked up at them and raised his arms over his head, waving them into an even greater frenzy.

This had dual purposes. One, it got the crowd on his side. And two, seeing Megatronus pantomiming victory before the fight had even begun would enrage any opponent with a shred of self-respect. Angry opponents were careless opponents. Careless opponents were dead opponents. The logic was flawless.

From the pile of body parts erupted not one, but three fighting bots. They were collectively one of Shockwave's combiner experiments, he could tell right away from the way they moved together—and these three were primitive, drones barely capable of what more advanced Cybertronians considered consciousness. One immediately changed into an all-terrain vehicle, its tracks studded and magnetic; it headed for one wall of the pit, looking for a higher vantage point to establish a crossfire. Megatronus kept focused on the other two, which sprang immediately at him. The first he knocked down with a blaster shot; the second he swatted aside with a sweeping backhand. Keeping the ATV in his peripheral vision, Megatronus pivoted to prevent the two bot-form combiners from flanking him. One of them reared up and sprayed a stream of corrosive fluid at his face; he ducked aside, feeling the spray of it burn on his shoulder. The second made another pass at him, its blade-tipped hands flicking out at him.

Megatronus caught the combiner's arm just above the bladed wrist. Another jet of acid spattered across his back. With a roar, he broke the arm off and flung it into the crowd.

This was a calculated maneuver. He wanted them to know that he was dangerous, that when you went to watch Megatronus fight he was always on the verge of bringing the entire arena down on all of their heads. He fought like he knew he would die and did not care, but also like he knew he could never die and so could take any risk without fear. The arm, sparking and leaking the residue of the vibroblade's Energon reservoir, spun into the second deck; some spectators lunged out of its way while others reached to catch it. In a klik, Megatronus saw the blade slash and eat through a spectator's arm; saw another in the crowd grab the arm near the break and fling it up into the deck above him; saw fights break out in the aftermath . . .

But he could watch it no further, because the bot on the walls was opening up on him with concentrated energy fire beyond what he would have expected in a Cybertronian so small. The blasts knocked him off balance momentarily, and the acid-spitter closed in to take advantage.

Megatronus took the next volley of energy fire across his back as he closed with the mutilated combiner. Always finish a kill was his philosophy. Two wounded enemies were still two enemies. He closed the distance between them in a leap and used his larger mass and greater strength to drive the wounded combiner into the base of a pile of debris. Acid streaked his back again but Megatronus ignored it. He had taken the best shot that the combiner could give and it would not kill him—at least not sooner than he could kill it and its wheeled comrade.

He held down the wounded bot, rammed the muzzle of his ion cannon into the joint where its neck met its multi-armed thorax, and blew it apart. Now the three bots would never be able to assume their combined form; this was another reason to finish a kill. A chittering sound reached him, even over the hysterical collective scream of the crowd at the match's first kill. Megatronus lifted the dead combiner up, swung it over his head, and flung it away to crash against the wall opposite the seating deck where he had thrown its arm. The acid-sprayer landed on his back in the next moment, its pointed nozzle looking for vulnerable points on the back of Megatronus's head and neck.

He was Megatronus. He had no vulnerable points. He reached back with both hands, grabbed the acid-spitter, and slammed it to the floor. Small pieces of it broke off, and Megatronus went in for the kill. This one he would do with his bare hands.

But surprises were yet in store. The combiner wriggled out of his grasp, then slithered with surprising speed across the broken terrain of the floor to join the ATV on the wall. The two of them then merged, combining into a single alternate form that leaped up into the air and hovered.

So, Megatronus thought. I was wrong. Even with only two of them, they can combine.

It stopped, hovering perhaps forty mechanos above the center of the pit floor. Extruded tentacular cables unspooled to catch on girders and keep the combiner up in the air. From there it rained energy blasts down on him from blaster-adapted legs, occasionally swooping lower to discharge globules of acid from its mouth. What strange forms the combiners were, Megatronus thought. To surrender their individuality and merge together like that. It repelled him. He hated them, all of them. Any Cybertronian willing to give up its own identity was not worthy of the name.

He changed form, adopting the alt-form he had learned soon after his creation, a tank adapted for heavy mining and demolition work. The combiner darted away as Megatronus's battery of proton blasters exploded across its carapace and severed one of its cables; it fell, swinging back down on the other cable toward the arena floor. Megatronus roared toward the higher end of the arena, closing with a speed it hadn't anticipated; it zigzagged through the pit, jinking so close to the balconies that the front-row audience alternately ducked away or reached out to grab it. Megatronus caught it up near the top of a debris pile that was the highest point on the arena floor, reassuming his proto-form as he collided with it and kept hold, one hand on an arm and the other clamped on its thorax. His optics momentarily flared out as it jammed an energy cannon in his face and fired. He tore the other cable from its body and they tumbled together down the flank of the now-burning pile of debris. The savage glee of the crowd vibrated in all of Megatronus's sensors.

Now was the time to end this. Megatronus reared up over the disoriented combiner and manifested twin maces in both hands. He stomped down on the combiner's back, holding it in place. It chattered, tried to divide, and failed. Its limbs scrabbled for purchase and leverage, but he was far too strong. Raising both maces, Megatronus let his gaze roam across the crowd, which was if anything more berserk than before. Combiners, he thought scornfully. Next they would send out Minicons for him to step on.

"Who defeats Megatronus?" he roared out, and struck. Lubricants and bits of combiner spattered him. "No one! No one defeats Megatronus!" He struck again, and again, butchering the combiner where it lay. Then he emptied his hands and raised his arms again. "I STILL FUNCTION!"

Striding from one end of the pit to the other, he pointed into the crowd. "Would you challenge me? You? Anyone! Any five of you, any ten of you, challenge me now for everything I have ever won! No one defeats Megatronus!" Back in the center of the pit, he kicked apart the remains of the combined Insecticon flyer and flung pieces of it into the crowd for trophies. "Remember!" he called out. "Remember that you saw Megatronus! It is the best day of your life! Remember!"

Their adulation rained down on him like Energon, like life itself. Never again will I be nameless, Megatronus thought.

MEGATRONUS! MEGATRONUS! MEGATRONUS!

Something odd happened as the chant intensified. The last syllable of the moniker started to fade out as the crowd made a collective choice to end the chant on a strong syllable. Megatronus listened, and felt a strange thrill as his name modulated, changed . . . transformed. He was renamed by his followers, given a name that no Cybertronian had ever carried. The arena shook with the force of the chant.

MEGATRON! MEGATRON! MEGATRON!

Yes, he thought. I will be Megatron.

And Cybertron will never be the same.

He raised his arms amid the smoke and debris of

the pit, and the shattered bodies of his opponents. No Cybertronian could oppose him.

Megatron was destined for great things. Soon he would no longer be a gladiator. Soon he would lead the gladiators.

He strode victorious out of the pit and into the complex of abandoned maintenance tunnels below a factory that had once churned out components for semi-autonomous mining machinery. Now most of the subterranean space in the factory complex was given over to the illicit but highly profitable gladiator tournaments. Gladiator mechas and Cybertronians lived, trained, fought, and were repaired here. The ones who died were turned into useful scrap.

Until perhaps an orbital cycle ago, all of this had been under the control of a syndicate of crime bosses who ran the gladiators like machines. Who was to know or care? The caste that produced workers in the factories of Kaon was beneath the notice of the higher castes. As long as raw materials were turned into finished goods, the engineering and government castes never spared a thought for their fellow Cybertronians who slaved in the refineries and smelters. The criminal syndicate took advantage of this in a number of ways. One was the creation of the gladiator circuit; another was the manipulation of results in that circuit.

Megatron had chafed under the control of the bosses for some time. Things came to a breaking point when they came to him one day offering a deal. You're the finest gladiator we've ever seen, they said. A real immortal. But the stands aren't as full. They won't be as long as everyone knows you're going to win.

At that point, in a room much like the one he stood in now, after a match much like the one he'd just fought in, Megatron had known what was coming.

We need someone else to win, the bosses said. Not every time. But once or twice. Starting next time you go into the pit.

It had been a moment of the sort that comes along only once, perhaps, in a sentient being's life. The moment, Megatron reflected, when you decided whether you were going to surrender control to someone else . . . or fight to the death to keep it.

He had decided to fight. Moments later, the bosses and their strong-arm bodyguards were in pieces, save one. Megatron sent him out to spread the word: The gladiator pits were under new management.

Now Megatronus was no longer. Megatron thought of that moment, that transformative moment, as he came into the infirmary and saw Soundwave and Shockwave waiting for him. "Soon you'll be leading more than gladiators," Shockwave said, coming over to examine Megatron's damage. Shockwave was Megatron's pet mad scientist, the kind of mind who would take two critically damaged gladiators and try to make one super-Cybertronian out of them. He had no ethical sense that Megatron had ever been able to detect, and Megatron did not trust him; but Shockwave was a believer in Megatron . . . at least for now. There would come a time, Megatron knew, when Shockwave would turn on him. Until then, the Cybertronian genius would be Megatron's most loyal ally.

Soundwave was a different matter. Spymaster extraordinaire, controller of a horde of Minicons so small that Megatron could crush several of them with a footstep, Soundwave was the only gladiator Megatron had ever fought who had a chance of beating him—they had met in a match to first wound rather than death; otherwise only one of them would still exist. He was nearly as single-minded as Megatron, nearly as dedicated. He possessed a suite of abilities that Megatron very nearly envied, with his multiple transformations and the triple Minicons that he contained within his proto-form and could eject into combat at any moment. These were Rumble, Ravage, and Laserbeak.

Megatron looked around and did not see any Minicons. That suited him well. He did not trust the Minicons, any of them. He was unsuited to subterfuge, disliked telling lies except when it was absolutely necessary, and would have much preferred to take whatever he wanted on Cybertron by straightforward force of arms.

Part of the reason he kept Soundwave and Shockwave close was that he trusted them to remind him when this was not possible. Megatron was mighty—he knew that—but he could still benefit from associates whose abilities complemented his.

"Minimal scarring from the acids," Shockwave pronounced. "The energy weapons had little effect. As is typical, Megatronus, you emerge from a battle with few signs of ever having been in a battle. What fascinating prototypes I could create from you."

"Megatron."

Shockwave stopped in mid-reverie, blinking and returning to the real world from his imagined army of Megatron-inspired supermechs. "What?"

"You heard the crowd. I am Megatron."

Soundwave and Shockwave looked at each other. "All hail Megatron!" they said.

CHAPTER FOUR

Orion Pax looked up at the stars, and between him and the stars the twin points of Moon Bases One and Two. The other near-Cybertron object, Trypticon Station, was out of sight on the other side of the planet. He walked the swooping streets and bridges of Iacon, pondering some of what he had heard Megatron say.

Freedom is every Cybertronian's right!

Perhaps. But what did freedom mean? If there were no castes, if Cybertronians were not organized and channeled into productive lines . . . if every Cybertronian simply decided what he wanted to do, the entire planet would descend into chaos. Orion Pax remembered being taught that freedom consisted of being free to contribute to the tasks that were appropriate and necessary to the caste you were born into. Unlimited choice, rather than leading to freedom, led to the paralysis of confusion.

This was the teaching of . . . who, exactly? Sentinel Prime had never said it out loud, but he had overseen the rise of the caste system, preserving Cybertron when individuality threatened to tear the civilization of the Cybertronians into contending splinters.

Who does the caste system benefit? The higher castes! Who do the higher castes live off? You.

Orion Pax climbed a tower to an observation deck from which he could see all of Iacon. The contours of Cybertron, the living expression of Primus, arced away in all directions. Canyons leading to the interior, where Plasma welled up from the Well at the center of Cybertron, split the surface. Far, far to the west he could see the highest peaks of the Manganese Mountains. To the north, over the horizon, was Six Lasers Over Cybertron.

Thinking of the amusement park, Orion Pax felt a twinge of anger. He had never been there. It was the preserve of the higher castes. Only rarely did lower-caste Cybertronians pass through its gates, and Orion Pax had not yet been one of those fortunate lower-caste individuals.

Individuals know what is best for them! Who but I know what I need? Who but you may decide what is best for you?

I would like to go to Six Lasers, thought Orion Pax.

But if anyone walked up to Six Lasers and demanded to get in whenever the desire struck, the park would be overwhelmed. Structure was necessary. And individuals would never impose structure on themselves. Would they?

Surely not. Sentient beings banded together and made decisions for the collective good. Not all of those decisions would benefit every individual.

He was tangled up, uncertain what he should be thinking or feeling.

What I need, thought Orion Pax, is a conversation that doesn't happen inside my own head.

* * *

"What we should do," Jazz said, after Orion Pax had tracked him down and met him at Maccadam's Old Oil House, "is go to Kaon and see the gladiator fights for ourselves."

"Are you serious? They're illegal. It's not even legal to see one, I don't think."

"That doesn't seem to stop any of the people who do it," Jazz pointed out. He drained off his can of Visco and waved at the bartender for another. "We could go, you know. And if some authority discovers us, if we get arrested or questioned, I'll claim it's a cultural investigation. That is what I do, you know."

This much was true. Orion Pax had met Jazz because he was a cultural investigator, charged—more or less—with making sense out of all of the communications and other data that Orion Pax harvested from the Grid every day. Jazz came into the Hall of Records looking for this or that bit of history often enough that he and Orion Pax crossed paths regularly. They had developed a friendship. Orion Pax was a little intimidated by Jazz's carefree attitude toward life and authority. His caste was enough higher than Orion Pax's that he could get away with more—but it was also true that Jazz was more interested in getting away with things than Orion Pax ever had been. Where he saw an opportunity to bend rules, he bent them, and always just a little bit further than was perhaps prudent.

He sipped his own Visco. "Kaon is all the way on the other side of the planet. I've never been anywhere near there." He realized as he finished speaking that he had meant the words to come out as dismissive, but they sounded wistful.

There was a great deal of Cybertron that Orion Pax had never seen. He had heard its citizens speaking from every nook and cranny, every tower and station of the planet; he had put their conversations and transmissions into useful categories so that people like Jazz could come into the Hall of Records and use the work of Orion Pax as raw material to fashion theories with.

He felt a sudden kinship with the workers in the factories. They made machines. He made data. Were they so different?

As soon as he mentioned this to Jazz, the cultural investigator laughed. "Yes, Orion. You're different. Your work won't kill you. And when you can't do it anymore, nobody's going to throw you into a heap and turn your broken body into datacubes or image matrices."

Jazz's words hit Orion Pax like a physical blow. "You're not pulling any punches," he commented.

"Those who are fortunate should know how fortunate they are," Jazz said. Then he sipped at his Visco and waited for Orion Pax to get his thoughts in order.

"I wonder if I could get in contact with him," Orion Pax said after a silence. The Visco, as it always did, invigorated him, filled him with possibilities.

"With who? This Megatron?" Jazz shrugged. "Possibly. Why would you want to?"

"You don't find him interesting?"

Jazz laughed. "I find everything interesting. This is what I was made to do, find things interesting. Listen, Pax. If you want to go to Kaon, let's go to Kaon. I can get travel passes for research. I can claim that I need someone like you to harvest data. Should I talk to the Archivist?"

Orion Pax considered this for some time. "History moves in cycles," he said after a while. "This much I've seen just rooting around in the archives."

"I thought you weren't supposed to be rooting around in the archives," Jazz said. "Careful you don't step outside the boundaries of your caste, my friend."

"How can I not?" Orion Pax asked. He drank off the rest of his Visco. "I have a mind. I can think, and analyze."

Jazz waited the perfect amount of time before responding. "If you say so."

"Easy for you to joke. You can do whatever you want. I'm a data clerk." Orion Pax leaned over the table toward his friend. He trusted Jazz implicitly, and could say things to him that he would never say to anyone else. "Where is it written that I have to stay a data clerk? Is there some ledger somewhere that the Primes keep, out in one of the Spiral Arms? Is my name in it next to the designation Data Clerk? I don't think so."

"You sound a bit like your gladiator friend," Jazz said.

"He's not my friend." Orion Pax thought about it. "But perhaps it is time that I talked to him."

He knew how the Grid worked. He spent his days wading through its matrices and intersections. If there was one thing Orion Pax had learned as a consequence of this, it was how to get a transmission across the Grid without anyone but the intended recipient knowing about it. During his next shift, in the dim silence of the data-mining section in the Hall of Records, Orion Pax did his job, but while he did his job he also was formulating a plan to get a secret transmission through to this gladiatorial insurgent Megatron.

Different possibilities for what to say overwhelmed him. He thought about it for the duration of his shift; then, as he was due to leave, he decided on something simple.

What you say is interesting, but more people are hearing than you realize. Let's speak.

He attached contact information to it, using a dead-end bit of storage space that wasn't coded for anything in the current Grid configuration. Then he sent it off and stayed late, combing the Grid for more signs of what Megatron might be thinking, doing, saying . . . or planning.

The next day he met Jazz at Maccadam's again. "He answered," Orion Pax said.

" 'He' being this Megatron, I take it. What did you say to him?" Jazz asked.

"That he had more of an audience than he might have expected."

"And what did he say?"

Orion Pax shook his head in amazement. "He said, 'You are more right than you know. I am also more right than you know.' "

Jazz laughed long and loud. "Confidence," he said. "No shortage of it in this one, is there?"

"Then he agreed that we could meet," Orion Pax said.

This put a serious look on Jazz's face. "Are you ready to take the chance on this? I was flippant about it before, but it's something you should consider. The consequences for you are potentially much worse than for me."

"I'm ready," Orion Pax said.

Alpha Trion tapped the tip of the Quill against his desktop. Before him, scrolling in text on a screen, was the substance of a conversation between his clerk Orion Pax and the gladiator-turned-revolutionary. A loaded word, *revolutionary*, but it seemed to fit, if Megatron's side of the conversation could be taken at anything like face value.

OP: In my caste, I may read and I may index, but I am forbidden to analyze.

M: How do you know where to index if you don't analyze first?

OP: I try not to ask myself questions that don't have answers I can do anything about.

M: Who has told you that you can't do anything about the answers? I never even had a name. I went out to die for the pleasure of strangers. Now I am Megatron, and I will fight when and where and for what reasons I please.

OP: Fight who?

M: Those who would tell me . . . like they tell you . . . that we do not have the right to determine our own fates. Interesting that even in Iacon my words are being heard.

OP: It is my task to hear all words.

M: But you don't answer all of what you hear. And

surely you don't answer all of what you hear on
channels that you hide for fear of being eaves-
dropped on.

OP: No.

M: A great many Cybertronians would love to have
Iacon as their home. Yet you are there and still
unsatisfied. What does that tell you?

OP: We should meet.

M: Should we? Why would I meet you?

OP: If you have goals beyond Kaon, you're going to
need to tailor your message so it will resonate
beyond the castes who smelt ore and die in the
pits.

M: Or the rest of Cybertron should learn to understand those castes. Even you do not, and you
consider yourself one of us.

OP: Then show me what I do not understand.

Alpha Trion closed his eyes. It was beginning. The
Covenant had seen it clearly, and now he was beginning to see the dim outlines of it. The days of Orion
Pax, data clerk in the Hall of Records, were drawing
to a close. New days, of upheaval and strife, were on
the horizon. This much was certain.

What was uncertain, Alpha Trion reflected, was
how much he could do to influence the coming events
in the correct direction. Orion Pax was raw, and
young, and not the one he would have chosen.

Yet it was not given to him to make the choice. He,
like every other Cybertronian, would have to experience the future only at the moment of its becoming
the present.

Over the next cycles, Orion Pax kept up his correspondence with Megatron. These conversations honed Orion Pax's own sense of what he believed regarding castes, individuality, and free will. According to Megatron, their dialogue was also refining his ideas. "You force me to think clearly, librarian," Megatron said via videolink several cycles after their first interaction. "A leader needs this."

Orion Pax thought that some of Megatron's ideas were still unclear. What exactly, he asked, did Megatron intend to do? Were they going to take their grievances to the High Council? What sort of plan was contemplated?

"I have other associates considering these questions, too," Megatron said, and he would say no more.

This made Orion Pax nervous—for good reason, according to Jazz. "You need to be very sure that you know what you're getting into here," his friend said. "I'll stand by and watch, whatever happens; but you could be letting yourself in for serious consequences. Right now you're just talking; the minute you do

more than that, there are laws involved. Are you prepared to break laws?"

Because Orion Pax didn't have a good answer for
this question, he asked it of Megatron.

"Who makes the laws?" was Megatron's answer.
"Did anyone consult you? Did anyone consult me?"

Orion Pax had no answer for that, either.

"Listen, my friend," Jazz said. "What would happen if anytime one of us felt left out of the law-
making process, he started a revolution? Can you
imagine what this place would look like?"

"No," Orion Pax said. "We're a long way from
that. We've got the opposite, don't you see? Nobody
ever says anything. Who decided that we should be in
castes? What do our leaders say about it now?"

Nothing, was the answer to that. Sentinel Prime
was not a visible leader; the High Council busied itself with the minutiae of governance and avoided the
big questions. Across Cybertron, argued Megatron—
and Orion Pax had to agree—Cybertronians had
grown lazy, satisfied with what was handed to them.
"Is this the same race that built the Space Bridges?"
Megatron asked rhetorically. "Are we still alight with
the AllSpark? Then why do we let others speak for us,
act for us, decide what we will and will not do?"

There was something different about him. Orion Pax
could see it as well as any other sentient being who
spent time in contact with Megatron. He was difficult
to ignore, and when he spoke of individual freedom it
was easy to think—no matter how many Cybertronians might be in his audience—that he was talking directly to you.

Still, Orion Pax had never met him in person. He wasn't sure the risk was worth it. In truth, he wasn't sure what the risks were.

Megatron began to encourage him. "If you would understand Cybertron, librarian, you must see Kaon," he said.

"Maybe if you saw Iacon, you would understand Cybertron better yourself," countered Orion Pax.

"Oh, I will see Iacon. Have no fear of that," Megatron said.

Something about the tone of his voice made Orion Pax want to change the subject. The last thing he wanted to do was provoke a fight with Megatron when he was just beginning to understand what Megatron's ideas meant . . . and what he, Orion Pax, had to contribute to the discussion. He believed some things in common with the hard-bitten survivor of Kaon's pits, but in other ways he felt that despite their commonalities, there were fundamental differences in the way they approached the question of freedom and will.

"Why Megatronus?" he asked. He had heard Megatron answer the question before, in slightly different ways. He moved along, refined his ideas and rhetoric. Orion Pax realized he was witnessing the growth and rise of a genuinely important leader . . . but of what? And where would he lead?

"I assume the name of one of the Thirteen because—although only one of them ever called himself the Fallen—they all fell away from their original mission. They all failed their future, which is our present. I took that name because the principles I believe in have fallen. Freedom has no caste, so there is no place for it in Cybertron today. History makes some bots villains for doing what they thought was right; if that happens to me as well, so be it. I can only do what is the right thing to do." Megatron cycled through his alt-form weapons as he spoke. At the periphery of the screen Orion Pax could see some of Megatron's inner circle. He only knew two of them, Soundwave and Shockwave. Soundwave carried Minicons, which made Orion Pax nervous. Minicons made him think of surveillance and treachery. Shockwave was cold and formal, a dedicated scientist out of place among the bulk of Megatron's followers.

It seemed, to judge from the single example of Shockwave, that Megatron was beginning to realize his goal of bringing different castes together. Scientists and steelworkers—let alone gladiators—seldom mixed unless one was giving the other orders, and that relationship, Orion Pax could see, was reversed here. Megatron was clearly in charge.

"In the pits of Kaon there is no second-guessing," he continued. "There are no shades of gray, no fine distinctions. You find those in the Hall of Records, perhaps, but not here. Down here you make a decision and commit to it with every atom . . . or else you die."

Orion Pax looked around. He was alone in his wing of the Hall of Records, and had done what he could to insulate this channel from the normal data-harvesting protocols that applied to traffic into and out of the Hall. Still, he spoke quietly. "You really think the Thirteen thought about their actions this way?"

"It doesn't matter to me," Megatron said. "Megatronus has been gone for a long time. I am here. You are here. What we do is not up to Megatronus, or to Liege Maximo, or any other myth. What we do is up to us."

"Who is us?" Orion Pax asked a few solar cycles later.

"Whoever wants to be," Megatron said with a laugh. "When you're taking on the world, you can't be choosy about who wants to be on your side."

"So you have followers in Kaon," Orion Pax said. "Where else?"

"That's the kind of question a spy would ask."

"If you were worried about that, we would have stopped talking a long time ago."

"Perhaps, perhaps not. Soundwave says I should worry that you will betray me." Megatron laughed. "I say back to him that if I thought you were going to betray me, I would meet you in the arena and settle things like warriors. Would you fight me in the ring for your principles, librarian? Can you tell your principles from mine?"

"I think I can," Orion Pax said. "And I would fight anyone for them."

As he said it, he realized it was true. Always Orion Pax had known that there was a larger world beyond the mundane horizons of the work he did and the caste he was part of. Hearing Megatron speak had lit a fire inside him that was not Megatron's fire, but Orion Pax's. It was as if his Spark had never come to its full brightness until it had struck against the revolutionary ideas of this criminal gladiator.

"Then I will tell you. I have followers in Blaster

City and across the Badlands to Slaughter City. I could make the spaceport at Hydrax mine tomorrow," Megatron said, as Orion Pax fit those place names into a map of Cybertron in his mind. "And across Cybertron, there are pockets of Cybertronians who hear me. They will follow when I call them into action."

"Which will be . . . ?"

"When the time is right. Remember, librarian. We have still never met. Until we can look each other in the face, we are discussing things that might never happen, the way we look up at the pieces of a Space Bridge and ask ourselves what it would be like if we could cross again to Velocitron or the Hub. We are friends, having a friendly conversation about things we believe."

Friends, thought Orion Pax. As unlikely as it might have seemed, this was correct. He was becoming friends with an agitator, a criminal, and possible traitor to the Council.

But in a society that was most of the way along a descent into stasis, what else could any right-thinking Cybertronian do?

"Tricky question," said Jazz when Orion Pax asked him later. "I've started to look into these things. Your friend Megatronus—or Megatron—has an interesting history."

"I know about his history," Orion Pax said.

Jazz said, "I know you do. But I did not and I thought I would look and see what I could find. What do you think he wants, Pax?"

Orion Pax thought about this question for a long time. "He wants the Cybertron that used to be," he said eventually. "The Cybertron where you were not doomed to a Guild and caste the moment you emerged from the Well of AllSparks. The Cybertron where any Cybertronian could become anything. The Cybertron that looked to the stars, that fought the Quintessons, that challenged itself to reach out and see how far its grasp could extend."

"That's what you want," Jazz said. "It's time you stopped pretending otherwise."

Again Orion Pax took some time to think. "Yes, it is," he agreed.

"Good. I won't say you're wrong. I will tell you, my friend, that this is a dangerous line of thought. How do you think the upper castes are going to react to this idea? Do you think they want a return to the days when a Cybertronian's success was based on merit and dedication?" Jazz laughed at his own sarcasm.

"If I can't make myself do what's right," said Orion Pax, "how can I expect anyone else to?"

Jazz nodded. They looked up into the endless black of the sky. "Fine," Jazz said. "Just so you're not surprised when you find out that everyone else isn't likely to hold themselves to the same standard."

"Did I tell you that Megatron said he'd fight me if he thought I was going to betray him?" Orion Pax said.

"Very funny," Jazz said.

"He did."

"Then watch your back," Jazz said. "If he brought that up, he's already half-convinced himself it will eventually happen."

Orion Pax laughed. Then he said, "I better get practicing and learn how to fight."

* * *

And he did, carving out time every solar cycle to practice with others of his caste. He worked on the altform weapons he could create from his proto-form, the ion cannon and Energon blasters. And he learned the ins and outs of the sword and axe that he could carry or manifest as another partial alteration. As he fought these mock battles he thought of Megatron, who for most of his existence had fought such battles for the stakes of his life. Jazz joined in, and together they battled, honing their skills. Orion Pax found he loved the clash and exhilaration of a fight. Often at the end of a session, his circuits abuzz with the energy of battle, he dreaded returning to his workstation in the silence of the Hall of Records.

Only his thirst for knowledge, both of the past and of all the things about present-day Cybertron he had never thought worth knowing, kept him coming back.

That, and his responsibility to his caste.

There the conflict inherent in his friendship with Megatron presented itself most clearly. It was because he was friends with Megatron that he had a rekindled interest in what was happening around him in this Cybertron that he lived on and experienced with other Cybertronians—yet if he kept any loyalty to his caste, that brought him into conflict with Megatron, who would abolish all castes immediately upon gaining the power to do so.

And wouldn't I as well? Orion Pax asked himself. The answer was: perhaps. He understood Megatron's reasons, and perhaps even more than the gladiator did Orion Pax wanted the freedom and initiative that would come with the end of caste and Guild.

Where they differed, Orion Pax suspected, was in method. He believed the change could be created through political means: spreading new ideas, watching them catch fire, attracting enough followers to their vision that eventually the High Council and Sentinel Prime would have to take notice. That was the vision of Orion Pax.

Sometimes he was concerned that Megatron did not have as much patience as he did. Orion Pax was beginning to attract followers of his own, though. Messages were appearing that mentioned him and not Megatron, or mentioned Megatron only as secondary to him. He was, despite his best efforts at remaining concealed, becoming known.

Things were going to come to a head very shortly. It was time, at last, to meet Megatron face-to-face.

Orion Pax looked at the screen of his workstation. He dictated a note to Alpha Trion asking for time free of work. On his way out of the Hall of Records, the Archivist contacted him directly, but Orion Pax did not answer. He could not think of what to say, could not take the chance that Alpha Trion would convince him not to go.

He saw clearly what needed to be done. All that remained was to do it.

CHAPTER SIX

The first thing Orion Pax thought about Kaon was that he had never seen anything like it. Of course he had seen images, but experiencing the place with all of his sensory arrays at once, getting the totality of the experience . . .

He had come to Kaon in his alt-form, rolling down through Kalis and near the Well of AllSparks, source of every living Cybertronian. Then he crossed the Torus States and entered the Sea of Rust, with the Sonic Canyons to the south. Skirting the Canyons, Orion Pax entered the Badlands and watched as the groomed, civilized surface of Cybertron was replaced by rugged, broken territory. Metallic ridges and sinuous canyons filled axle-deep with rust were the norm; in places ancient ruins sprouted from the formations. Orion Pax knew that the Badlands had been the scene of great deeds and immensely important moments in the history of Cybertron, but he had never gained access to the records that might have told him what those deeds and moments were. So he rolled on, drinking in all of the information he could by observing the environment around him.

Once, he imagined, this had been an industrial area but not a wasteland. Now it was hard to see it as anything but a dead remnant of a civilization irrevocably in decline.

That, however, was what Orion Pax was out to change. He and Megatron together could spearhead that change.

The city of Kaon sprawled across a plateau three times the surface area of Iacon. Over it hung a perpetual cloud of smoke and heavy-metal compounds. Whereas the architecture of Iacon reached up and out, defined by towers and arches, stepping-stone ridges of residential blocks and marvels of engineering, Kaon in contrast was like an endless tumble of blackened rubble, immense mechanical structures collapsing onto one another, and newer generations of the same built upon them. It looked as if it had been bombed from orbit, then pieced back together by blind Minicons. In alt-form, Orion Pax rumbled through the outskirts of Kaon, returning to protoform when he got toward the center of the city, where the roads became tangled and overhung with conduits, catwalks . . . it was impossible to keep oriented without satellite and Grid interface. You couldn't see in Kaon. There was no way to understand where you were in relation to the rest of the city. In Iacon you had a sense of space and location.

What must it have been like to live here from the moment you came out of the Well of AllSparks?

Walking now, Orion Pax looked for the building Megatron had described to him. It was to the south of Kaon's center and in between two slag pits so deep that Orion Pax could not see to the bottom unless he came right to the edge. The building itself was a pyramidal black monument, squared at the top for a landing pad. Inside it, Megatron had said, was an abandoned cyber-hydraulic works. It was the perfect venue for gladiatorial matches as well as black-market production of optics and auditory components. Those degraded fast in the heavily polluted atmosphere of Kaon, and especially in the gladiatorial arenas, where injuries to sensory arrays were extremely common in surviving combatants.

But it was below those workshops that the real action took place. For nearly half a hic below street level, interconnected subterranean levels of support mechanisms, workers' housing, materials storage, and refinery pipelines formed a perfect series of spaces for gladiatorial matches. There were more than a dozen places like it just in Kaon; twenty more in Slaughter City; more yet in various outlying settlements in the Badlands and right up to the eastern terminus of the Sonic Canyons.

Here, though, was the heart of the gladiator profession. All the fighting Cybertronians from other districts came here to make their names—literally, in Megatron's case—and now that Megatron had thrown out the criminal syndicate that had controlled the pits, he was in the process of turning the gladiators into the seeds of an army. Orion Pax approached the pyramid as if it held the secret of a Cybertron he had never known existed.

At the side door, two Cybertronians—one slightly smaller than Orion Pax, black and white with eyes like red searchlights, and one enormous, four or five times his mass and carrying a mace the size of Orion

Pax at least—appeared to block his way. "Match entrance is at the other side," the small one said.

"You must be Barricade," Orion Pax said. He turned to the big one. "And you're Lugnut, right? Megatron told me you might be out here. I'm here to meet him."

"Just strolling through beautiful Kaon to meet the boss, are you?" Barricade said. "Funny. He didn't say anything about that to us."

"You sure?" Orion Pax glanced at Lugnut, who wasn't speaking. He thought he understood. Lugnut would watch whatever happened until one of his superiors told him to act.

The trick with beings like that was to convince them you were one of their superiors without them ever knowing you were trying to convince them.

"Lugnut. He must have told you," Orion Pax said.

Lugnut looked surprised that anyone was talking to him. "Could be," he said. "I don't always—"

"Shut up," Barricade snapped. He glared at Orion Pax. "You don't know what the boss said to who."

Orion Pax said, "I know what he said to me."

Standoff. Orion Pax could feel the tension. Barricade couldn't stand the idea of being shown up in front of Lugnut; he was that easy to manipulate. Or was he? Was he making this easy to test Orion Pax?

Kaon was a long, long way from the House of Records in Iacon.

"Listen," Orion Pax said. He thought he'd already made his point. "I'll stay here with the big guy. You go ask the boss. Easy, right?"

"I don't need you to tell me what's easy and what isn't," Barricade said. But he was already moving to go back inside. Perfect. "Lugnut," he added with the door open. "Don't let this mech go anywhere."

Mech, thought Orion Pax. He's got to put me in my place. Gladiators wore their emotions on their sleeves, it seemed. He wondered if he should have reacted to the insult, or if a reaction would have been too provocative. Then he started thinking that he was being too deliberative, overthinking everything he did, overanalyzing everything others did.

What else? Megatron would have said. What else are you going to do when you've been told for your entire existence that you can't analyze, can't think for yourself . . . and then you get the chance?

Yes, Orion Pax thought. And on the heels of that thought, another: He might have said it even before Megatron.

It occurred to Orion Pax that he was on the verge of becoming a revolutionary. It was, in fact, a revolutionary act just meeting Megatron, whose reputation was already spreading. There were rumbles around the Grid that Sentinel Prime was "concerned," and that the High Council was "considering action."

If he himself kept on with his present course of action, Sentinel Prime might well express concerns about him. A data clerk from the Hall of Records, drawing the attention of Sentinel Prime! Or the High Council!

It was hard to imagine.

Still . . . what else could he do? Every Cybertronian deserved the right of self-determination. Orion Pax believed this, and his friend Megatron believed it as well.

As if summoned, Megatron loomed in the pyramid's

doorway. Behind him glowered Barricade. "I see you've met some of the indigenous semi-intelligent life," Megatron said. They clasped hands. "It is good to see you in person, my friend."

"And you," responded Orion Pax. Friend. There was a word he had not used much . . . perhaps only with Jazz, and some of the now-forgotten fellow students in his first training sessions out of the Well of AllSparks, when they had initially learned how to assume alt-forms, and learned what their natural alt-forms would be.

Inside, the pyramid was largely hollowed out. The internal space was crisscrossed with girders and catwalks, and much of its floor lined with spectator seating. Only the farthest corners appeared to still be used for manufacturing.

"We have a separate aerial tournament that takes place here," Megatron explained. "I fought here a few times. Mostly underground, though."

"You're running it all now?" Orion Pax prompted.

"Barricade takes care of the day-to-day details, and Shockwave handles keeping the gladiators healthy and putting them back together." Far off in the dimness, Orion Pax heard the skitter of tiny servos he always associated with Minicons. Megatron chuckled. "Soundwave spies on everyone," he said. "Even me, and especially you. This is how he demonstrates his loyalty."

They fell into a conversation then, as Megatron gave Orion Pax a tour of the pyramid and the uppermost subterranean levels. They passed through a training facility where ranks of Cybertronians did martial exercises under the direction of a drillmaster.

Not far from there, a level down, was a vast machine shop in which armor and weapons were coming together under the skilled and watchful eye of warsmiths.

"This is all for the gladiator pits?" Orion Pax asked.

"It might be," said Megatron. "Depending on what else might require the services of a well-trained fighting force."

A thrill sparkled through Orion Pax's circuits then. "My idea is that we advance our cause by spreading the concepts of freedom and self-determination," he said. "We talk, we argue, we convince. Sentinel Prime is slow to react; the High Council will dither endlessly unless a problem walks directly into their chambers and demands to be solved. I don't think armed insurrection is going to be necessary."

"Maybe that's what it looks like from Iacon," Megatron said.

"It does." Orion Pax persisted. "You came up through the gladiator ranks. Every problem looks to you like it can be solved by fighting."

"And every problem looks to you like it can be solved by reading," Megatron came back.

"Sounds like a compromise is in order," Barricade interrupted. He had only just caught up with them after disappearing for a few cycles on some errand. "And around here, Orion Pax, compromise means agree with the boss."

"Whoa there," Megatron said. "This is a scholar, from Iacon. He's not an ore hauler or smelter you can threaten. Orion Pax is a friend. He is my friend, and the movement's friend." He locked optics with Barricade, whose ruby spotlight gaze was the first to drop.

"Understood, boss," he said. "No offense meant."

"None taken," Orion Pax said.

"Still," Megatron said. "We have talked and talked and talked. And here, in this pyramid, where so many like me have fought and died, we have talked and talked of freedom. It is time to act. Some Cybertronians loyal to me are out searching the planet for some of the artifacts of the Primes; if it is granted to us to find them, that will be a sign that our cause is just. And others . . ." He trailed off as if uncertain how to go on.

"Others what?" asked Orion Pax.

"Our ideas have taken root in different ways, my friend. Some of the more combative and fiery citizens of Kaon do not believe that ideas spread by talking. They believe that ideas spread by action."

"Then we need to distance ourselves from them before they do anything stupid," Orion Pax said immediately. "Violence at this stage will be counterproductive."

"Counterproductive? Not wrong?" Megatron said.

It took Orion Pax a moment to notice that the great gladiator was teasing him. "Of course, wrong," he said. "Megatron, if a bunch of firebrands go around Cybertron destroying things and putting our names on those acts, our ideas will be tarnished as well. We'll be written off as radicals. We'll be defined by the worst excesses of our followers."

"Perhaps," Megatron said. "Another way to look at it is that if we truly believe in self-determination and free will, we must respect the right of our followers to disagree with our methods and choose their own."

In a philosophical sense, of course, this was true. But Orion Pax knew—he could tell, could feel it right down to the Spark in his body—that their philosophical discussion was not going to stay philosophical for long.

A time was going to come when he would have to insist on doing things his way. But that time had not come yet. Not here, on Megatron's home ground, among Megatron's followers, who did not yet know that many of Megatron's ideas in fact came from Orion Pax.

Of course, the reverse was also true. "So you are with me, librarian?" Megatron asked.

Orion Pax looked around at the inner circle of ex-gladiators and other low-caste Cybertronians. He did not fit in; yet he was not afraid. "I am with your ideas," he said. "They are my ideas as well."

"Excellent," Megatron said. He turned to the gladiators who had paused in their work to watch them. A more brutish lot of Cybertronians, thought Orion Pax, could not have existed outside Slaughter City. And these were the Cybertronians who would usher in the new age of free will. "Cybertronians!" Megatron called out. "My friend Orion Pax! Together we will lead all sentient citizens of Cybertron to a new age, a restoration of our former greatness!"

MEGATRON! MEGATRON! MEGATRON!

Megatron leaned close to Orion Pax as the chant washed over them. "Soon they will chant your name, too," he said.

"As long as they hold to the ideals," said Orion Pax, "they can chant whatever they want to."

Megatron laughed. "We need a name for our movement and its followers," he said. "Something in line with what other great movements in Cybertronian history have been named."

Orion Pax had in fact been thinking about this for as long as he had taken seriously the idea that he might have some effect on the future history of Cybertron. The archives at Iacon were full of long-gone and forgotten movements that incorporated their beliefs in their names, one-word distillations of complex philosophies . . .

"Autobots," he said. "For we seek autonomy, and see it as our basic right."

"Interesting. I, too, had thought of a name." He looked as if he was about to say more, but Shockwave approached and said something quietly enough that Orion Pax could not hear it. "Ah," Megatron said. "Come with me, librarian. Something is about to happen that you will want to see."

CHAPTER SEVEN

Investigators would later determine, from a detailed analysis of disruptions in the Grid, that the string of synchronized explosions that ripped through Six Lasers, Uraya, Polyhex, Stanix, Blaster City, and several sites in the Sonic Canyons took place less than a cycle apart.

"It is clear that these attacks were carried out at the behest of the criminal gang leader and underground gladiator who calls himself Megatron," stated High Councilor Halogen as the rest of the High Council looked on. Halogen was the longest-serving member of the Council. His district included Blaster City and the entirety of the Badlands. For more orbital cycles than any Cybertronian cared to remember, he had agitated to annex the Hydrax Plateau and its lucrative spaceport to his district. For this reason, few Cybertronians tended to believe anything he said, on the grounds that anything he said concealed an agenda that would eventually lead to an attempt at that annexation.

* * *

In Blaster City, an armaments factory filled a steel canyon, its exhaust portals and smokestacks coming just level with the surface. Once raw materials were mined out of the canyon; then when they were exhausted, the factory was built in the space they left behind. When the bomb went off, attached to a reservoir containing plasma fuel for the arc torches used in the construction of highly heat-tolerant weapon barrels and magazines, observatories on Moon Bases One and Two recorded a flash that momentarily whited out their lenses directed at that portion of Cybertron.

From the ground, it looked as if a column of energy had erupted from the canyon, reaching toward the sky and spreading into a torus of expanding heat and light. Bits of debris as small as the casing of a conduit junction and as large as the entire cooling stack, which had until that moment stood radiating away the heat from a small fusion reactor, rained down across multi-hics of Badlands and the unfortunate Cybertronians who happened to be working, scheming, or just passing through.

In Blaster City, Sparks were cheap. No one cared about life or death. And no one knew how many Cybertronians disappeared when the armaments factory vaporized.

The people who watched did know one thing, though. Cybertron's Council militias had just lost an important source of munitions.

When Megatron heard of the attacks, Orion Pax was speaking to him on a secure Grid link. Orion Pax had tested it himself using the security apparatus available to him in the Hall of Records . . . and then Megatron had put Soundwave to work adding another layer of security. "If you ever need something hidden, or need something to disappear," Megatron said, "Soundwave is the bot you should talk to."

"I'll keep it in mind," Orion Pax was saying, and that was when reports of the bombs started to flood the Grid.

"By the AllSpark," he swore. "What is this?"

On the videolink, he watched as Megatron registered the events. Then he turned back to face the link. "Orion Pax," he said. "It is time for me to speak out. Cybertron must know that this is not how our movement will operate, and they need to know it now. You are in Iacon, correct?"

Orion Pax nodded.

"I need an open channel, one that cannot be interrupted. I need it to feed to all of the caste aggregators and directly to the Council's group input. Can you do this?"

Even as Megatron spoke, Orion Pax was constructing the necessary parameters. Legally this task belonged to one of the programming castes, not his own data caste, but Orion Pax was coming to full realization of just what his actions already meant for his existence within the caste system.

"It's done," he said, and opened the link for Megatron. Then Orion Pax watched as, for the first time, Megatron stepped out of the shadows and into the public consciousness of Cybertron.

"I had nothing to do with these attacks, but I do not deny the possibility that the Cybertronians who carried them out were partly inspired by my belief that every Cybertronian has the right to self-determination." Megatron swept a powerful arm in an arc over the assembled crowd, taking in a cross-section of castes and occupations. "I pity the loss of life, but how many of those who died took pleasure from watching me fight for my life in the gladiatorial pits below Kaon? How many other Cybertronians died for their pleasure? Now those Cybertronians, whose lives were your pleasure, are telling you that they reclaim their lives! No Cybertronian shall tell any other Cybertronian what can and cannot be done!"

Megatron was in control of a much larger network than Orion Pax had understood. This was a situation he had not expected . . . had Megatron choreographed the entire thing because Orion Pax was in Kaon, on Megatron's home territory, to witness it from the inside?

"I am Megatron. I lead all those who choose to follow me, and I repudiate all those who perform despicable acts in my name. I do not fight with bombs but with logic. I do not believe in killing, but in the arena of ideas. Let the perpetrators of these attacks feel the full weight of Cybertronian justice." Megatron stepped closer to the feed, his visage filling the frame as his expression grew cold and menacing. "If I find them first, my justice will be swifter and more final."

The Sonic Canyons were said—by some of the more pious and conservative Cybertronians—to be the ears of Primus, his means of keeping track of events in the universe his creations inhabited. The great multiversal computer, Vector Sigma, was popularly said to be installed in those canyons as well, although it had been long orbital cycles since any Cybertronian had directly interacted with Vector Sigma. Most of them did not know for certain that Vector Sigma was still active or functional—or had ever existed.

A series of explosions tore through the far northwest terminus of the canyons, where, legend had it, an ancient entrance to Vector Sigma's interface had once existed. No one, initially, could be certain whether it was an attempt to collapse the venerable computer or a forced entry into the interior of the Canyon walls.

In other words, was someone trying to destroy Vector Sigma or access it? Or what else might be inside the Sonic Canyons that only a bomb might reveal? In the chaotic aftermath of the explosions, all possibilities were on the table. Even those who knew for a fact that Vector Sigma was housed in the subsurface expanse built below Iacon listened to the conspiracy theories with interest.

Across the Grid, the upper classes twittered in outraged tones. Was nothing sacred? What did these scum desire, that they would strike at the very foundations of what made Cybertron Cybertron?

This Megatron, they said. He was behind it, no doubt about that. We've heard enough about him to know.

The Council should do something.

This Megatron, he should be in prison. Next it'll be the resorts he destroys, or the museums, or the Hall of Records. He should be in prison.

Or, perhaps, we would all be better off if he were dead.

*   *   *

Orion Pax could stand it no longer. He hacked into the media feed using a priority code from the Hall of Records. "This is Orion Pax," he said. "I am a data miner at the Hall of Records in Iacon, working under Alpha Trion himself. And I am here to testify that Megatron is not responsible for what is happening."

The data channels around him exploded with feedback. In that instant, Orion Pax ceased his former existence as a simple data clerk and was reconstituted as outlaw/terrorist/revolutionary/crackpot. What he heard and saw over the feedback channels—before he instructed the Grid to isolate and focus on the Council-moderated lines of communication—shocked him.

The moment he spoke in support of Megatron, he might as well have been Megatron. In the public view of Cybertron, Orion Pax and Megatron were now the co-leaders of the movement that was setting off lethal explosions all over the planet.

"No," he said. "I have known Megatron. He did not do this. Neither did I. All of you must listen. You must understand."

In the back of his mind he could hear Megatron saying: *They will never understand because they do not care to understand. As long as their situation is better than ours, understanding is the last thing they want.*

Orion Pax hoped this would not turn out to be true.

Around him, Soundwave and Shockwave and Megatron's other lieutenants watched. An observer might have noted that they looked less than thrilled to have an outsider taking such an active role. Orion

Pax, in fact, noted this as well. Was there a way to handle it, to change it? He thought that the best thing he could do was prove himself capable. He did not care to be liked by Megatron's lackeys. He cared to be respected. He cared for the good opinion only of those who deserved his good opinion, and those who believed in what was right.

At Six Lasers Over Cybertron, the favorite roller coaster was the Plasma Curve. Lines for it extended around the entire setup of girders on which the magnetic coaster rails sat, conducting cars at speed and gravitational forces sufficient to leave riders dizzy and delirious enough to want to ride again. There were seventy-one of these girders, sunk into the surface of Cybertron and anchored with welded bolts.

As Orion Pax created the channel for Megatron's first communication to the Cybertronian public, another feed exploded across the Grid, spilling across a giant screen in the pyramid's interior.

Thirty-six Minicons, their polished frames glinting in the garish light of the coaster's signs and logos, scattered across the bases of the girders. They formed two concentric circles, one spaced around the outside girders and the other clustered near the center of the Plasma Curve's course. Above them the track whined and groaned as the next set of cars whipped through the first turn. Waiting Cybertronians looked up, ignoring the Minicons. All they thought about was their turn on the Curve.

Then, simultaneously, the thirty-six Minicons detonated thirty-six fusion bombs. The enormous steel edifice of Plasma Curve collapsed in a blinding flash of unleashed energy and mangled Cybertronians. As it hit the ground, its riders—coming into fatal contact with the intense electromagnetic energies on the tracks—exploded as if they, too, had carried bombs.

It was this scene that Megatron spoke over, and Orion Pax knew no one would hear.

The truth would not matter.

Yet still, he thought. It matters to me. I will fight for it. I—perhaps I alone—can make them see.

"I have to return to Iacon," said Orion Pax.

Megatron clasped his shoulder. "Do not leave angry, brother. What has happened was the will of Primus—else it would not have happened. We are the vessels of our Creator's will, are we not?"

"We have our own will," Orion Pax said. "The code of Primus is what guides us to know when we should and should not exercise it."

The two Cybertronians looked at each other. "We are friends," Megatron said. "We will do great things together. But we must also realize that once we set events in motion, they will not always unfold according to our plans. That, too, is the nature of free will, is it not?"

"It is." Orion Pax admitted this reluctantly, feeling somehow cheated of the chance to make an important point because of the way Megatron had framed the discussion.

This was the great orator's gift. Megatron, the champion gladiator, had been rousing crowds since early in his career. Orion Pax, the peerless data clerk, had never needed to. He resolved then and there to pay closer attention, and to learn his own set of oratorical skills. Megatron could not always be allowed to speak for him, or for his ideas about the movement they were spearheading together.

The central settlement of Polyhex looked out from the flank of the ancient fortress of Darkmount. A plume of magma rose from Cybertron's interior here, creating what the locals knew as the Upper Pool, in a caldera around which the bulk of Darkmount had been built. Once that fortress had protected the natural smelter from the primitive life forms spun off from the initial creation of the Cybertronians. These malformed vehicles of dying Sparks clustered around the molten Lower Pool until they were destroyed and their bits of Spark returned to the Well of AllSparks. Now the Darkmount fortifications were a ruin—albeit an inhabited one, which clustered around the Upper Pool—and the Lower Pool was the focus of a small settlement of artisan manufacturers. They used its endless heat to fuel their works, which in turn adorned the living spaces of the higher castes.

Farther from the smelting pools, some of the more adventurous high-caste Cybertronians built their dwelling places on the opposite side of the valley from Darkmount. These were the lovers of art, the dilettantes, the socialites who drew the admiration of other socialites by living in remote areas and rocketing in alt-form from party to party in Cybertron's great cities.

In between them and the fortress itself, at the head of the valley, was the city of Polyhex. The bomb that went off there destroyed a cliff face that collapsed in a slow-motion cascade into the Lower Pool, carrying a number of outrageous homes with it. The casualties were few, but of prominent castes. Among them was the renowned artist Chromatron, who died in the middle of creating a projection model of Megatron, whose face he had seen for the first time on a Grid feed the day before.

Megatron watched Orion Pax go. "Brother," he said, knowing Orion Pax could not hear. "You must understand that I did not wish this. The world looks different from the bottom of the pits than it does from the stacks in the Hall of Records."

Behind him, Soundwave and Shockwave stood silently until the great door of the pyramid had boomed shut behind Orion Pax. Then Soundwave said, "Should I have him followed?"

Stanix was one of the radial nodes in the great architecture of information that Cybertronians had for gigacycles called the Grid. Feeding from the central servers and the great pool of data at the Hall of Records in Iacon, each node served as a backup and distribution point for communications that did not need approval or routing through the central processors.

The node itself was built into a crenellated ridge at the eastern edge of the city of Stanix itself. Above it sat the forbidding Fort Scyk, a training site for the Council militias and local civil-defense regiments. It was at Fort Scyk where the first generals of the militia had conceived of the idea of formalizing the castes.

And it was at Fort Scyk where a bomb destroyed the headquarters of the current militia magistrate.

His name was Gauntlet. He took pride in the history of the site, and in the history of the militias of Stanix. He was a believer in caste and had never considered a life outside the military caste into which he had been channeled the moment he emerged from the Well of AllSparks.

Gauntlet had observed the initial classified communications from Iacon about this Megatron character. He was one more low-caste malcontent looking to disrupt a system that had served Cybertron well since time immemorial. That was Gauntlet's firm opinion. He was waiting for the Council to reach the same conclusion and to take direct action against the cesspool of crime that Kaon and the Badlands were becoming.

He looked forward to taking part in those actions. Gauntlet's singular regret in his existence thus far was that he had never seen large-scale combat.

The bomb, carried by an anonymous Minicon, detonated just below the parade-ground reviewing stand on Field Rho, in the northwest corner of Fort Scyk. It blew that corner of the fort out and down the side of the ridge. Its electromagnetic pulse caused cascading failures in the Grid node located inside the ridge itself.

One hundred and eighty-three Cybertronians were killed by the explosion, the collapse, or EMP damage to their processing systems. Among them was Gauntlet.

Alpha Trion watched fires bloom across the face of Cybertron. The sight brought him near to despair. He had seen it before. He had fought in a war on Cybertron, a war that pitted brother against brother and threatened the fabric of the planet and the universe.

Now, it seemed, another such war was at hand.

A screen carrying a feed from Uraya displayed another iteration of what he was seeing across the planet. Wreckage, scattered and damaged bodies. Over the feed played an anonymized voice claiming responsibility for the attacks.

ON BEHALF OF THE LOW-CASTE, THE FORGOTTEN, THE DOWNTRODDEN. NOW WE TREAD ON YOU.

Orion Pax roared across the Badlands, exhilaration warring in his heart with a sense of foreboding that he could not ignore.

Once we set events in motion, they will not always unfold according to our plans.

But what exactly were Megatron's plans?

Don't think like that, he told himself. Megatron knows how to do things his way. Orion Pax knew another way. The two of them together would achieve great things. Today was a misstep, a mistake. Necessary? Orion Pax did not want to think so. But the undeniable lesson of the day was that Megatron was right about one thing: The day's events had Cybertron talking about this new radical movement and its rebellion against the long-entrenched caste system.

Many Cybertronians, for the first time since they had awakened next to the Well of AllSparks, were just now realizing that their lives did not have to be the way they had always been.

He arrived in Iacon and returned to his proto-form while still in motion, hitting the street running in front of the Hall of Records. Alpha Trion was waiting for him just inside the door to the data-harvesting area.

"I need advice," Orion Pax said.

Alpha Trion nodded. "You need more than that."

They went inside.

"This will mean a war," Alpha Trion said.

Orion Pax nodded. He knew this.

"And," Alpha Trion said, tapping his Quill on the desktop as he did when he was about to say something that upset him, "you no longer have any choice but to be squarely in the center of it."

Considering this, Orion Pax found it impossible. He was a data clerk. He had never fought anyone beyond some desultory training with Jazz after first beginning to hear of Megatron. What use would he be in a war?

And was a war really the only possible outcome of the chain of events that had begun with these bombings?

Reconsidering, Orion Pax realized that the chain of events had begun much farther back than that. One might say that it had begun the first time he had initiated contact with Megatron. Or perhaps if Orion Pax had not done this, someone else would have. Perhaps the development of events became inevitable the moment Megatron assumed his name.

But why stop there? If you were going to believe in

inevitability, then Megatron's choice had been predetermined by the existence and actions of the Fallen, back in the age of the Primes. And what, in turn, had predetermined that fateful murder? How far back did you look for cause and effect before you had to acknowledge that certain effects had unknowable causes?

"It is difficult to assimilate, this idea that you have an unaccustomed role to play," Alpha Trion said.

"Yes," Orion Pax said.

"Megatron, too, might not find himself playing the role he expected," Alpha Trion went on. "What is your sense of him?"

"Why are you asking me? You've seen everything I have."

"I have not met him. Let us not pretend that your face-to-face meeting didn't take place."

Orion Pax was taken aback. He had never thought to deceive Alpha Trion, but he also would not have minded if the topic of his meeting Megatron had never been broached. "No," he said. "No point pretending about that. I do not regret meeting him."

"Then I repeat my question. What is your sense of him?"

"He is a leader, and he has many followers," Orion Pax said. "More than anyone would believe, I think. He believes in things that I believe in as well. He has the best interests of Cybertronians at heart. That is my sense of Megatron." After a pause, expecting a response and getting none, he added, "What is yours?"

"What I think about Megatron is this." Alpha Trion flipped open the immense book on his desk, but closed it without looking at a page. "He believes what he professes to believe. You may count on that. What you must consider is whether his methods may ultimately undermine his ideals."

For some time Orion Pax was silent. Alpha Trion let him think. Eventually he asked, "What conclusion have you reached?"

"Whatever Megatron may believe," Orion Pax said, "I think that I must be there to act as a check on his methods."

"Do you think he ordered those bombs?"

Orion Pax shook his head. "No."

"What makes you think this way?"

"I wish I could argue more effectively," Orion Pax said, "but my reason in the end is this: If Megatron had ordered something like that, he would want every Cybertronian to know he had done it."

Alpha Trion was nodding. "Yes. If Megatron is undone, it will not be due to a failure of his ideals, but a failure of his ego."

But who without ego would ever lead? Orion Pax wondered.

"Know this, Orion Pax," Alpha Trion said. "In times of war, much is proven about the true nature of those who fight. It may be that you will not learn the truth about—"

"Yes," Orion Pax said. "About Megatron."

Alpha Trion stared at him until Orion Pax grew acutely embarrassed about his interjection. When the Archivist spoke again, his tone was sharp. "Only a fool interrupts his elders. The war that comes, if it comes, will teach you a final truth about yourself."

*   *   *

He emerged from his audience with Alpha Trion to find—amazingly—Shockwave waiting for him out in the public-access area of the Hall of Records. "Librarian," the mechasurgeon said. "You would perhaps do me the honor of accompanying me on a tour. I know little of Iacon, having spent most of my time in less savory circumstances."

Orion Pax didn't have to try hard to get the subtext. "What would you want to see?"

As they walked together toward the front door, Shockwave showed him a location on a small screen that unfolded from the outside of his forearm.

"I think I know where that is," said Orion Pax.

The Observatory of Iacon was the finest surface-based astronomical facility on the planet Cybertron. It was one of Orion Pax's favorite places, and he went there whenever he could to remind himself of the destiny that awaited bold Cybertronians who dared reach beyond their planet toward the stars. And it was there that he led Shockwave, and there that Megatron met them, in the shadow of the great Solar Telescope.

Orion Pax was nervous and a bit angry. "Things are getting out of control," he said.

"The kind of thing that needs to happen is not the kind of thing that can be controlled," Megatron said. "We all need to know this. Not every Cybertronian is going to wait and talk forever. Some will act."

Something about Megatron's tone alarmed Orion Pax. He spoke slowly, knowing that Shockwave would distort anything he said if he wasn't careful. "Are you saying you knew it was going to happen?"

Megatron, too, chose his words carefully. "I am saying that I heard something was going to happen."

Shock flooded through Orion Pax. He realized in that moment that there was far, far less common ground between him and Megatron than he had previously thought. They shared goals, yes; but it was becoming increasingly clear that they did not share methods. Perhaps they never would.

"I defended you!" Orion Pax said.

"Listen, brother," said Megatron. "I knew this was going to happen. Yes. I did not try to stop it. Why not? Because I could not have. I had no control. What are we fighting for, if not the idea that we do not have control over the lives of our fellow Cybertronians? I do not want them to conduct terrorist attacks. I don't want innocent bits of the Spark to be extinguished. But here is a hard truth." Megatron turned and beckoned Orion Pax over to the wall of displays showing the carnage at the explosion sites. "The hard truth is this: I can distance myself from this, and by doing so become more credible. If those groups, whoever they are, continue to be more extreme than I am, I begin to look rational and reasonable by comparison. This moves us forward, brother. Do you not see that?"

Orion Pax did see it. But he did not like it.

"Would you like to know something else that you probably had never considered?"

"I have a feeling you'll find a way to tell me," Orion Pax said.

Megatron walked toward the door. "My turn to play tour guide," he said. A few cycles later Orion Pax, stunned, was ringside at a gladiatorial pit in the subterranean heart of Iacon itself.

* * *

"Did you think that only Kaonians enjoyed these sports? Or only those of the lower castes?" Megatron prodded him.

In the pit, two creaking Cybertronians—clearly discards from some industrial enterprise—faced off against a swarming army of Minicons. More Minicons than Orion Pax could count were already lying crushed and broken on the pit floor, which unlike the Kaonian pits was made of welded steel. One of the larger Cybertronians, the name Hydrau painted across the backs of his shoulders, was torn and leaking from dozens of tiny wounds. The other was in better shape as they fought back to back with vibroweapons, the blades clearly customized from a scrapyard. Orion Pax turned away. Once again the presence of Megatron had taught him something about Cybertron that he hadn't necessarily wanted to know.

"You don't need to take your caste grievances out on me," he said. "The caste system hasn't helped me any more than it has you."

"Again, that's where you're wrong." One of the large gladiators went down as the Minicons severed the connections in his right leg. They swarmed over him as the other, Hydrau, swept them away with great sparking arcs of his vibroblade. "Your caste is safe. You observe. You move data and put it in places where your betters decide if it has been put in the right place." Megatron tapped a knuckle against his own chest. "My caste dies. We die in industrial accidents when molten alloys pour over us, or when energy leaks from a conduit and vaporizes our processors, or when liquid nitrogen shatters our limbs, or when a crane spills a cubic kilounit of raw ore and crushes us to junk. We die. You watch. Do not compare the two."

He returned to watching the match. "*Hydrau!*" he roared, raising an arm. The other large gladiator was dead, but the Minicons had been too eager to take him down; while they focused on finishing him off, Hydrau had decimated them. He was now facing off against barely a double handful of them, with his back against one wall of the pit. One of the Minicons struggled under his foot until he leaned on it and its skull popped with a shower of sparks.

HYDRAU! The crowd picked up the chant. HY-DRAU! HYDRAU! HYDRAU!

And incredibly, across the pit, shouting and thrusting fists into the air along with the rest of the audience, Orion Pax saw Jazz.

He was with two other Cybertronians whom Orion Pax didn't know. One yellow and black, one clearly a Seeker, red and silver and all sharp angles. Jazz? Orion Pax couldn't believe it.

"Friend of yours?" Megatron asked, following Orion Pax's line of sight.

He nodded. "His name is Jazz."

"Never know who you're going to find down in the pits," Megatron said. He laughed and clapped Orion Pax on the shoulder. "Come on, friend. One of the things about getting free of caste is that you get to see the world as it is. Sometimes that means seeing things you wish weren't there."

The crowd erupted in a thunderous scream as Hy-drau finished off the last of the Minicons, holding it up and snapping pieces of it off until it fell limp. Flinging it away, he leaped onto the top of the barrier separating crowd from pit and stood, rocking back and forth.

HYDRAU! HYDRAU! HYDRAU!

"Might be some competition there," said Megatron with a smirk.

"Competition for a hardened survivor of Kaon?" Orion Pax made a great show of disbelief. "Surely none of us weak, soft Iaconians would have a prayer against the scourge of the subterranean Badlands."

"Oh ho, his sense of humor returns!" Megatron looked delighted. On the wall-spanning holograms that hung over the pit, Hydrau soaked in the admiration of his audience . . . and then those images disappeared, replaced with multiplied vistas of fire and destruction.

The crowd fell silent, then a confused murmur spread through them. Orion Pax looked at the holos. A factory exploded. Groups of Cybertronians ran in formation through an intersection, and four of them were cut down by heavy energy-cannon fire from out of the frame. The rest ran on.

"That's Altihex," someone said nearby.

"But what's happening?"

On one of the feed screens, Orion Pax could see that the Altihex militias had responded. Pitched battles raged throughout the city. Other Grid feeds spawned on every available bit of wall, and different perspectives on the news and events flooded in. From his perch on the pit wall, Hydrau looked first annoyed and then shocked.

"Looks like civil war, doesn't it?" Megatron said.

Orion Pax spun to face him, enraged. "You sound happy."

"No. I will mourn the dead just as every other Cybertronian will." Megatron pointed at one of the screens, where civil-defense forces were concentrating their fire on a pair of Cybertronians. They blew apart in a flare of ion discharge, their weapon reservoirs exploding out into the air like the visual ghost of their invisibly escaping Energon. "Those two. I mourn them. You are merely shocked by their deaths. That is a difference between us, Orion Pax."

It was true, Orion Pax realized. He saw the images of destruction but they did not connect with him emotionally . . . because he was still arguing for or against free will like a data clerk. He was analyzing, because he had at last taken his chance to analyze, but he had never yet taken his chance to feel.

"What are we coming to, Megatron?" he asked, as Altihex began to burn.

"The place we were always coming to, my friend," Megatron said. "Power is never given up. It must be taken. And we are going to take ours."

He started moving toward the door. Reflexively Orion Pax followed. "Now it is time for us to join them," said Megatron.

"Join the fighting? Why?" Orion Pax asked.

"No, not join the fighting. Not yet." Megatron paused for Orion Pax to catch up. "But we have to go to Altihex, because Altihex was one of the last known locations of the Matrix of Leadership."

CHAPTER NINE

All Armorhide had ever wanted to do was make people laugh. He was from an artists' caste and therefore permitted an amount of social latitude generally forbidden to more socially integrated castes. Comedy being his chosen art, he had found an audience in Altihex—specifically in the Great Hall of the Altihex Casino. An orbital station, slung in a fixed path visible from Iacon and the other great cities of the north, Altihex Casino was a haven for those who fled convention. It teemed with artists, social malcontents, those who preferred to view the workings of a society from the outside. These were Armorhide's people, and it was his life's work to give them a moment to forget the mundane cares of caste and isolation on a planet that wandered through space, cut off from all other Cybertronian settlements since the collapse of the Space Bridges how many cycles ago . . .

He was telling a joke about the Space Bridges, an elaborate story that involved the prices charged by an invented force of entropic toll collectors. The joke was failing, and it began to go worse as he improvised a faster way to wrap it up. The crowd laughed because it was his crowd. He had performed for them in Altihex's Great Hall dozens of times. They would cut him a break on a bombed joke once in awhile.

But he was frustrated because tonight—of all nights!—the great distant leader Sentinel Prime was in the audience.

Sentinel Prime!

The most important night of his life, and his timing was off. Even his old material, guaranteed to get a laugh, wasn't doing the job. The audience must have known Sentinel Prime was there, and they were nervous, too.

Then a couple of things happened at once.

The first was that Sentinel Prime, Keeper of the Castes, Marshal of the Armies of Cybertron, the leader to whom (it was rumored) Cybertron itself had granted the Matrix of Leadership—he laughed. At a joke about Armorhide's last failed joke, no less.

The second was that the entire wall that faced the exterior of the station blew out with an enormous rush of air, preceded by the unmistakable sound of explosive charges detonating.

Starscream assumed alt-form reflexively when the explosions sounded through the Great Hall—but then he froze the change and returned to his proto-form, hauling Sentinel Prime out of the way of a collapsing column. The station's artificial gravity wavered with the initial blast. Then atmosphere poured out into space, sucking a number of audience members with it.

Through the holes in the wall came a number of Cybertronians, some still finishing their return from alt-form. One of them flipped a device up onto the wall. It crawled immediately up to one of the speakers wired into the Hall's general audio system.

"We are Decepticons," boomed a voice from the speakers. "We claim Altihex in the name of no castes, in the name of free Cybertron—in the name of Megatron!"

Claim Altihex? Starscream thought. Was there a ground force operating as well?

The voice thinned out as all of the atmosphere evacuated from the Great Hall. Starscream leaned over and touched his head to Sentinel Prime's. "Leader," he said. "We must—"

Rocket fire and the boom of energy detonations cut him off. Invading Cybertronians, some still in the middle of reversions to their proto-forms from Seeker variations, continued to pour through the hole in Altihex's outside walls.

"I will fight!" roared Sentinel Prime, the words vibrating into Starscream's audio sensors from the inside of his head. "Who are these Decepticons? Who dares? Who is this Megatron?"

A fusillade of ion bolts hammered into Sentinel Prime's torso, knocking him spinning across a row of seating. Starscream fired back, suppressing and covering as Sentinel Prime got to his feet. The leader looked shocked—and, Starscream was surprised to note, afraid. Of these? This rabble? Contemptuously Starscream blew one of them back out the hole they'd come in through, and then he followed Sentinel Prime up one of the aisles, beating an orderly retreat along with the rest of the audience that hadn't been damaged or destroyed by the initial penetration.

He shoved Sentinel Prime ahead, staying in physical contact with him. "Leader, we will protect you. Now is not the time for you to fight."

And Sentinel Prime went along. Starscream felt contempt for him now, not just for Megatron's cannon fodder enlisted to pull off this operation. Sentinel Prime's time was long past. He did not know it, but Starscream did. So did Megatron.

And so did two of his subordinates, Skywarp and Thundercracker, waiting in a mechanical access corridor where the atmospheric pressure was still maximal and the power was still on. Starscream shoved Sentinel Prime in ahead.

"These are my trusted lieutenants," Starscream said. "They will protect you until we can sort all of this out."

Sentinel Prime nodded. "Go, Starscream. If you can find help, do so. If not, at least spread the truth about what has happened here today."

Once he had been a great warrior, had Sentinel Prime. Starscream knew the stories. Now he had lost his nerve, had been complicit in the freezing and slow death of Cybertronian society, the death of a thousand castes. It was time for new leadership, who would rebuild what had been lost and forgotten. This operation, the taking of Altihex, was a statement to Cybertron and simultaneously the first tangible sign that the Decepticons were more than just rhetoric and arena-style posing.

Skywarp and Thundercracker would take good care of him, deep in Kaon, out of the way. Where he belonged.

Distant explosions and alarms echoed throughout

the torus shape of Altihex. There was never going to be enough resistance to trouble the Decepticons; that was part of why they had chosen this time and place for their first overt act of revolution. Starscream reached the evacuated Great Hall without encountering any resistance. The only motion in the Hall was the comedian whose poor jokes had mercifully been cut off by the attack. He rumbled back and forth on the stage, targeting random fixtures in a fury. When he spotted Starscream, he locked in with a shoulder-mounted rocket launcher.

Starscream had neither the time nor the inclination to fight. He assumed alt-form and thundered away, the comedian's rockets exploding silently in his wake. He had a meeting to attend, far down below and all the way across the planet in the Badlands, and if the burning of Altihex was any indication of the way the future was going to go, he didn't want to be late. There were some decisions to finalize . . . and Starscream had some plans of his own to set in motion. Megatron was not the only Cybertronian with a vision of what Cybertron could be.

By the end of the invader's proclamation in the Great Hall, no sound could be heard save the distant alarms whose vibrations carried up through the floor and Armorhide's feet. He looked around, hanging on to one of the stanchions supporting the stage lights. An invasion? Of Altihex? And it started here, during his show?

Not funny.

Everyone evacuated the Hall in a blaze of panicked

defensive firing as the invaders pressed in—ignoring
Armorhide completely.

This wasn't funny, either.

It took only a few cycles. The invaders blasted
through one of the interior walls, their goal clearly to
destabilize the station. Armorhide, like most permanent residents of and frequent visitors to Altihex, had
a sensor array specially retrofitted to handle contin-
ual and drastic shifts in pressure and temperature. As
his sensors recalibrated themselves now, he watched
the last of his audience disappear. Sentinel Prime was
one of the last out the main doors into the station's interior, shepherded by the menacing figure of his
guard. Who had not laughed at a single joke in Armorhide's routine.

Something unusual was going on here—unusual
even beyond the fact of a splinter cell of renegade Cybertronians attacking and killing other Cybertronians. The whole scenario had an air of planning about
it, as if there had been something specific about Altihex and about the Great Hall that had made them
targets.

Armorhide was just a comedian. He never wanted
to think about politics. But this was a time when all
Cybertronians needed to confront what needed to be
confronted.

Who could he tell? There were no guards at the
hole in the outside wall. Not all of the Decepticons—
was that what they had called themselves?—had been
Seekers. They must have come in some kind of vehicle.

Keeping an eye out for their possible return, Armorhide went to the hole and stuck his head out into

the void of space. On his left, he saw stars, and little pieces of the station floating away. Down below, he saw the signs of war in the Torus States, centered in Altihex proper. Explosions bloomed, and the contrails of Seekers crisscrossed the skies over the city.

On his right, he saw a short-range surface-to-low-orbit vehicle magnetically tethered to the station.

"Perfect," Armorhide said, even though there was no one there to hear, and even if there had been they wouldn't have because of the vacuum, and if there had been someone there he wouldn't have said anything because he didn't want other Cybertronians thinking that he talked to himself. Except . . .

"Get on the ship, idiot," he told himself, and he did. Someone in Iacon needed to hear about this. If he could get through the chaos on the ground in the Torus States first.

The Badlands stretched endlessly around Megatron and Starscream as they met face-to-face for the first time. "The operation at Altihex went well," Megatron said. "You played your part perfectly."

"It was an easy part to play. I have been close to Sentinel Prime in a protective capacity for some time." Starscream wished they could see Altihex from the Badlands, but the only near-Cybertron objects in view were the moon bases and the shimmering string of the single Space Bridge that still remained. No one knew where it led, or whether it still worked. Perhaps no one would ever find out.

Although Starscream wanted to. He wanted to lead the Cybertronians out into the universe again . . . and perhaps leading the Decepticons would be the first step toward that goal.

The first step toward leading the Decepticons, of course, was to ensure an alliance with Megatron, and to make sure that this alliance was on the best terms possible. Starscream had gone along with the plan to remove Sentinel Prime because it put him in a position to bargain. The final nature of that bargain was yet to be determined.

Megatron saw him looking up toward the sky. "Altihex is ours. Now every Cybertronian knows that the Decepticons are a force to be reckoned with, and that our opposition is weak, disorganized, and unwilling to resist," he said. "When the new history of Cybertron is written, I am the one who will write it. What part do you want to play?"

"You cannot threaten me, Megatron," Starscream said. "If you want a war, you might get it; but if you want to win a war, you're going to need me and my forces. The Council will deploy plenty of airpower, and right now you've got a bunch of gladiators who don't know any more about high-altitude combat than they do about the chemistry of star formation."

"A standoff, then," Megatron said. "Fair enough. I can leave now, and you can make your own choice. But I warn you: The next time we see each other the offer may not be the same."

"What I will do is go to Trypticon Station," Starscream said.

"Trypticon?" Megatron said. "And what will you do when you get there?"

You don't know, do you? Starscream was delighted. As long as he knew something Megatron didn't, he

could keep angling for the best position . . . and, ultimately, the shortest route to leading the Decepticons
himself. "Protect it," he said. "There is much at Trypticon that would be dangerous for Cybertron if it fell
into the wrong hands."

Megatron faced up to Starscream. They locked optics, neither backing down, but Starscream knew this
was pure bravado on Megatron's part. Still, he played
along with the necessary charade. "And you suggest
that my hands are the wrong ones?" Megatron said.

"I suggest," Starscream said, "that Cybertron needs
change, but that it does not need annihilation. I will
watch over Trypticon to make sure that one does not
lead to the other."

Megatron looked for a moment as if he would fight.
Some of his armaments systems flickered, but he held
himself back. "I will ask you plainly," he said when
he had regained his temper. "Starscream, are you
with us?"

"I'm not against you, Megatron," Starscream answered. "I don't think I'll say more than that. The
Council might yet be listening."

"Still hedging your bets? That's a good way to lose
no matter what happens. The High Council would
never imagine that a low-caste gladiator could have
any ambition beyond the next battle," Megatron
scoffed.

"Holding a grudge still?" Starscream shook his
head. "Megatron, if you are going to fight you must
fight with a clear head. Most Cybertronians—even
the ones who disagree with you—don't care one way
or another about the caste system. Would you set

them against you because they don't share your obsession?"

"I would set the universe against me if it meant the lines were clear," Megatron said. "Beware, Starscream, that you do not find yourself on the wrong side of that line."

He backflipped into the air, assuming alt-form in the same maneuver and thundering away. Starscream watched him go. Then he composed a message to all Seekers he knew he could trust:

Rendezvous at Trypticon immediately.

Puzzled, Megatron read the intercepted message. Trypticon? That pile of semi-sentient junk? What could be up there that Starscream thought was so valuable that he would rather sit on it than take part in the war for Cybertron?

It was time for some research.

And for that, Megatron thought, he was going to need the librarian.

CHAPTER TEN

In the aftermath, as the dead were counted and the Grid thrummed with outrage and speculation, Orion Pax consulted with Alpha Trion. "Sentinel Prime was on Altihex," Orion Pax said heavily.

"Much time has passed since it mattered where Sentinel Prime was," Alpha Trion said. The Quill left afterimages as he ticked it metronomically back and forth, thinking.

Once again, Orion Pax thought, Alpha Trion surprises me with his lack of . . . what? Compassion? No. It was Orion Pax who had no feeling for all of the institutions—caste, leader, and so forth—that defined Cybertronian society. This was an odd feeling to get from the Archivist in charge of the Hall of Records, the being entrusted with organizing the history of the civilization.

Orion Pax wrote it off to the stress of the circumstances. "My concern," Alpha Trion said, "is that Megatron, having gotten a taste of armed rebellion, will find it to his liking. Did you know that the gladiator tournaments across the Badlands—including Kaon—have shut down? All of their warriors now clamor to join these Decepticons." He stood and looked out the window from his official study over the great cityscape of Iacon. "Orion Pax, did he know? You have seen that he denies it. You supported his denials of the terrorist bombings."

Alpha Trion turned to look Orion Pax in the face. "What is your intuition about this?" he asked. "Is the Altihex takeover the brainchild of a rogue splinter cell, or is that a cover to keep Megatron safely distant from actions he has ordered?"

Orion Pax did not know the answer to this question. He believed that Megatron's ideals matched his. But he had also seen Megatron's personality, the quickness of his anger, the sharpness and aggression even of his wit. It was not impossible, he decided, that Alpha Trion was correct, that Megatron had indeed gotten a taste of violence and found himself unable to stop indulging that taste. Perhaps he had always been this way; that would explain his initial entry into the gladiatorial pits. Or perhaps the pits had changed him somehow.

Ancient history, Orion Pax thought, and useless. Then he realized what an unusual sentiment that was for a data clerk in the Hall of Records. He couldn't help but smile.

"I see your expression, but I detect no humor in the situation," Alpha Trion said. "What answer do you have to my question?"

"Only that I do not know, and that my smile is a recognition of irony rather than an indulgence of humor," Orion Pax said carefully. "I apologize if it came off differently."

"You know this Megatron better than anyone in

Iacon. If you were advising the High Council, what would be your advice?" Alpha Trion asked.

"If I were . . ." Orion Pax trailed off, unable to quite believe the idea that he might actually advise the High Council. But the more he considered the proposition, the more sense it made. He did know Megatron, and could offer some useful insights . . . but more useful yet would be if . . . "Archivist," he said respectfully. "What if Megatron and I both appeared before the High Council? I would take it upon myself to be a go-between and explain my understanding of the situation, but they need to hear his grievances directly from him."

Alpha Trion considered this idea. A squadron of Seekers streaked over the towers of Iacon, not one of the mandated commercial routes. Orion Pax wondered where they might be going, and at whose bidding. "Perhaps," Alpha Trion said eventually.

"Will you contact the Council on my behalf?"

"There are specified times for specified castes to bring their grievances before the Council," Alpha Trion said.

"Slag the specified times!" Orion cried out. "Even now, with Altihex destroyed and Sentinel Prime gone missing, with Megatron about to lead Cybertron into civil war, you want to talk about caste?!"

"You mistake me. I have never wanted to talk about caste. I thought the castes were a poor idea when they were instituted," Alpha Trion said. "But they exist, and must be dealt with, especially when one is contemplating an audience that will deeply disturb the High Councilors. If you're going to get anywhere with this idea, Orion Pax, you're going to need to think instead of just act."

For a moment Orion Pax considered the irony. Megatron accused him of thinking and not feeling; Alpha Trion accused him of feeling and not thinking. Perhaps, he mused, this meant he had found—or was finding—some correct middle ground.

"What must be done, must be done," he said. "I thank you for speaking to the Council. If you will do it."

Alpha Trion sighed. "I will do it," he said.

And it was only after Orion Pax had left Alpha Trion's office that one of the Archivist's lines recurred in his mind: *I thought the castes were a poor idea when they were instituted.*

How old was Alpha Trion? Could he be . . . ?

Impossible, thought Orion Pax. The Thirteen were all dead, if they had ever even existed. Long gone, long since. It would do no good to grasp after such myths now.

He arranged a meeting with Megatron, not in Kaon but in the vast unused portions of the spaceport at Hydrax Plateau. Once this had been one of the busiest points on Cybertron, as shipping traffic blasted off for the Space Bridges that interconnected Cybertron with the dozens of worlds Cybertronian explorers had discovered. What a sight it must have been, thought Orion Pax. All of the different races coming and going, organic and mechanical mixing and interchanging ideas, technologies . . . but now it was mostly quiet. The vast majority of its takeoffs and landings were of automated, semi-sentient vessels returning raw materials from the Trypticon Asteroid Belt. The only piloted space traffic that came and went from Hydrax was the steady stream of resupply vessels sent to Moon Bases One and Two, and the occasional fresh crew sent up to replace the skeleton staff at Trypticon Station.

Which was what Megatron wanted to talk about as soon as they met, in a hangar that once had contained semi-sentient spacecraft but now stood empty, its door open and roof collapsed. Ruined machinery and spacecraft parts made the hangar interior feel something like a gladiator pit, missing only flames and rabid spectators. They met warily, keeping an eye out for security forces who might fire first and ascertain identities later.

If Alpha Trion thought war was inevitable, Orion Pax reasoned, then sooner or later someone was going to have to seize the Hydrax Plateau and the spaceport. He wondered if Megatron had already formed a plan for this—or, perhaps, if one of the breakaway factions of the Decepticon movement was planning it for him.

"Librarian," Megatron said. "I need you to find something out for me."

No, Orion Pax thought. We are doing this my way for once. "First we need to decide what we're going to do, Megatron," he said. "The Altihex situation makes us look very bad. Sentinel Prime himself has disappeared. The invaders claimed to be Decepticons, operating under your instructions. This is going to be difficult to explain."

"Yet, you were about to say, explain it we must," Megatron finished.

"That's right."

"You said Altihex makes us look bad. Us. How us?"

"You and I are associated. I spoke up for you, and now whatever happens associated with your name, or this Decepticon term . . . that is associated with me as well. And I don't like it. This is not the way I would have done things."

"No, it isn't. But this is the way that things are being done, and it's working. All of Cybertron is talking about caste and privilege now."

Orion Pax couldn't believe what he was hearing. "Really? They are? You must mean all of Cybertron except for the millions of Cybertronians on every channel of the Grid who are screaming for your head because of the violence. Are you that out of touch?"

"I'm in touch with what needs touching, brother," Megatron said.

"When you're in shackles before the Judge of the High Council, we'll see if you feel the same way."

"Who's going to put me there? You, brother? I don't think so," Megatron said. "You can disdain my methods, but every cycle that goes by without you stopping me means that when it comes right down to it, you approve. You want things done just as I do, but you don't want to contemplate what must happen to get them done."

Orion Pax's temper started to boil over. He knew Megatron was testing him, seeing how far he could push Orion Pax without breaking their friendship. We do believe many of the same things, Orion Pax thought. What I told Alpha Trion was true. It is important not to let these kinds of disagreements get in the way of the larger vision: a caste-free Cybertron, populated by Cybertronians who chose their own paths from the moment they manifested next to the Well of AllSparks to the moment that each individual Spark returned to its maker.

"And you," he said, "rely on me to get you things that you can't get as well."

Megatron nodded and clapped Orion Pax on the shoulder, smiling, his sneering commentary already forgotten. "Of course I do. And one of those things—the most pressing thing for our movement—is to find out what Trypticon Station contains."

"Because of this Starscream? He's a Seeker officer, like any other. What makes you think he knows anything?"

"Can't tell you," Megatron said with a shake of his head. "It's better you do not know. One secret to a successful rebellion is compartmentalization."

Orion Pax didn't know what to say to this.

"Just like I don't want to know what you had to do to get us an audience before the High Council," Megatron went on. Seeing the expression on Orion Pax's face, he said, "Yes. I know. How do I know? You don't want to know."

"You know because you have Soundwave's Minicons sneaking all over Cybertron finding things out," Orion Pax said. "I'm not a fool, Megatron."

"No," Megatron said. "You're not. And you're not as naïve as you appear to be sometimes. I'll have to keep that in mind."

These last words came out in a contemplative tone that made Orion Pax curious as to what Megatron was actually thinking. He was not curious enough to ask, though, if it meant distracting the conversation from the critically important topic of appearing before the High Council. That, Orion Pax was sure, represented their best chance for stopping the violence before it escalated further and creating the best possible platform for the reforms they proposed.

"We can appear before the High Council in five megacycles," Orion Pax said.

That would also give him plenty of time for a preliminary search through the Records to see what they might have to say about secret projects on Trypticon Station. Not that there were any. This was a mad flight of fancy, Starscream's way of angling for a role in the rebellion—or, perhaps, of suppressing it. What if they went to Trypticon and found a reactionary force established there, ready to put them in custody and try them for treason?

"Yes," Megatron said. "We should appear before the Council and make our arguments there. I do not wish anarchy, brother. But you will notice that before, when we were just talking to each other beyond the sight of the Grid and the hearing of the Council, nothing changed. Now when they can ignore us no longer, we will have an audience in the Grand Conference Chamber with the entire Council. See the relationship?"

"This is what you were talking about when you said that the existence of terrorists would make you more palatable, isn't it?" Orion Pax sighed.

"Yes, brother. And it's working."

There was no denying that, Orion Pax thought. "Well," he said. "That will console all of the dead in Altihex and Six Lasers."

"If their deaths mean we get a hearing before the High Council instead of an all-out civil war," Megatron said, "then in the future we will know it was a worthwhile sacrifice."

"But it's not a sacrifice they chose, Megatron. Isn't this all about self-determination? It's a little too easy for you to sacrifice other people to your goals."

Megatron considered this for some time. "Yes, brother," he said. "Perhaps it is. This is one reason that I am glad for your friendship. You keep me conscious of these things that otherwise are too easy for me to forget."

CHAPTER ELEVEN

Crystal City had stood for teracycles, a monument to the union of Cybertronian ingenuity and aesthetics. It shimmered and glowed as the various materials of its composition caught different spectra of light, creating a prismatic show that was visible for dozens of hics in any direction. During certain atmospheric conditions, even the citizens of Iacon could see it shimmering like a mirage just over the horizon. It was a monument both to achievement and to the aristocracy of Cybertron that demanded beauty along with function.

Scientific research went hand-in-hand with artistic innovation here. Soundwave hated the place. To him it reeked of self-indulgence.

"Rumble, Frenzy, eject," Soundwave said. The two Minicons he had brought with him spun down to the floor and awaited instructions. "Operation Matrix Quest, parameters as in previous briefing," he said. "Do not let anyone see you. If anyone does see you, ensure that they tell no one."

A series of chirps was the Minicons' answer. They could talk, but on a mission—especially a mission in which timing was critical, as it was here—they tended to communicate via coded bursts. They skittered away into the shadows and Soundwave returned to the surface, standing sentinel against the possibility that they would all be discovered. He preferred to avoid a standup fight; the chance of losing was too great. But for this, the risks might be worth it. He kept in touch with the two Minicons via a direct videolink that played as if on the interior of his own optics.

For a moment he considered opening up and ejecting Ravage and Laserbeak. Too dangerous, he decided. The more of his Minicons he sent in, the more likely it was that he would lose one. And on this mission, he might well lose one, because he was after the deepest secrets of Crystal City.

Not even Starscream, who had spent much of his scientific career in the labs contained within these endlessly refracting walls, knew every secret of the City. No one did.

Except, perhaps, Omega Supreme. And it was Omega Supreme who worried Soundwave. He hadn't come all this way to get rendered into his component molecules by one of the Guardian's missiles. Not even for the liberation of Cybertron . . . however that was going to be accomplished. Soundwave thought he had Megatron convinced of his loyalty, but the truth was he was waiting to see how things progressed. His skills would be useful to the High Council and the Cybertronian defense forces as well—and they would be useful to whatever other groups emerged to compete for the future of Cybertron.

Orion Pax, for example. Soundwave felt strongly that Megatron was underestimating the librarian.

Time would tell, however, and right at that moment time was something Soundwave didn't have. He moved back outside the security-sensitive perimeter surrounding Crystal City and waited for his Minicons to send their first set of rendezvous signals.

Frenzy reported in exactly one cycle later. Nothing out of the ordinary. On the half-cycle, Rumble followed up. Everything in his sensory perimeter was normal as well. Soundwave started to wonder what he was looking for. No—he knew what he was looking for. He started to wonder whether it could actually be in Crystal City, if two Minicons could sneak around without even registering an automated probe of their credentials. Either things were not as they once had been in Crystal City, or the object of his search was long gone.

It occurred to him to wonder whether it even existed anymore. There was no way to know short of laying one's hands on it.

Had the civilization of Cybertronians grown and developed past the Matrix of Leadership? Was a fragment of a long-broken mythical sword really worth pursuing and handing to a chosen leader as if it made a difference to that leader's quality? Soundwave was not superstitious. He never had put much stock in the old stories of Cybertron, in the Primes' (the Thirteen's) legendary actions and that sort of thing. He knew how the minds of sentient beings worked. He had spent his existence thus far finding things out about Cybertronians that they didn't want anyone to find out. If you did that for a while, very quickly you lost whatever superstitious leanings you might have had.

The workers inside Crystal City were the scientific elite of Cybertron, the planet's most advanced thinkers and engineers, capable of marvels. Yet, thought Soundwave, the Space Bridges still floated in their orbits, dead and slowly disintegrating. What use was a scientific elite if it devoted all of its time to refining previous achievements without ever pursuing new greatness of its own? If the Matrix was in Crystal City, Soundwave thought, some academic was probably using it in an experiment about color preference or something equally stupid.

Twin datastreams flowed from Frenzy and Rumble as they made their way deeper into the center of Crystal City, and from there down into its subterranean laboratories, where most of the real work took place. Beneath Cybertron's surface, experiments encountered much less interference from stray cosmic rays and ordinary background radiation, as well as the everyday electromagnetic noise of a highly advanced technological civilization. If the Matrix—or anything else important—was in Crystal City, odds were it would be in the downstairs parts.

Seeing advanced materials experiments, Rumble reported. *Weapons system integration using energy feedback from chassis-based absorption panels.*

Noncritical, Soundwave thought. He sent a narrowcast burst reply: Continue search. Report only mission-critical information. Where was the Matrix?

Or at least something he could take back to Megatron and use as leverage to cut a better deal. He was willing to be the Decepticon spymaster that Megatron seemed to want. Compiling knowledge, especially damaging knowledge, was one of Soundwave's fa-

vorite pursuits. But spymasters eventually fell victim
to one singular problem: Their principal employers
started to need not just the information a spymaster
provided, but information on the spymaster himself.
So the position brought with it the certainty of rivals.
Soundwave didn't want rivals.

And if he could nail down the location of the Matrix so some of Megatron's fanatical ex-gladiators
could storm its location, he would have enough in the
way of good favor to see him through whatever this
war would bring.

Briefly he wondered if the High Council could
make him as good an offer. Unlikely, it seemed. They
were determined to keep everything the way it was.
Soundwave didn't particularly mind the way things
were, but if they were going to change—and Megatron was going to make sure they were, with or without the librarian—Soundwave wanted to be on the
right side as it happened.

Frenzy reported in. Large portions of subsurface
labs cut off. Warning signs everywhere about intru-
sions from the Underworld—explore or continue reconnaissance?

Recon is primary, Soundwave sent. Focus.

Underworld incursions. Interesting. Who knew
what might be down in the Underworld after the teracycles that had passed since the last exploratory expeditions, or the ending of the tradition that every
Cybertronian had to make the Underworld run from
the Well of AllSparks to Crystal City. That, thought
Soundwave, was one more step on the way to soft-
ness and decline. When the younger Cybertronians

survived that run, they emerged tempered and ready for whatever Cybertron might need from them.

Now they posted signs and fretted about what was on the other side of long-unopened doors. If Megatron could restore the swashbuckling spirit of Cybertron, Soundwave thought, any amount of collateral damage would be worth it.

Simultaneously Rumble and Frenzy reported in a local-area communication intercept. Someone, deep inside Crystal City, was talking about Megatron. The transmission was heavily encrypted, but the parts of it that Soundwave could parse at the moment filled him with dread. Someone down there foresaw that Megatron was a dire threat. And it sounded like that someone was taking a step that Soundwave had been hoping would not be taken.

It sounded as if the scientists in Crystal City were awakening their guardian. They were awakening Omega Supreme.

"Frenzy, Rumble, back now," Soundwave commanded. Both Minicons pinged that they were on their way. Soundwave almost couldn't wait for them. If Omega Supreme was going to stand up for the existing order on Cybertron, Soundwave suddenly wasn't so sure he wanted to be a revolutionary after all.

The archives in the Hall of Records were far from silent on the contents of Trypticon Station. Constructed in the distant past as a simple space station, orbiting on the same orbital plane as the twin Moon Bases, it had more recently been re-created . . . could this be true? Orion Pax thought. Who had done this?

Was the entire station sentient? Had it been given a Spark?

Why?

The records hinted that something had been sequestered deep within Trypticon at about the time it had been raised to sentience. Wherever Orion Pax looked, though, he encounted dead ends. Records had been altered or removed. Security barriers had been erected for which he had no clearance. He went to Alpha Trion in the end, not so much because he wanted Alpha Trion to know what he was seeking but because no matter what else he had become, he was still a clerk of the Hall of Records. Problems with the data architecture were very disturbing.

"Archivist," Orion Pax said at the door to Alpha Trion's study. He waited while Alpha Trion finished writing something in the book on his desk.

When the Archivist looked up, Orion Pax spawned some of his findings on holoscreens along the study's wall. "There has been a great deal of data manipulation surrounding the topic of Trypticon Station," he said. "Particularly where its Spark is concerned. Why was it made sentient? What are these references"—he indicated several documents on a screen near the door—"that indicate something of critical importance has been hidden on the station?"

Alpha Trion examined the records closely. He glanced back at his book, one hand falling on it as if he wanted to flip through its pages. Then he shut the book instead and turned back to Orion Pax.

"I do not know what is concealed therein, Orion Pax," he said. "But I do know that Trypticon was created—re-created, I should say; given Spark—to serve as guardian for something that an ancient version of the High Council thought needed to be hidden."

"Do any members of that Council still survive?" Orion Pax asked.

Alpha Trion was looking out the window again. "Sentinel Prime," he said. "If he yet survives. But what is in Trypticon Station, what must be so jealously guarded, I do not know."

Something in the tone of Alpha Trion's voice made Orion Pax want to pursue the question. "There are further references to Seekers being given charge of the task of guarding," he went on, prompting his elder.

"Yes," said Alpha Trion. "Ask them what they know."

Ask them what they know . . .

Orion Pax did not know any Seekers. He saw them flying overhead. He knew that some of them were designed for atmospheric and some for space operations. He knew that among their leaders was Starscream, whose name Megatron had mentioned and who was seen protecting Sentinel Prime in Grid-harvested security video of the Decepticon attack on Altihex Casino. And he knew, thanks to the few communications about Trypticon Station that had not been tampered with in the Grid, that Starscream and some of his officers were now at the station.

What they were doing, he did not know. Nor did Orion Pax know how to contact him or what he might ask to get the beginnings of an answer instead of a curt refusal.

Was there some superweapon stowed deep within

Trypticon to prevent its misuse? Or hidden knowledge, an artifact of the Primes left behind for future
Cybertronians to use when the time was right and the
need was greatest?

The Records were silent. So was the Keeper of the
Records, Alpha Trion, when Orion Pax most needed
him to speak.

None of it mattered until he and Megatron had offered their vision to the High Council and seen what
future their ideas had in the eyes of Cybertron's ruling
body. Orion Pax returned to his workstation and
took up once again—possibly, he considered, for the
last time—the tasks and responsibilities of his caste.
He read, he assimilated, he categorized, he indexed.

And he considered what he might say to Megatron,
who would surely ask about this search. Had he
found anything worth knowing? And if he had, did
that mean he might have found something he should
keep from Megatron?

Orion Pax considered the possibility that he might
need to keep secrets. It was something he had never
done. It made him uncomfortable, but also—he was
honest enough to admit this—he knew that if he had
secrets worth keeping, he was more than just a data
clerk in Iacon's Hall of Records. *Great events find
great Cybertronians,* he had read somewhere in one
of the versions of the Covenant that circulated
through the Hall's archives. *And other times, great
events make great Cybertronians.*

Which was happening now?

CHAPTER TWELVE

Orion Pax did not speak to Megatron again until Alpha Trion let him know that the High Council had scheduled a special session at which the questions of anti-caste agitation and Cybertronian civil liberties would be raised. When he told Megatron, Orion Pax was expecting excitement. What he got was satisfaction. "Well done, my friend," Megatron said. "You see? You have connections you never even knew were connections, by virtue of your caste. How do you think the Council would have reacted if it were I asking them for a hearing?"

"I don't know," Orion Pax said. "But I do know how they will react to you if you show up in the Chamber more interested in airing your grievances than finding a way forward."

"I'm just a gladiator, librarian. I will speak the way I know how to speak."

Orion Pax laughed. "It's been a long time since you were just a gladiator. Maybe it's time to stop pretending you're simple and naïve. When you walk into the Council Chamber, you need to present yourself as the leader of a legitimate movement. If they think you're just a gladiator, they'll cut you off in a nanoklik and you'll never get a second chance."

Megatron paused and thought this over. "I can count on you for advice, my friend. I'll think this over." After another pause, he asked, "Can I count on you to speak for me?"

"Yes. You can count on me to advocate what I know we both believe."

"Then I will see you in a few megacycles," Megatron said.

"Agreed," said Orion Pax. "Don't make too much of an entrance. One thing you have to know about the Council is that they hate to be upstaged."

The High Council of Iacon met in a chamber built in the shape of an idealized Spark, with radiant arms running in three dimensions away from a central space where the Council stood at a long, slightly curved row of podiums. Each member had a gavel, and each could signal to the moderator a desire to speak. The gallery was in several balconies rising vertically away from a viewing area on the floor. There was not an empty space to be seen; Cybertronians of every shape and size packed the floor, Minicons struggling for good sightlines among the hulking Lightning Strike Coalition, the combiners grouped together near a back corner, and the multiforms who flitted and flickered around the periphery of the chamber, or hung from the edges of balconies, or hovered above the dais. It was an active scene, but order prevailed. Militias of the High Council had segregated pro- and anti-reform spectators, and created another subdivision to keep officials and policy makers away from those who were there purely out of interest in seeing the theater of a Council debate. Orion Pax stood along the wall, approximately halfway between the Council dais and the back wall of the chamber, where the thirteen entrance doors symbolized the guiding spirit and philosophical oversight of the Primes.

Today the moderator was Halogen, who according to legend had known some of the Primes personally and had seen Cybertron through every disaster since the disappearance of the Fallen. His long experience and perspective—or so Alpha Trion had suggested to Orion Pax—would lead him to be open-minded about the prospect of abandoning castes and returning to a more open social system such as the one that had existed in the aftermath of the War of the Primes.

"On the other hand," Alpha Trion had added, "there are a number of other Councilors who will be against this from the beginning because they are against anything that disturbs the status quo."

This made no sense to Orion Pax. "Why? If nothing ever changed, we might as well have never emerged from the Well."

"Why? Interesting question," Alpha Trion said. "Consider this. If you are on the High Council, and you think of the High Council as the status quo, how are you going to see challenges to that status quo?" He saw Orion Pax figuring it out. "Yes. You are going to see them as personal challenges. This is what your gladiator friend, and you, are going to be up against in the Chamber. Bear it in mind."

And Orion Pax was, as he entered the Chamber for the first time and took in its grandeur. Here, all of the luminaries of Cybertron past had proclaimed their ideals and testified their beliefs. He was humbled to join those ranks, and still somewhat amazed that the Council had agreed to hear the ideas of a data clerk and a gladiator who imagined a new way forward for Cybertronian society.

Of course he had Alpha Trion to thank . . . and the more he saw Alpha Trion's name appearing in the Archives and put it together with landmark events in Cybertron's history, the more Orion Pax started to believe that there was more to the Archivist than met the optic. Orion Pax was no fool, and if Alpha Trion was just an Archivist, then all of Cybertron was going to have to rethink its ideas about the denizens of the deepest, darkest libraries and repositories of knowledge.

Without Alpha Trion, Orion Pax thought, I would not be here.

And, paradoxically, now that he was in the Council Chamber, Alpha Trion was not there. He had elected not to attend, he said, because he did not want the Hall itself associated with the argument that would take place. Orion Pax could not help but wonder if this was some kind of test. He could imagine Alpha Trion saying to him: *There. I got you your audience. Now it is up to you and your gladiator friend to see what you may make of it.*

All the while, Orion Pax thought, Alpha Trion would be observing on a Grid feed, his Quill tapping and scratching, tapping and scratching . . .

The moderator, Halogen, tapped his gavel on his podium, and the business of settling in for the Council session concluded. "We are here," Halogen growled, "to take up a question of the gravest consequence, for it is a question that has brought our society from peace to the edge of civil war in a very few megacycles. The Council first states without reservation that it deplores the acts of violence that have so far taken place. Those must be answered for, and one of our goals today will be to discern who should answer for them.

"Further, the question of the legitimacy of castes will be addressed. The Council feels that the caste system was instituted legally and that Sentinel Prime has overseen its continuation in a prudent way. Were he here, he would be able to speak for himself, but this brings us to a dire reality. There are those among us who would prefer terror and violence to discussion and consensus."

Halogen began to play to the number of Grid feeds whose lenses were visible all around the chamber. "Sentinel Prime, the Council believes you to be alive and well. We call upon your captors to renounce their ways, release you, and present themselves to the machinery of justice! Regardless of the merits of an argument, it must not be prosecuted by lawless behavior."

"Hear! Hear!" cried out a smaller Councilor from his podium at the end of the row.

Ratbat, as he was known, was widely known to be corrupt and beholden to the established interests represented in the upper echelons of Cybertronian society. It was said of Ratbat that he never believed anything for more than a cycle at a time unless he was paid to. Orion Pax had never spoken to him.

A few other voices picked up and echoed his approbation. Halogen gaveled for order. "I beg of you to contain yourselves, fellow Councilors," he said severely. "Or else how may we demand of our audience that they keep themselves in check?"

After a pause, he went on.

"It is said that the former gladiator now known as Megatron is responsible for the disappearance of Sentinel Prime. This is a most troubling accusation and must be addressed. It is further said that the Seekers and their commander Starscream have been co-opted into Megatron's unsavory operations. This, too, must be addressed despite the recent relocation of Starscream to the space station Trypticon." Halogen paused. "Introductions are wearisome. Let us begin to hear from the citizens. First the High Council, under penalty of confinement and further justice, commands the Cybertronian of Kaon known as Megatron to present himself."

An anticipatory murmur and buzz spread through the Chamber as everyone present—including Orion Pax—looked around for Megatron. Very few of them had ever seen him in person, but nearly all had beheld his likeness via the Grid.

He was nowhere to be found—and then he was, materializing as if out of nothing to stride down the center aisle onto the floor and present himself at the Witness Podium before the Council dais. "I am here at the request of the High Council," he said.

Halogen and the other Councilors took a long time to look him over. "Are you the Kaonian industrial worker and so-called gladiatorial champion who assumed the moniker Megatron?" asked the Council Secretary, a powerful Seeker named Contrail.

"I am."

"By what authority do you claim this name?"

"By my own and no other."

The audacity of this answer caused a ripple of surprise, tinged with approval and condemnation in roughly equal measure, to spread throughout the audience. Halogen banged his gavel and the sound subsided. After a moment of imperious staring at the unruly gallery, Contrail went on. The tone of his voice had acquired a new edge. "Are you not aware that names are presented at the Well of AllSparks and nowhere else?"

"I am aware of that tradition," Megatron said. "I do not recognize it as the only possibility."

"Let us not quibble over the protocols of how a citizen chooses to identify himself," interjected Ratbat. "Surely there are more interesting questions to address."

"And just as surely, the protocols of this Council should be observed," said Halogen.

Ratbat nodded and spoke no more. "Your testimony before the Council," resumed Contrail, "is commanded to be truthful and complete."

"And so it shall be," Megatron answered, "although I fear that the complete truths I have to offer will not please those members of the High Council who demand obeisance rather than the interchange of equals."

Again the gallery muttered and whispered, and again Halogen gaveled them into silence, and again Contrail glared at anyone who dared to meet his eye. Orion Pax gazed right back at him. He had not spoken, had not made a sound, but he was not going to be cowed by anyone. The days of hierarchies on Cybertron were over—or if not over, waning. Orion Pax could look around the Chamber and see that just from the postures and attitudes of the audience. He wondered if the Councilors saw it, too, and if they were already performing the internal calculus that would let them allow the changes Megatron and Orion Pax called for. In all probability, if they did so, they would frame it as their own action, arrived at for their own reasons. Orion Pax knew this and had decided that he would accept any amount of grandstanding if it meant that their goal was accomplished. But he did not know how Megatron felt on the topic.

It seemed that he might be about to find out.

Contrail nodded at Halogen, signaling that the identification and swearing-in of the witness had concluded and that the testimony could begin.

CHAPTER THIRTEEN

"In the beginning," said Megatron, "I had no name."

He paused to let that sink in. There was no sound in the Council Chamber.

"None of us did. We spoke to each other, down in the mines and the smelters, by electronic signature. We indicated each other by function. We assigned each other nicknames. I was D-16, named for the sector of the mine where I conducted demolition operations. And then I saw my first match in the gladiator pits." Megatron had spoken exclusively to the Council so far. Now he extended an arm backward and up, picking out the crew of industrial bots in the second balcony. "That is where I first learned how life was for the lower castes that none of you ever take a nanoklik to consider. Each Cybertronian in that balcony has seen more Cybertronians die himself than the total of you in the rest of the gallery. Our lives are worthless!"

His voice rose to thunder out this last sentence. Reflexively Halogen tapped his gavel. "Until," Megatron said over the echo of the tap of the gavel. "Until we decided we had worth. We, the lower castes. We, the bots who die in subsurface mills and factories creating all of the things that you up here take for granted. We learned that we were individuals by facing off against each other in the gladiator pits in Slaughter City and Kaon, and how did we know we were individuals?" He waited for a moment to let the question sink in. The Chamber was silent again as gallery and Council alike awaited Megatron's next flourish.

"We knew we were individuals because as we killed our opponents in the ring, we saw in their deaths the realization that they were individuals. And so we knew we were, too. In killing, we understood life. In being the most disposable of commodities—a gladiator, whose remains are thrown into the junkpile to be picked over and scavenged, the healthy pieces sold off to brokers in Iacon and Crystal City—in being disposable, we discovered that we had value. Someone would pay us for what we did. Someone would cheer when we killed, and roar in anger when we died.

"So if our lives had worth—even to others just as worthless as we were—then we had the right to names," Megatron finished. "And that is how the sequence of events started that led to me being here before you today. My friend Orion Pax, I thank you for helping our cause gain this platform; and to the High Council, I express my thanks for your time and attention."

And with that surprisingly conciliatory ending—or that was how it came across to Orion Pax, in any case—Megatron fell silent, awaiting questions. They were not long in coming.

"In what way are you linked to the terrorist bombings of Six Lasers and other sites a few megacycles ago?" asked Contrail.

"I had nothing to do with those actions," Megatron said. "An issue like this one raises intense passions. I myself feel passionately about it. The difference between me and those who would bomb Six Lasers is that I channel my passions in a direction that I think will be better for all Cybertronians. I disavow any act that does not ultimately herald a new and better era on Cybertron."

A clever phrasing, Orion Pax thought. He remembered his conversation with Megatron in which Megatron had pointed out that the existence of extremists made him look reasonable by comparison. Here was the proof, that he could stand here in front of the High Council and make pronouncements about the value of individuality while Guild representatives shifted noisily in the front rows of the floor area.

"Clearly you are exceptional, especially for one of your caste," Contrail parried. "Are you not responsible if your rhetoric excites those unfortunates without your willpower, though? Do you not have the same kind of responsibility that this Council and its members have, if your leadership position is to be taken seriously?"

"What you have to worry about is what will happen if my leadership is *not* taken seriously," said Megatron.

"It would seem that we have seen that already," interjected a new voice, the rumbling Drivetrain. One of the patriarchs of the group loosely known as the Constructicons, Drivetrain originated in the middle castes associated with building and civil engineering. His influence on the High Council was the result of long service and gradual acceptance among the other members, who by and large came from higher castes associated with science, arts, and government.

"I will say it again. I had nothing to do with those bombings or with the attack on the Altihex Station casino." Megatron stood resolute.

Orion Pax couldn't decide whether to admire him or be scandalized that he could stand up in front of the High Council and ignore the truth. He saw motion at the back of the gallery and noted that Soundwave had entered, a Minicon perched on either shoulder. The Minicons scampered down Soundwave's arms and disappeared into the crowd.

"You will say it again, and I will disbelieve it again," Drivetrain said. "Would you have me believe that your co-conspirator, a data clerk in the House of Records, masterminded an invasion and kidnapping using a force of bots who identified themselves as Decepticons and specifically proclaimed their allegiance to you?"

"Decepticon?" echoed Megatron. "An interesting name."

"You would think so," Drivetrain pressed him. "Since it was you who coined it, was it not?"

Megatron drew himself up to his full height. He was larger than most Cybertronians, and the diffuse light of the Council Chamber made his combat scars seem silvery, almost luminous. "I would say that you should implicate neither me nor my friend Orion Pax until you have facts. What other bots might have said means nothing to me. But if the term *Decepticon* is to be laid at my feet, I accept it!" he said. "Sometimes deception is necessary, when those who should listen to the truth will not, and will only understand once they have been lied to and forced to see their own lies."

"Very well, Drivetrain. You have provoked him," Ratbat said. He looked around, making a show of waiting for other Councilors to speak. None did. Orion Pax thought in that moment that all of it was a charade, that they were never going to get anything from the Council . . .

That if there was to be a war, it had been decided before any of them had entered the Chamber. Perhaps even before Alpha Trion had succeeded in gaining them the invitation.

A shouting match had erupted while Orion Pax was distracted by Ratbat's unctuous blathering about choice and collective good. "What the High Council has so far failed to understand is that it is our right!" Megatron boomed over the sound of Halogen's gavel. "Each and every Cybertronian has a right to question the Council's actions, and to demand change when those actions fall short of the Council's mandate." With that, apparently a parting shot in a salvo much of which Orion Pax had missed, Megatron paused.

"What say the Guilds?" croaked the ancient Halogen.

"Representative of the Guilds, Sigil speaking," said a Cybertronian even more ancient and doddering than Halogen. They had emerged from the Well on the same day, it was said, and had ever since backed each other whenever conflict arose.

"Speak, Sigil," the High Council droned in unison.

"The Guilds claim the right that is theirs." Sigil indicated the assembled heads of the Guilds, who administered the castes and exercised absolute control over which newly born Cybertronians were routed into which castes. "For thousands of orbits and more—since the disappearance of the Primes, in fact—the Guilds of Cybertron have guided the populace in their decisions about life and work. Without the Guilds, there would be no developed civilization. There would be no Space Bridges. There would be no Hydrax Plateau spaceport. There would be no Moon Bases. There would be no Teletraan-1, and no city of Iacon to house it."

He turned to address the Council, after having played to the gallery during the first part of his speech. "Can one criminal . . . one gladiator with the deaths of how many innocents on his conscience . . . can this killer be suffered to undermine what Primus himself decreed when he created this planet and seeded all Cybertronians on it through the Well of AllSparks?"

The Grid fed his words out across Cybertron, and the planet itself seemed to be listening. In the Sonic Canyons, a hush fell over the repair crews working on Vector Sigma's interface. As he spoke, Sigil seemed to gain strength.

"The Guilds have overseen the prosperity of all Cybertronians, and created a framework within which any individual Cybertronian can find his role in our society. If every criminal malcontent is given the chance to upend what we have spent megacycles working to maintain, then I fear for the future of our civilization. I fear for Cybertron itself."

A rumble of approval and discontent swept through the Council hearing chamber. Halogen gaveled the audience back to silence and pointed the gavel at Orion Pax.

"Here is another come to testify," he rumbled. "What say you, Orion Pax, clerk at the Hall of Records in Iacon?"

"I say first that Sigil makes no friends among unhappy Cybertronians because he is as pompous as any Spark ever has been," Orion Pax said. He was angry at Sigil's mischaracterizations and he had decided that, with everything there was at stake, it would be useless to hide it.

He had a reputation of being level-headed and calm. With any luck, his show of anger would register with the Council and bring home to them the degree to which many Cybertronians sympathized with the burgeoning anti-caste movement and, specifically, with the charismatic figure of Megatron.

Moving from his spot next to the wall, Orion Pax worked his way through the crowd and down the center aisle, speaking as he walked and as other members of the audience made way for him. He thought he could see subtle signs of encouragement from many of them, and he knew he could see simple hate on the faces of some.

"You claim for the Guilds the power to determine the lives of every Cybertronian," Orion Pax said. "Is this what the Thirteen would have wanted? Is it any coincidence that as the Guilds rose in power and the castes became entrenched, Cybertron lost contact with the rest of the Transformer worlds? As you confine each Cybertronian into a smaller and smaller

space, with less and less room to go and see and do
what he might want, you create a world in which no
one knows how to look beyond anymore. No one
knows how to imagine."

"I can imagine an end to this session," Ratbat
called out. Laughter boomed through the chamber.
Orion Pax looked around, fearing that he had lost the
goodwill of the audience . . . and that was when he
saw Jazz, squarely in the middle of the lowest balcony, his bright colors standing out. Jazz put one
hand out and made a fist.

Be strong.

Orion Pax turned back to the Council. He had considered the possibility of delivering a speech, and even
given some thought to what he might say, but now
that the moment had come he had no idea how to
begin.

So he began simply. "Fellow Cybertronians, members of the Council, hear me. Megatron speaks
harshly but true. He has seen the truth of life for
many Cybertronians whose lives are all too often invisible, and if he is angry, it is anger born of love for
an ideal and Spark-deep pain at our failure of that
ideal.

"The recent attacks were savage and inexcusable—
yet they were only symptoms. The unrest spreading
across Cybertron will not stop with these attacks because it is the natural expression of a people who for
too long have been held in check, their potential forever unrealized because of the false constraints of
caste and Guild.

"It is natural for a being born with Spark to know
that it should be free. And it is natural that Cybertron-

ians, who are born to change from one form to another, should want to be able to change their roles within Cybertronian society as a whole. If castes and Guilds fight change, they fight our own nature—and the nature of Cybertron itself. The absence of change is not stability. It is entropy. Only dead things stay the same.

"No Cybertronian is simply the mechanical sum of his parts. From the smallest Minicon to the mightiest combiner, from the simplest data processor to the scientists who teach us the laws of the universe, each of us contains a living Spark that makes us *who* we are, not simply *what* we are. The Spark within us awakens us to the possibility of freedom. It makes us alive to the idea that we might choose what we shall become—as each of you did, Councilors. Why should we not? One bot's freedom can never be given or taken away by another. This goes against the very nature of the Spark, the very nature of Cybertron itself.

"In the past, in times of great need, noble Cybertronians rose to become Prime and lead our civilization out of crisis. Most recently, Sentinel Prime—once one of this chamber's honorable Elite Guard—united all Cybertronians against a dire threat. High Councilors fought alongside smelters and data clerks then, to drive off an invader. What did this invader want? To enslave us, to turn us into property, to deprive us of our fundamental Spark-given right of self-determination. Have we driven the Quintessons off only to enslave ourselves by caste and Guild? And will we crush this new movement toward freedom, sacrificing freedom for order? I say no. Order achieved through force can never be a true peace. *There can be no true peace through tyranny.*

"The time has come for all Cybertronians to be united again, and I say we need a new Prime to unite us. We do not need a Prime who moves us as if we were parts of a great machine, who demands that we be drones and slaves as the price of a peace that is only stasis. The Guildmasters and Keepers of the Castes do that more than adequately, and look where they have gotten us. Cybertron needs a leader of the free, a Prime who recognizes that all Cybertronians are autonomous robots, owned by no one but themselves, masters of their own fates.

"I will say it again. Autonomous robots!

"We will remember this moment, in this Council Chamber, as the moment where free robots broke the welds of oppression that had taken the beauty of the Spark away from us. We are all autonomous robots today—Autobots, if we need a name to rally around—and we Autobots declare that a Spark once freed will never again stand to be oppressed.

"You must choose a new Prime today. Choose well, for a Prime might either lead Cybertron to a new golden era in our history, or stand by as the dark energies of anger and resentment explode into planet-wide chaos and war.

"Members of the Council, the choice is yours. I wish you wisdom."

He knew he had spoken well because when he finished, the Council Chamber was silent. Even those bots Orion Pax knew to be his enemies were forced to consider what he had said. The knowledge of this overcame him in the nanokliks immediately following that last sentence; Orion Pax raised both arms, fists clenched, and thundered, "For Cybertron! Autobots!"

Over the pounding of Halogen's gavel, the crowd erupted. AUTOBOTS!

"For freedom! Autobots!"

AUTOBOTS!

It started high up in the gallery, beyond where Megatron's oldest and most loyal followers were clustered. AUTOBOTS! And from there it spread. AUTOBOTS! AUTOBOTS! AUTOBOTS!

This time it took nearly a full cycle before Halogen and the other Councilors could gavel the gallery back to silence. And Orion Pax noticed something odd. When he caught Megatron's eye, he was expecting approbation. Instead he saw anger on his friend's face, and did not know why. Surely, brother, he thought, it is more important to accomplish our goal than it is for us to agree on every mote of our method?

He did not know if that was what had angered Megatron, but Orion Pax knew his friend, and he knew that they would have words. If not during the course of the High Council hearing, then after. Megatron clearly had something on his mind, and he was not a Cybertronian who kept his emotions to himself.

At least not for long.

"There is more to this scenario than whether you, Orion Pax, and you, Megatron, will call your followers Autobots or Decepticons," Halogen said when at last he had gaveled the Council Chamber back into something resembling silence. "Your actions thus far have set this planet on a course of war. Megatron," he went on, leveling his gavel at the great gladiator, "it matters not a bit whether you told your Decepticons to abduct Sentinel Prime or not. What matters is that your Decepticons abducted Sentinel Prime. And Orion Pax, it matters not whether you and Megatron have argued over methods or philosophy, because your actions have contributed as much to the current crisis as his have."

This stung, but Orion Pax knew he must accept it. Humility comes before greatness, it said somewhere in the Covenant, and where humility has not paved the road, greatness may not walk it.

"Yes, Councilor," he said.

This seemed to satisfy Halogen—more, at any rate, than Megatron's haughty silence had. "The question of freedom has lain dormant for far too long. We, this

Council, must accept our share of the blame for this. I stand before you, citizens of Cybertron, and I express my regret for my failure to see and acknowledge the pent-up anger caused by the perpetuation of the caste system."

"Councilor," Ratbat interjected. Four other Councilors echoed him, among them Contrail. Ratbat went on. "Surely you do not wish to upend the caste system that is serving us so well and so stably right now."

"Ratbat, you fail to understand that the upending of the caste system has already happened. It happened with the detonations at Six Lasers and the Sonic Canyons and the other places where innocents lost their lives at the hands of zealots. And it happened at Altihex Casino, where our leader—our detached, disaffected, disinterested leader—vanished with apparently no fight whatsoever."

This drew a roar and tumult of disapproval. "It is time to see what is before us!" Halogen cried out. "We have been willfully blind for far too long."

Orion Pax and Megatron stood together, listening. They glanced at each other. Orion Pax could still see the anger in his friend's face, but he saw also that they were still allied, still working together. Whatever the Council said, the movement would continue.

And the Council said that they had already won.

"Without leadership our civilization must surely founder," Halogen went on. "This High Council, with its thirteen competing voices, may deliberate and consult, but in the end a single individual must make decisions. Sentinel Prime would have done it but he is . . ."

"We do not know where Sentinel Prime is," Sigil said.

No, Orion Pax was thinking. We do not. And it may be that we do not find him until long after all of this is settled. We cannot count on anything, he realized. No existing structure can handle the problems we have raised.

He glanced over at Megatron, and could tell from his friend's expression that they had reached the same conclusions—but had very different reactions to it. Megatron looked as if he could gleefully have presided over the permanent and total destruction of every institution of Cybertronian civilization. Orion Pax wanted to be free. But if there were no Cybertron, if there were no Iacon or Hydrax or Sonic Canyons . . . then what good would freedom do?

"Silence!" commanded Halogen. "This is not the time for commentary from the gallery. The High Council speaks here, and will speak until it is done." He paused, recovering his temper. "In the absence of Sentinel Prime, we must take collective steps where we would prefer to have individual initiative."

"What are you getting at?" Megatron called out. "If the times are as dire as you say, they do not permit elaborate speeches. Let us hear what you have to say, plainly and directly."

Halogen stared at him in a silent fury of affront. In that gaze Orion Pax could see everything that was wrong with Cybertron, everything that his awakening made him want to change. Who cared about the protocols of the High Council, about Halogen's sense of decorum, about the grand theater of waving gavels and shouted dissents from the gallery? None of that was real. None of it mattered.

Because somewhere in a pit below the surface, perhaps in Kaon, perhaps even in Iacon . . . a nameless gladiator was dying.

"Then I will speak as plainly and directly as I may," Halogen said.

Megatron started to speak again, but Orion Pax reached over to put a hand on his shoulder. "Let's hear what they have to say," he said quietly. After a tense moment, Megatron relaxed.

"There have been attempts to discover the Matrix of Leadership," Ratbat said. "We suspect that elements of these Decepticons are responsible."

"What seems at least as likely is that any band of malcontents claiming the name Decepticon can be linked to these searches," Contrail said. "How are we to know the truth about what Megatron himself, or Orion Pax for that matter, might be planning?"

"Orion Pax has disavowed the name Decepticon," Halogen pointed out.

"Who then is mobilizing spies to dig through old ruins and sneak past security in Crystal City?" The voice came from the gallery. No one could tell immediately who had called out, but Orion Pax recognized the voice. It was Megatron's spymaster Soundwave.

That's what is happening here, Orion Pax thought. Someone is maneuvering me into a position and waiting for me to agree to occupy it. Soundwave had never trusted him, not from the moment they had met inside the great gleaming pyramid in Kaon, the nerve center of everything that had made Megatron who he was.

Whatever happened, resolved Orion Pax, he was going to have to make sure that he never turned his back on Soundwave.

"The Matrix of Leadership, more than any other remnant of the Age of the Primes, defines Cybertronian society by marking the leader of the Cybertronians, irrevocably and irreversibly." Halogen stood a little off to the side of his podium, allowing the entire gallery to see him in full instead of as a head-and-shoulders bust behind a piece of furniture. "But the Matrix does not grant itself to whoever might find it. On the contrary, it has a tendency to discover those who have the innate qualities necessary to claim it."

"And none of the searchers thus far have found it. Which means," added Ratbat, "that it has not permitted itself yet to be found."

It was unlike Ratbat to mention mythology, or anything more far-reaching than the events of the next megacycle. What was he doing suddenly seconding Halogen's excursion into the nature of the Matrix of Leadership? Orion Pax was suspicious. He saw that Megatron looked as if he wasn't quite sure what was going on, either.

Unaware of what anyone in the Chamber thought, Halogen pressed forward. "This body, the High Council of Cybertron, has realized that events in our cities are spiraling out of control. Part of this is due to a lack of leadership, which explains the sudden surge in the number of expeditions searching for the Matrix of Leadership. But, as we have explained, the Matrix will not reveal itself to just anyone."

Contrail stepped forward to stand at Halogen's shoulder. "There is a way forward. We have consulted with the Archivist of the Hall of Records and he has revealed to us some things that we did not know."

"Get on with it," muttered Megatron. Only Orion Pax could hear.

What were they getting at? Orion Pax couldn't tell from all of the ceremonial verbiage. Yes, the Matrix of Leadership was lost. Yes, someone was going to have to find it, especially in the absence of Sentinel Prime. But what did this have to do with the question of castes, and of individual self-determination among the forgotten classes of Cybertronians?

Orion Pax had never been a great observer of the High Council, but he didn't think they were known for this kind of uncertainty and dithering. They looked like they had been caught doing something wrong, and were trying to make it right without ever admitting that it had been wrong.

Halogen regained control. "The Matrix of Leadership is on Cybertron though it has not been seen in these many billions of cycles. According to the Archivist, Alpha Trion, it may be found in these turbulent times, and if found will lead all Cybertronians through to a new age on the other side."

Halogen leveled his gavel at Orion Pax and Megatron. "Yes," Megatron said softly, so softly that Orion Pax wasn't quite certain he had heard.

And then Halogen said, "Orion Pax, upon you we place the quest for the Matrix of Leadership."

Silence fell, so absolute that Orion Pax only then realized how much ambient noise there was in a room full of Cybertronians unless they stood absolutely still. It was as if the High Council and its Chamber and everyone within had suspended every function, frozen themselves in space and time, as the implications of the High Councilor's words became clear.

Orion Pax could not believe that they might be saying what it seemed that they might be saying. "Excuse me?" he said, knowing that when Halogen spoke again it would be to clarify a misunderstanding. Next to Orion Pax, Megatron's stillness was the stillness of decommissioned factories in long-dead cities.

As one, the High Council set their gavels down and saluted. No, Orion Pax started to say—but he did not, because he could not interrupt the High Council and because he realized that it was not his place to refute the beliefs of his people. Perhaps the Matrix of Leadership was mythical, perhaps not. He believed it was not because he trusted what he had read in the Hall of Records.

He trusted that he knew the true history of Cybertron, except those portions of that history that time or circumstance had hidden from him.

And in the end, he trusted that the leaders charged with acting in Cybertron's best interest would do that. If he believed that, he must let them speak.

"The Matrix of Leadership is yours to seek, because from this moment forward," said Halogen in a voice that filled the Chamber even over the astonished outbursts of the gallery, "you are Optimus Prime. Unite Cybertron and all of the Cybertronians. Usher in this new era you have spoken of so eloquently."

The Archivist knew, Orion Pax thought. Is this what he knew? Is this what they were talking about?

How could he have known?

There was a pause, crackling with tension, for a single nanoklik. Then the Chamber of the High Council exploded into a welter of reactions: scandalized shouts from the Guildmasters who could not believe that the Council would thrust such a responsibility on an unknown data clerk; robust cheering from Orion Pax's fellow clerks; an avalanche of venom from the gladiators who had trooped all the way from the Badlands anticipating a coronation of sorts for their leader Megatron.

Orion Pax stood stunned. He looked around, unable to process the enormity of what had just happened. Optimus Prime? He was now Optimus Prime?

What right did a data clerk have to be called Prime and to seek out the Matrix of Leadership?

As soon as he had formulated the question, another presented itself: What right did he have to refuse?

The High Council held its salute for a full cycle, then dropped it and stepped back behind their podiums—save Ratbat, who stayed on top of his. Halogen gaveled for order and motioned Optimus Prime forward. "In time of great need," he said over the slowly diminishing tumult, "Cybertron turns to those in whom the spark of greatness truly blazes. Optimus Prime, you must see us through the turbulent times that are to come."

Optimus Prime approached the witness podium. When he reached it, painfully aware of the intense scrutiny he was under, he paused. Then he said, in as level a tone as he could muster, "But I am not worthy of this."

"A fine show of humility," said Megatron. His voice was low and cutting, a growl intended only for Optimus Prime, who looked at him, shocked. He had not noticed that Megatron had come to the podium with him.

"A fine show of humility!" Megatron said again, louder this time. He turned, playing to the gallery. "My friend Orion Pax came here saying that he wanted to play peacemaker, that he did not want isolated acts of violence to escalate to civil war! He asked me to come under the banner of friendship and trust. He brought all of us here flying the false flag of reconciliation—when what he really pursued was power!"

Thunderous reaction greeted Megatron's last shout, his supporters standing in massed ranks at the front of the balconies and the partisans of Optimus Prime rallying to points opposite Megatron's followers on the upper balconies and down on the viewing floor.

Optimus Prime pivoted around and raised his arms for quiet, instinctively, not expecting it to work—but to his astonishment it did. "I did not want this," he said. "I still do not want it. If I had my preference I would remain a clerk, reading the data brought to my station by the Grid.

"But I believe in Cybertron. I believe in the history that I read as a clerk. I believe the stories that say that when Cybertron needs someone, that someone will always be found, and that someone will light Cybertron's darkest hour.

"I do not know if I am that someone. But I respect the High Council, and I respect our traditions, and if they say I am . . . I will try to fulfill the role expected of me."

He lowered his arms and looked around the Council Chamber. Then he looked at Megatron.

"Brother," he said. "You believe me. Don't you?"

"Optimus Prime," Megatron said. A long moment stretched out as under Megatron's gaze Optimus felt like Orion Pax again, just a clerk who had gotten involved in events far too large for him to handle and far too important for him to comprehend.

Then Megatron dropped his gaze and said, "It doesn't matter whether I believe you now, brother. I believed you before. We embarked on this course together. We will see it through together. If the High Council believes you are the next Prime, that is their prerogative."

Optimus Prime began just for a nanoklik to think that Megatron was overcoming his shock and surprise—but Megatron surprised him instead.

Turning back to the gallery, he called out, "Optimus Prime! Does it not have the ring of leadership? Of heroism? Does Cybertron not call out in its hour of need and find . . . a data clerk?"

"Brother," said Optimus Prime.

"Brother no more!" thundered Megatron. Then, to
the High Council, he went on. "This . . . travesty . . .
is one more in a long line of injustices that at last provoked the invisible castes of Cybertron to take up
arms. Blame them if you must, but blame yourselves
as well. You see a people chafing under the yoke of
caste and Guild, and what do you do? You send out
militias. Those bots do not yield to your militias, and
what do you do? You call for a new Prime. A new
leader. A new autocrat," he said, picking up volume
again as he turned back to the gallery. "A new autocrat to keep the High Council safe behind their podiums and keep Cybertron safe for the Guildmasters
and caste overseers who keep the lower castes down
in the pits!" Pointing up into the balconies, he roared,
"Will you yet stay in the pits?"

NO!

"Will you fall into place behind this Optimus
Prime, this creature of the High Council, who would
keep you there?"

NO!

"You see, brother?" Megatron said, twisting the
last word as he looked back to Optimus Prime. "They
do not want your control. They want to be free."

"I do not wish to control them; I believe, as you do,
that freedom is the right of all sentient beings," said
Optimus Prime.

"Lies!" Megatron's face was contorted with rage,
the pitch of his emotion nearly causing a partial
transformation.

LIES! came the echo from the balconies.

"No!" roared Optimus Prime. "I do not want to
lead, but I will if I must. And if you will break away

from all the laws of Cybertron and from all the traditions of the Primes, then lead I must. I would rather work with you, brother, and change what we both know needs changing. But this is not the way."

"You do not tell me what the way is," Megatron said coldly. "I found the way when you were still a drone filtering data out of the Grid. What you know of the way forward, you learned from me. And what you learn from this day on, you will also learn from me. The High Council calls you Prime? I defy them! I lead the Decepticons of Cybertron, and I fight for the freedom of all Cybertronians!"

Halogen's voice cut through the building rumble of discontent. "You will yield!" the High Councilor said. "This is not your bully pulpit, Megatron—and you will not deform this Chamber with your posturing."

"And this is no longer your Chamber, Halogen," returned Megatron. "Must you not defer to Optimus Prime, whom you have anointed leader? Well, I refuse to acknowledge him as my leader—and I defy you! You have betrayed the ideals you proclaim!"

Rounding on Optimus Prime, Megatron added, "And you, brother. You have betrayed the ideals you professed to me from the first. I should have known."

"You will not speak to the Prime that way," Halogen began, but he never finished because Megatron finally lost the last of his patience. His arm transformed in mid-arc, revealing the muzzle of a fusion cannon that flared actinic blue with a blast that destroyed Halogen's podium in a hail of shrapnel.

There was a stunned pause in the Chamber. Such a weapon had never been seen before.

Then several things happened at once. The Elite
Guard, a formidable body of twenty-six heavily
armed bots, appeared from every part of the Chamber to lock into a tight perimeter around the Council
dais on which the podiums stood—twelve now instead of thirteen, with a smoking gap between two
sets of six. Ratbat scampered up on top of Contrail's
shoulder. And the ratcheting sound of weapons being
unholstered or Trans-readied echoed throughout the
Chamber as Megatron's followers readied a fusillade
from the upper balconies. On the floor, Autobot-
sympathizing Cybertronians snapped to readiness,
suddenly bristling with missiles, cannon barrels, and
hand weapons that flickered and hissed with latent
energies.

"Stop!" Optimus Prime commanded.

If every armed bot in the Chamber let go at once, he
thought, the building would not survive it—never
mind the casualties among some of those most important to see Cybertron through the coming war.

Because Optimus Prime was beginning to realize
that whatever his intentions, whatever his ideals, he
was not going to be able to prevent Megatron from
going his own way.

And taking his followers with him.

Optimus Prime stepped between Megatron and the
focused firepower of the Elite Guard. "You will not
fire at him," he said. "Not in the Council Chamber. If
I am Prime, and I command this, you must obey."

After a pause, the Guard lowered their weapons.

Yes, thought Optimus Prime. I have this authority.

"Well done, Prime," Megatron said behind him.
The scorn in his voice rankled Optimus Prime, but he

did not respond to it. "And what if I told my gladiators to fire on you?" he pressed. "Do you believe they would hesitate because you are Prime?"

"I believe any Cybertronian must believe in the ideals of Cybertron," Optimus Prime answered without looking back. "If I must be destroyed because I believe in those ideals, then so be it."

Another silence, briefer than the last but equally tense. At the edges of the balconies, the weapons of the gladiator corps bristled like a sensory array on the planet-side facet of an orbital station. Another array of barrels and antennae spread around the perimeter of the Council dais. The third, from the Autobots, primarily answered the focus of the Decepticons, but some of them aimed their weapons past Optimus Prime toward the Elite Guard.

A standoff. Optimus Prime felt a deep foreboding sense of certainty that it would not be the last.

He waited, not looking back at Megatron. "Decepticons," Megatron said. "Stand down. For now."

With a cascade of ratcheting echoes, the Decepticons hid their weapons and stood in quiet ranks, awaiting their next instruction. Optimus Prime turned to face his friend. "I would value your advice," he said. "And your friendship."

"I would have valued yours as well, before your betrayal," Megatron said. "But now you have been chosen. You have fallen into the trap they laid for you, and already I can tell you love being in their trap."

Megatron took a step back and gave a signal to the gladiators—no, not just to them, Optimus Prime saw. A number of bots on the floor reacted, too, making preparations. "You see how many of us there are, just here? How many others do you think await you out in the Badlands, or in the subsurface levels? How ready are you to die?"

"I am ready to do what needs to be done. No matter how many Decepticons you drag up from the pits," Optimus Prime said, letting his anger get the better of him.

"And no matter how many Autobots you haul out of the libraries and the art galleries," said Megatron, his voice cold with fury, "my Decepticons will meet you. You have the backing of the Council, but we will see who claims the Matrix in the end."

He assumed his alt-form then, and every Decepticon in the Chamber did as well. Those that were wheeled or tracked tore through the back wall of the Council Chamber, leaving the wall collapsed behind them and the two bottom balconies hanging at an angle. Winged Decepticons hovered in the domed space over the Council dais, blades and engines thrumming as they awaited final instructions.

Debris rained down on the dais and the viewing floor as remaining bots ducked or, if a little bolder, swatted the chunks of steel and concrete aside as they fell. Megatron accelerated through the hole in the dome and was gone, followed by the Seekers who had declared for him. With them, Optimus Prime noted, went Contrail, with Ratbat hunkered down in his cockpit, that hangover from the era of Quintesson slavery.

Optimus Prime watched them go, heavy thoughts on his mind. Megatron had committed himself. There was no way back now.

*   *   *

In the quiet of his study, Alpha Trion rested a hand on the Covenant and said the name aloud but softly: "Optimus Prime."

The High Council had followed his advice. Now it only remained to be seen whether they—and the rest of Cybertron—had the courage and the strength to follow this new Prime.

And that, Alpha Trion considered, was still not a part of the Covenant he could understand. That particular future was murky, unsettled. What would become of Cybertron? The answer lay in the fortitude and will of two individuals: Megatron and Optimus Prime.

Which was, given the ambition and ideal that had driven them to this point, exactly the way it should have been.

Yet still Alpha Trion worried. Perilous times were ahead.

After the War of the Primes and the wrenching aftermath, I never expected to see Cybertron torn apart in this way again. I watched the Golden Age of Cybertron emerge and flourish. I watched our civilization reach out to other stars, and I felt certain that Primus could watch over us, his creations, with pride. Then I watched as the Golden Age peaked and began a slow decline into stasis . . . and where stasis comes, decay is never far behind. The Space Bridges carried fewer and fewer ships, and grew less and less reliable; the societies of Cybertron calcified along lines of social and vocational existence; what had been great about our civilization was lost. We staggered forward, one foot in front of the other, forgetting the aspirations that once had guided us ever upward and outward.

As the castes solidified and the Guilds arose to entrench themselves in the totalizing bureaucracy of this new Cybertron, I receded. Last of the Primes, final holdover from the previous great age, I took up my position in the deepest reaches of that monument to history, the Hall of Records at Iacon. Ages passed.

Cybertron perpetuated its state of monotony and social stratification. I kept records, I scratched the Quill I now hold in my hand over the diminishing number of empty pages in the Covenant of Primus.

And I tried to decipher those pages in the Covenant that addressed the approaching future. Unease was my constant companion then, and a sense of foreboding that kept me from taking pleasure even in those rare moments when some new bit of knowledge or understanding came from the depths of the archives . . . or from the analytical skills of the army of clerks deployed to monitor the billions of transmissions that stormed through the Grid with every passing cycle.

Entropy, or the consciousness of it, was my other companion. This was one reason why Orion Pax, with his dedication and tireless focus, stood out from the other clerks. He seemed to resist the robotic monotony of the data-harvesting enterprise; instead the size and scope of the task invigorated him.

Yet it was not for this that I came to realize that he was to become the next Prime.

It was a combination of observation, research, and raw . . . it is difficult for an archivist such as myself to say this . . .

Intuition.

Orion Pax seemed different. He was humble but certain, rigorous in completing his assignments yet unafraid to deliver results beyond or contradictory to the stated parameters.

And when he first began to discern that a few gladiators in the forgotten savagery of Kaon's pits were beginning to grow into something more—Orion Pax might have been expected to do one of two things. He might have ignored the data as irrelevant, thus confirming the caste bigotry that those gladiators hated. Or he might have passed on the information without comment to his superiors, who might also have ignored them out of caste bigotry or suppressed the dissent without investigating its origins.

Orion Pax did neither of those things. He investigated, analyzed, synthesized—and when that still did not satisfy him, he went to those who were dissatisfied. He learned.

He empathized. Unencumbered by the prejudices of his age, he chose to see clearly.

When I proposed to the High Council of Cybertron that Orion Pax was the Prime referred to in the Covenant—the Prime who would fight valiantly against the forces that would divide Cybertron in a civil war among Transformers—I felt certain I was correct, but I felt equally certain that the Council would not agree. In that I was wrong. Fortunately wrong, for if the High Council had not anointed Orion Pax the next Prime, the Autobot movement might have failed utterly. As it is, prospects for the survival of the Autobot resistance must be characterized as uncertain at best.

In the cycles following the confrontation in the Chamber of the High Council, the Decepticon uprising has spread quickly across the face of Cybertron. If the Decepticons succeed in their goal to take over Cybertron and subject it to their particular brand of anarchic tyranny, I fear that my identity will not remain secret for long. Should I be discovered, the records I leave behind will survive me. For this reason I am going to synthesize what I know about the events of the civil war as they unfold. I follow the example, in short, of the Prime I taught at first by my example.

The first battle of the war was contested at Fort Scyk, overlooking and protecting the city of Stanix. The Decepticons, led by Megatron himself at the head of a formation of Seekers, attacked without warning. The fort's garrison, grown lazy and bored with ages of monotony and caste rigidity, were overwhelmed almost immediately.

On the Grid feed from the top of the administrative complex in Stanix, the Decepticon assault first looks like a rain of meteors that stipple the walls of the fort with fire and cascading bits of molten wreckage. Then that feed cuts out as the Decepticons destroy the communications infrastructure of Stanix while their advance forces continue the assault on Fort Scyk.

The garrison fights bravely, but they receive no help. From inside the fort and along its walls, the bots rally to their positions under the pitiless lenses of the security cameras. The Decepticon Seekers, even without their leader Starscream, rain missiles down on the defensive positions. The return fire brings down some of the Decepticons; those who survive the crash and can reassume proto-form join the militia garrison in savage hand-to-hand combat. Defensive fire is a new rain from the walls.

The Decepticons fight hard but carefully. What they want is to take the fort and use it, not raze it. They eliminate the garrison, slowly at first and then much faster when their land-based bots arrive and mount an armored assault on Fort Scyk's main gate.

The gate explodes under the impact of an air-to-surface bunker-buster missile, delivered—I discover later—from space. Starscream is involved after all. Decepticon ground troops pour through, their gladiator instincts sharpened with military training administered in the pyramid at Kaon. They fight like seasoned warriors, which they are. The garrison never has a chance.

The officer of the militia in charge of Fort Scyk broadcasts alerts and alarms, but no help comes. No help was ever going to come. Optimus Prime is making the first difficult decisions of his leadership. He is recognizing that soldiers die, and that leaders of armies must sometimes allow them to die for greater goals.

If he cannot rescue the militia at the fort, Optimus Prime can at least use the time gained by the Decepticon assault. While they are occupied, he can rally his existing forces and do whatever time permits to rally undecided Cybertronians to the Autobot cause.

"Jazz," he says later, when he knows that Fort Scyk has fallen and its garrison has been destroyed, "I never wanted this."

"You didn't turn it down, either," Jazz points out.

They are in the Hall of Records. I can see them and hear them anywhere in that building, and it is a place Optimus Prime will return to as long as it exists. "How could I turn it down?" Optimus Prime responds.

"Might have been better than accepting a burden you know you can't carry," Jazz says.

"I can carry it." Optimus Prime says.

Jazz nods. "I believe you can. But not unless you stop grieving over every soldier who is going to die in this war. You'll never survive that."

"Jazz." Optimus Prime turns on his friend, a fierce light on his face. His passion is awakening, his consciousness developing to encompass the enormity and importance of his role. "I will grieve every Autobot and every innocent who dies. That is what separates me from Megatron."

"Only that?" Jazz asks.

Optimus Prime has no answer.

The Siege of Hydrax Plateau follows closely after the fall of Fort Scyk. The spaceport that sprawls across the plateau will be key to the war; both sides know this and, because of this knowledge, this battle is the first in which each side commits all the resources it can muster. The Decepticon ground forces come from two directions: the east, from Fort Scyk, and the south, from the Badlands that stretch all the way past Slaughter City to Kaon and beyond. It is Decepticon territory, all of it, even the treacherous and shifting surface of the Sea of Rust. The Autobots have no supply lines, no support from the uncommitted local population . . . What they have is will, and belief.

It is never going to be enough, but they fight as if it will.

The advance from Fort Scyk is blunted and turned back by a regiment under the leadership of the sergeant of the Council Guardians, a freshly pledged Autobot known as Ultra Magnus. Daring, strategically ingenious, and courageous to the point of recklessness, Ultra Magnus hammers back the Decepticon forces—literally, for his favored weapon is a hammer so charged with energy that its every blow releases electromagnetic pulses on a frequency that damages the sensory apparatus of his enemies.

Coming from Kaon, the Decepticons are not prepared for this weapon. Nor are they prepared for the battlefield savvy of Ultra Magnus. Despite having the advantage of numbers and better supplies of Energon, the Decepticon advance stalls. Meanwhile, a separate thrust, up from the south, cuts through that quadrant's Autobot defenders.

In this battle, Optimus Prime fights for the first time, kills for the first time, sees the deaths of friend and enemy on the battlefield for the first time. He is willing—too willing—to fight to the death. Only the influence of his old friend Jazz convinces him to make an intelligent retreat, saving his forces for later.

The first Decepticon he kills in his role as leader of the Autobots and potential savior of a free Cybertron is a former industrial drone, a low-caste worker named Drixco. Fighting through the main battle line with hand-to-hand expertise learned in the Blaster City arenas, Drixco is carving the Autobots to bits with his vibroblade. He meets Optimus Prime in a split between two angled iron planes, oxidized already with the heat of discharged armaments.

Optimus Prime looks up from a battle chart he has just received from Jazz, who immediately rejoined the battle, holding back a Decepticon advance over a ridge at the southwestern hook of the Hydrax Plateau. Streaking energy discharges crisscross the skies overhead. The Autobot position is precarious. Drixco vaults the dying body of an Autobot—who before the war was a maintenance worker at Six Lasers, and joined the Autobots because of the Decepticon attack on the park—and Optimus Prime sees him coming. He levels his ion cannon and blows Drixco apart, never knowing his name. Never knowing his reasons for pledging himself to the Decepticon insurgency. Never knowing Drixco's origin because all that mattered in the moment was his end.

After killing this anonymous Decepticon, Optimus Prime will realize that once and for all he has committed himself to the course of war.

He would have preferred—he always said this to me, and I believe it—he would have preferred to reason with the opposition, but that was never possible. And having killed once, he nearly felt that the killing was itself evidence that he was on the wrong side. For what right side in this conflict could demand the killing of fellow Cybertronians?

I do not think Optimus Prime has yet found that answer, or ever will.

By the end of the Siege of Hydrax Plateau, the leading members of Ultra Magnus's unit have already become known as the Wreckers, and Ultra Magnus has cemented himself as an indispensable link in the Autobot force.

None of this makes a difference to the course of events. In the end, the spaceport falls, and the Hydrax Plateau with it, and most of the Eastern Hemisphere of Cybertron falls into Decepticon hands. It will remain there, with the exception of a few skirmishes and brave but temporary incursions, for the duration of the war. The only unusual intelligence reported by the few Autobot spies who survive within the perimeter of the Decepticon territory is that Starscream seldom makes an appearance at the station. Apparently he spends most of his time with his Seekers garrisoning one of the Moon Bases and keeping an eye on Trypticon Station. It is not clear to anyone why this should be so.

Shortly after the Decepticon takeover of the spaceport, the Satellite Command Center at Polyhex falls to Megatron's forces as well. It is early days, but the Decepticons seem better organized and more willing to fight. It is possible that they have more support from the unallied sectors of the population. What is coming to Cybertron?

Perhaps I should not be surprised that Polyhex falls so soon after Hydrax and Fort Scyx. After all, Polyhex is the home of, and still the nerve center of political support for, the Minicon High Councilor Ratbat.

The next great loss of this war has come. Crystal City is no more.

I remember when it was built, by some of the greatest scientific minds of Cybertron—including Shockwave, now gone to the Decepticon side. It was his innovations in materials science that created Crystal City's signature stressed-crystal material and enabled the construction and use of it on a large scale. The first time I went there, it seemed a place fit for the Primes. I was saddened that I alone of the Primes remained on Cybertron.

And now it is destroyed. Megatron has invaded the heart of Cybertron's civilized area. He has gutted the beacon of our science. I fear for the future.

There is a new group within the Decepticons, calling themselves Constructicons. The ancient art of combining is as old as Cybertron itself but the Decepticons, under the guidance of Shockwave, have taken it to new and terrifying heights. Before the Grid submatrix in Crystal City failed, they announced themselves in a way as flamboyant as it was destructive—through the combined multicomponent form calling itself Devastator.

I believe Devastator has seven component Constructicons, but from the surviving records this is not certain. What is certain is that the combination into the Devastator form is terrible for the component Constructicons, diverting some of their intelligence to the maintenance of the combined form. The sum is thus less intelligent—though unimaginably more powerful—than any one of the parts.

Devastator loomed out of the periphery of the light spill from the Refracting Gardens of Crystal City, one of the most beautiful of all our civilization's creations. Larger than any mobile Transformer I have ever seen, it brought havoc, too, like no Transformer I have yet seen. It tore Crystal City's outer wall into glittering shards, a vast spray of shards that glittered as though electrified. Then it savaged the city's militia without much more trouble than it had had with the wall.

Behind it poured in the other Constructicons. I have seen combiners before, but this was the first time I had seen so many bots used to create such an awesome killing force. I have since learned that the scientist Shockwave had something to do with this Devastator's reconfiguration. I cannot say I am surprised, but I can say I am uneasy; if Shockwave creates too many more combiners like Devastator, I am not sure how the Autobots will stand against them.

The destruction of Crystal City was the most beautiful thing I have ever seen. The prismatic displays of its buildings and sculptures as they shattered under energy fire or the kinetic assault of fist and foot . . . it was like nothing ever seen in the universe before. The city is gone, and I mourn its passing, but if it was to be destroyed I am glad that its destruction was captured for future iterations of Cybertronians to see. Never has optic beheld such a display of colors, such a fusion of art and violence.

The Sensor Towers, observatories containing instrumentation designed for every spectrum of energy, collapsed in a flowering upsurge of silver, set off by the raging flames at their bases as the doomed defenders of Crystal City laid down heroic fire to slow the invading Constructicons as long as was possible.

But all was to be in vain, for behind the Constructicon vanguard came Megatron's legion of ex-gladiators. They fought as if their enemies were not just the Autobots protecting the city, but the city itself. Watching the feed from the Grid, I saw more than once a Decepticon disengage from the Autobot defense so it could assault the buildings and infrastructure of Crystal City itself.

Inside the warren of laboratories that ran below the surface, honeycombing the upper strata of Cybertron's crust right to the border of the Underworld, the fighting was fierce, single Autobot valiantly resisting individual Decepticon. Behind the bulldozing Constructicons, Megatron's forces burrowed ever deeper, rooting out the last resistance where they could.

And where they could not? There the Decepticons simply demolished entire quadrants of the city, collapsing them into mass entombments of the noble Autobot defenders.

I wonder if Megatron ever hesitated at such moments and considered how far from his ideals he had already fallen. It seems that he must have, since once he was so passionate about the value of every Cybertronian's life, no matter what caste or guild. How many lives has he extinguished now? How many more? I search the Covenant for answers, but it will not be definitive, and what hints I discover therein bring me to the edge of despair.

The Autobots have won their first incontestable victory in this war.

I pause to read those words again. Long have I wished to be able to write them.

Leaders on both sides have known for quite some time that as the war spread and the expenditure of munitions increased, new sources of energy would have to be found—or existing sources controlled. This led Optimus Prime and Megatron both to focus on controlling Kalis, with its Energon stores and the enormous subsurface fusion reactor upon which power supplies for Iacon depend.

When it became clear that they could not hold Crystal City, the Autobots began to fall back. Courageous and doomed volunteer units drew the main invading Decepticon force ever deeper into the labyrinth below the city while the Autobots rescued what they could from the laboratories and fell back toward the core of their ever-diminishing territory. They rallied at Kalis, knowing that if they could not at least arrest the Decepticon advance there, the war was lost.

Unlike the endless battles over the Hydrax Plateau and Crystal City, the Kalis contest is over with startling speed. Partially this is because—for reasons that are unclear—the Seekers under Starscream's control never join with the wheeled and tracked divisions of Megatron's force. Autobot strength in the air is poorer than Decepticon when Starscream's units are present; without him, that element of the battle tips in Optimus Prime's favor. This has proved telling in the battle for Kalis, as aerial support and suppressing air-to-ground missile fire enabled the Autobot defenders to consolidate their positions before Megatron could execute his standard plan of identifying a single weak point and pouring his forces at it until the Autobot lines broke.

This time the Decepticons suffered devastating losses before they could even get close enough to the perimeter of Kalis to engage the Autobot defenses directly. Here, it seems, a weakness of the Decepticons might at last have been identified. So many of their crack soldiers come from the gladiator corps, armed with only hand-to-hand weapons, that slowing their advance to melee distances results in quickly multiplying Decepticon casualties.

Optimus Prime identified this opportunity, and Starscream's absence enabled the Autobots to make the most of it. The result—I write it yet again—has been a clear and undeniable victory for the Autobots.

As well as their tactical victory over the Decepticon force as a whole, the Autobots won a number of critical individual battles—none more important than the brutal defeat inflicted on Bruticus Maximus by Sideswipe, Jazz, and Optimus Prime himself. By the time it was over, Bruticus had spontaneously decombined, and several of his individual Constructicons were badly damaged enough that some among the Autobots claim they will never be able to combine again. Sideswipe has gone so far as to claim that he tore the head from the focus of the combination process, the Constructicon known as Onslaught. To this observer, such claims (especially coming from the excitable and angry Sideswipe) smack of hyperbole, as much as I might wish them to be true.

What is doubtless true, however, is that the Decepticons were thoroughly beaten and driven back. Kalis remains in Autobot hands, and at least for the immediate future, Optimus Prime will have enough Energon at his disposal to keep the fight alive.

Beyond the immediate future, the outlook is less clear. Already the heady aftermath of Kalis is mixed with dire news from the south, out of the city-states of Tarn and Vos. It seems that Starscream's absence from the Battle of Kalis was part of a broader strategy . . .

I wrote before that Starscream was intentionally absent from Kalis. With time to reflect, I am now uncertain whether this reflects consensus among the Decepticons or an effort on Starscream's part to gain more control over Decepticon strategy. What seems clear is that Starscream is manipulating circumstances in some way.

The cities of Tarn and Vos, south of Kaon, have been troublesome for as long as they have existed. Somewhere in the archive, perhaps, one might find the reason for the feud that has erupted periodically between the two; but whatever the original cause, the feud is alive and well. Previous leadership, during the relative peace and bonhomie of the Golden Age, gave each city something to pacify it. Tarn was made the location of the State Games, the focus of Cybertronian sporting greatness; at Vos was installed the Cybertronian Air Command.

Tarn surrendered itself to the Decepticons with minimal resistance, its leaders even offering to root out Autobot sympathizers so the Decepticons could focus their energies elsewhere. Megatron, seeing an opportunity to create a model Decepticon city-state, installed the savage and ruthless Shockwave to oversee Tarn in the aftermath of its surrender. True to form (and angry at being removed from his experimental paradise in the ruins of Crystal City), Shockwave brutally suppressed every faint sign of discontent. Dissenters became fodder for his experiments, with results horrific enough that I will not reproduce them here.

At approximately the same time, with Starscream on unknown business at one or both of the near-orbit Moon Bases, Decepticon forces under the direction of Shockwave assumed control of Vos. Then, possibly as a way to curry favor with Megatron by demonstrating his absolute ruthlessness, Shockwave provoked both sides with a series of escalating minor attacks, for which he blamed resisting elements in either city. Finally he demanded that the elements of the Air Command remaining in Vos destroy those districts of Tarn he blamed for sheltering the resistance.

I have seen a barrage of photon missiles only twice. The first annihilated perhaps half of the surface area of Tarn, and with it any hope of an organized resistance. Almost before the fires had stopped burning, Shockwave captured the local Grid and used it to propagandize—Iacon had destroyed the city of Tarn in an unprovoked attack! See the savagery of the Autobots, who only wish to perpetuate the status quo of caste and tyranny!

And at the same time a second barrage of photon missiles—of unknown origin, according to Shockwave—destroyed practically every trace of the Air Command and the city of Vos. With its destruction, the military commanders who had formed the basis of Starscream's power are gone, and Shockwave positions himself as the second-in-command.

What Starscream's next move will be, I do not know. Clearly he will not let such a provocation pass unchallenged. Any dissent within the Decepticon leadership hierarchy serves the purpose of the Autobots. I encourage intra-Decepticon treachery.

I believe that an Autobot resistance still survives within Tarn. May they not fall prey to Shockwave's demented sense of scientific adventure. Also it seems that some of the surviving Seekers from the Air Command at Vos are presenting themselves to the Autobots, their trust in both Megatron and Starscream betrayed. This will prove useful in both military and propaganda senses.

And still Starscream spends most of his time in space. He has fought, yes. I have observed him over Hydrax and (briefly) Crystal City. Starscream is brave. Not even the most partisan of Autobots would suggest otherwise.

Neither would anyone suggest Starscream is not ambitious. He has a plan, I suspect. One wonders how much of it Megatron also suspects. Much of this story remains to be told; even the Covenant leaves it incomplete, insofar as I can tell.

In passing, because in light of the Tarn/Vos events it seems trivial, I note that Six Lasers Over Cybertron has been destroyed. No one seems to know why the Decepticons found it a worthy target, and there was never more than a token Autobot garrison.

The ruins of Crystal City have turned into fertile ground for Megatron. There he finds forgotten resources and technologies. Occasionally he discovers a bot who has not been seen for teracycles.

One such is Bruticus Maximus. Suspended with the other prototype combiners in a research field, Bruticus was considered a failed experiment. His components were of enough intelligence to be useful; but combined, the Bruticus-form was intellectually compromised, enough so to be considered a danger to allies as well as enemies. I have gleaned from the records that Shockwave himself was part of the original experimental team, and that it was Shockwave again who proposed raising Bruticus after he was sealed away. I would not be surprised if this is true, for Shockwave is as empty of morality and ethics as any Transformer who lives.

And it was the raising of Bruticus that led, indirectly, to the massacre at Nova Cronum, in which a generation of scientific minds was erased with no mercy or compunction.

Before that, the Decepticons turned their sights to the city-state of Praxus. It was here that Optimus Prime and the Autobots made their first all-out stand against the Decepticons. The smoke from that battle still hangs over the remains of Praxus. Neither side will ever know who won.

Early in the growth of the Decepticon movement, Praxus—with its progressive politics and its citizens' willingness to speak their minds—was a hotbed of pro-Decepticon agitation. Praxians were never a militant citizenry, however, and they were—I am certain—astonished and disappointed to see the self-aggrandizing turn that Megatron's efforts soon took. By the time Megatron began to view Praxus as a target rather than a base of support, Praxians were ready to fight against him.

It was this that turned the Battle for Praxus from an inevitable Decepticon rout to a war of attrition that ended in stalemate, with nothing left to fight over.

Everything that made Praxus a marvel of Cybertronian engineering is gone: the famous Assembly, where the great scientists presented their findings from their laboratories in Crystal City and Nova Cronum; the Helix Gardens, eternally turning in the invisible magnetic winds, their displays of genomic art and metalsoma showcasing the aesthetic brilliance of our Golden Age . . .

Gone. Burned away to nothing by the fury of ion

cannon and explosive missile, fusion bomb and vibroblade.

How many thousands died at Praxus, only the
Covenant knows. What is clear is that both sides
committed everything they had to the fight, and the
citizens of Praxus threw their support behind preserving Autobots against their former champions, the marauding Decepticons. All three parties—Autobot,
Decepticon, Praxian—paid a terrible price.

For the Autobots, two new leaders emerged who I
believe will prove useful to Optimus Prime in coming
battles: Prowl and Ironhide. The former militia and
police officer Prowl brings Optimus Prime experience
in urban combat operations; the barely contained
fury of Ironhide at the loss of his home gives the Autobots a pitiless edge that they will need if they are to
stand against Megatron. One of the eternal dangers
of war is that in defeating the enemy, you assume the
qualities of the enemy and thereby sow the seeds of
your own destruction. Ironhide walks the edge of this
peril without knowing it. He has, very slowly to be
sure but certainly, come to trust Optimus Prime as a
leader and warrior.

For megacycles, Autobot and Decepticon fought
back and forth over the rubble of Praxus. Neither
could hold an edge. Megatron's forces had the initial
edge in numbers and ferocity, but the Praxians went
over to Optimus Prime and in this battle, for the first
time in his leadership of the Autobots, Optimus Prime
stood and fought rather than fighting strategic with-
drawals in order to buy time for a more suitable
situation. Praxus was that situation. It was far

enough away from the pacified Decepticon territory that, for the first time, Megatron had the same supply-chain and Energon-replenishment concerns that Optimus Prime did. In fact it was at Praxus that the Autobots first had an advantage in Energon. Heroically, the Praxians denied themselves to the edge of death so that the Autobots could fight on.

Finally there was nothing left to fight over. Both forces, exhausted, fell back to positions on either side of the ruins. Scouts overflew their positions, looking for clues about whether the battle was to resume or be abandoned as a costly draw.

Knowing that they would never have a better situation to fight, save for an unthinkable confrontation within the city of Iacon itself, the Autobots stood ready to go on. Ratchet and the other medics made what repairs they could, and remaining Energon reserves were distributed equally, so that no Autobot would die unable to fight back.

The Decepticons, seeing that as long as a Praxian remained alive who would aid the Autobots they could not win on this ground, retreated. Their columns of Seekers, fearsome Constructicons, the hulking figure of Bruticus staggering from wounds that would have killed any five other Transformers . . . all vanished to the north and west, returning to the Badlands stronghold of the Decepticons. There they took some time to recover. So did the Autobots, falling back to the north and east in the direction of Iacon.

In the brief combat hiatus that followed, Megatron understood that the Battle of Praxus had taught him a lesson: No one was to be trusted when words turned to blows. If Praxus could turn against him—so said the captured Decepticons who were debriefed by Optimus Prime and Ironhide after the battle—then the time for converting the opinions of Cybertronians was past.

Henceforth, the captives warned, Megatron would fight without quarter, mercy, or interest in the support of the populations he sought to conqueror.

In other words, he had begun the final stage of the journey from revolutionary to despot.

And in reprisal for the stalemate at Praxus, Megatron sent a force into Nova Cronum, on the very borders of Iacon itself. I watched Nova Cronum grow over the ages, developing into a haven for philosophers and theoretical explorations. It was from the intuitive leaps of Nova Cronum that the applied discoveries of Crystal City were derived. Nova Cronum was the cradle of Cybertron's intellectual dynamism.

Now it is a ruined shell populated only by scavengers and ghostly memories, because in his fury at the Praxus outcome, Megatron slaughtered every sentient being in Nova Cronum, save those who would step forward and join the Decepticons on the spot. Those new conscripts have made a terrible choice, preferring to die on the battlefield rather than be massacred in their homes. And from a new command post set up in the ruins, Megatron oversees the next phase of his plan: a siege upon Iacon itself. He warns that there will be no quarter for any bot who resists.

Cybertron, why has it come to this?

* * *

Iacon itself has now been under siege for what must be millions of cycles.

As yet there has been no full-scale assault, for the city of Iacon possesses formidable mechanized defenses as well as its place in the forefront of Autobot identity. Every Autobot on Cybertron would lay down his life for Iacon, including myself. I have not fought in anger since a time that most Cybertronians consider mythical—but I would again, and gladly, and gladly I would die if it meant that Iacon would survive.

Yet it may not come to that, for thus far the ingenuity and bravery of Optimus Prime—combined with the tenacity of the Autobot forces under his command—have kept the Decepticons at bay.

The situation is dire, however. The subsurface power conduits traversing the distance between the great reactor at Kalis and the Capacitor Complex in Iacon are under constant threat. Teams of Autobots patrol below the surface, endangered not only by Decepticons but by increasing attacks from the creatures of the Underworld, which are perhaps emboldened by knowing that so much of the world above the surface has fallen into chaos.

In the city, at times the war seems far away—if one stays away from the Grid and ignores the convoys of alt-formed Autobots roaring from defensive position to defensive position as they respond to the Decepticons' constantly shifting probes. In places, art and music still happen. In the Hall of Records, a skeleton staff of clerks still harvests data, cataloging and indexing as Orion Pax once did. These are the invalid or damaged, who can no longer fight or who were designed without armaments. They are immensely proud that Optimus Prime rose from their ranks, and when he visited some cycles ago, it was as if one of the Thirteen had descended among them.

I permit myself these moments of humor. As I permit myself a small smile whenever I hear the clerks arguing about whether the Thirteen existed or are just another myth sprouted from the mists of antiquity.

Optimus Prime came to the Hall of Records seeking my counsel. It was immediately after the victory of Kalis. "Can we win, Archivist?" he asked.

We sat in my study, surrounded by the ebb and flow of data on the Grid. Below us, into the interior of the planet, stretched the Records and Archives, the entire history of Cybertronian existence. "Can we not?" I responded, to keep him talking.

"If I am destined to lose," he said, "and I keep fighting despite this destiny, how many of the lives lost are my responsibility?"

"Only a being that can see the future can answer such a question," I said.

The truth was that I had a very limited ability to do exactly that, because more often than not I could understand the material—if not the idiom—of what the Covenant had to say about the near future.

Yet I had no idea how to answer Optimus Prime's question.

"When I was a clerk I never had to worry about lives," he said.

At that I had to laugh. "It was never going to be any other way, Optimus," I said.

He looked at me, and then at the Covenant where it sat closed on my desk. Then he looked back at me.

For a moment I almost told him, almost unburdened myself of the secret I have carried for so long. But I could not. It was not his burden to bear, not when he had so much else that was more important. "I say that because I knew you were destined for something greater than being a data clerk," I said. "The caste system was rotting from within. Those of us willing to see knew that. All that was required was a few committed bots . . ."

"To start a war and trade castes for Decepticon tyranny?" he said, with a smile but not humor. "And along the way destroy the planet?"

"Cybertron will survive," I said. "It is larger and stronger than you can imagine. And if there has been war, perhaps it is because the alternative would have been worse. What if you had gone along with Megatron and then realized his tyrannical inclinations after it was too late to do anything about them? How much more costly and terrible would this war have been if it began when all of Cybertron was like Kaon? Or Tarn under Shockwave?"

For some time he did not speak. Always a thoughtful bot, was Orion Pax. He had not lost that quality upon his elevation to Optimus Prime.

"You spoke to the High Council," he said eventually.

I nodded. "But I did not have to. They would have reached their conclusion without me, if they had studied the situation."

"You do yourself an injustice, Alpha Trion," Optimus Prime said, using my name for the first time. "I think you know exactly how influential you are."

"I will recuse myself from this particular argument," I said. "And you, too, should avoid it. You have far more important things to do."

As he left my study, we were both stunned to see that the data clerks had come to the atrium outside, every single one of them. They stood in a double row, perfectly silent, having come just to see their former colleague and to pay their respects to what he had become.

For Optimus Prime it must have been a moment of intense and conflicting emotion. He has not spoken of it to me; since he left at that moment, he has been absorbed in the skirmishes around the perimeter of Iacon. The clerks glean every bit of data about his actions hungrily, as if it were Energon itself that they might nourish themselves with. Some of them would get up and fight if it were permitted, but as I have written, they are all either created not to fight or have been so damaged that field repairs cannot refit them for the battlefield.

And of course there is no immediate hope of rebuilding anything because the Tagan Heights area, and therefore much of the advanced industrial production of Cybertron, has been devastated in a long series of inconclusive battles, almost as long as the siege of Iacon.

From the beginning of the war, Autobot and Decepticon provocateurs waged a quiet war for influence over the factories and research laboratories of the Tagan Heights—and for the allegiance of their owners and the scientific elite that directed the research. As resources became scarcer and competition among the factories grew more intense and ruthless, the Autobot and Decepticon forces grew more aggressive in their efforts to control production. From there to open conflict was a short and inevitable step.

Ultra Magnus and his Wreckers have been crucial to the Tagan Heights saga, keeping the Decepticons at bay—at times, it seems, alone. Had they not been present when a reconstituted Devastator appeared on the battlefield again, the Autobots certainly would never have had the time to create their own combiner, the Protectobot Defensor. These two combiners have recently contested the battle largely between themselves, in the process reducing much of the industrial capacity of the Heights to ruins. Even the research facility where the combinatorial process for Defensor was perfected has become a casualty, blasted away by a frenzied series of blows as Devastators pursued a fleeing pair of Autobot Minicon saboteurs.

I do not know how long this war can go on.

Energon grows increasingly rare and precious. If many of the Tagan factories were not already destroyed, they would have had to be shut down for lack of power. It is all Optimus Prime can do to keep power flowing to Iacon. If Iacon falls, all is lost. The Autobot-controlled portions of Cybertron shrink yet more. We hold Kalis, and Iacon, and a few outposts elsewhere—but how much can be defended?

Tyger Pax is destroyed, and in an act so audacious that it borders on the suicidal, the Autobots have ejected the AllSpark from the body of Cybertron. It is gone, fired away into space. Orion Pax—sometimes I still think of him as my clerk instead of the Prime, the leader of the Autobots and herald of Cybertronian ideals, that he has become. So at times I call him

Orion Pax. Yet he is Optimus Prime. And he has another confidant, this brave enthusiast Bumblebee.

The Well of AllSparks seemed to have gone dormant for some time at the beginning of the war. Perhaps Primus, through the form of Cybertron itself, was expressing his displeasure, or his sorrow. This dormancy did not last, however, and when new Transformers began to appear, both sides in the war remarked that this generation overwhelmingly committed itself to the Autobot side. Among them was a fresh and invigorating youngster, known as Bumblebee. He has quickly made himself indispensable. Impetuous and aggressive, he longs for a leadership role. Yet he holds himself back, learning from Optimus Prime's two closest advisers: Jazz and the formidable Ironhide, long a skeptic of Optimus Prime's leadership qualities but lately one of his most dogged supporters. Those three form a triumvirate at the head of the Autobots—Optimus himself in control, of course, but the counsel and support of the other two is important to him. Bumblebee could have no better mentors.

And he will have none, for there will be no more Transformers created on Cybertron, not for as far into the future as I can see, or as I can decipher in the Covenant. Optimus Prime has ejected the AllSpark, to where no sentient being knows. And in doing so he has either saved the planet . . . or simply prolonged the inevitable here, and displaced the wrath of Megatron to wherever the AllSpark falls. I fear for the people of that place, if people there be.

This Bumblebee may yet be a great warrior for Cybertron. And perhaps the devastating experience he had at the fall of Tyger Pax will harden him, teach him, rather than break his will. The loss of one's ability to speak is terrible; when Megatron destroyed Bumblebee's vocoder, after Bumblebee had personally and heroically made sure that the AllSpark would escape Megatron's grasp . . . many a lesser bot would have quit the battlefield. Not Bumblebee. Silent now, he is testament to what is truly at stake here.

I do not think, upon reflection, that anything could break Bumblebee's will. This is something he has in common with Optimus Prime. It is the only thing that will save the Autobots, if anything will.

And now, perhaps, the definitive moment has come.

I believe that Megatron, no scholar by inclination but a keen student of treachery, has discovered exactly why Starscream had been so adamant about protecting Trypticon Station and keeping the Moon Bases within his sphere of influence.

With that discovery, the final phase of the Autobot-Decepticon War has begun. The Covenant predicted it and it has come to pass. The Decepticons will reach the height of their powers, and Optimus Prime will find his leadership qualities tested in ways he never could have imagined. There are hints in the Covenant that a long, dark time awaits Cybertron and that the fate of our planet will be decided . . . I cannot decipher it. Where?

Time will tell. Time, and the indomitable will of Optimus Prime.

. . . And with those lines, I consign myself fully to

the anonymity that has always been mine only in my fondest imaginings. In these times I cannot leave the planet that created me and has always been my home. But I can leave the role of Alpha Trion, perhaps. I can observe only. No longer will I influence.

Megatron had gladiators who would fight and kill
without question. He had officers who would admin-
ister captured territories, maximizing resource return
and minimizing the possibility of dissent or revolt. He
had planners who advised him well on topics related
to the battlefield.

But perhaps more important than all of them, he
had—thanks to the outlaw culture of Kaon and the
Badlands—a corps of data spies that outmatched
anything on the Autobot side.

This, like a number of the Decepticons' other unusual advantages over their Autobot adversaries, was
a result of what Shockwave likes to call invention.
His experiments are pitiless, cruel, and often devastating in their successes. This kind of inventive
attitude had created the Constructicons and the Com-
baticons, the multiform bots that even now were in-
filtrating Autobot positions and returning with
crucial information. It had, in previous generations,
created Trypticon itself. Or so the stories went. Megatron had his busy data moles ferreting out the truth of
those stories as well.

He was sick of fighting this war. It was time for the hostilities to end so Megatron could get on with his work of rebuilding Cybertronian society in the image he carried with him in his mind.

It would be a Cybertron in which every bot knew what to do—not because a group of Guildmasters and caste arbiters told them what to do, but because the Decepticon triumph had meant that every Cybertronian had a chance to find out what he was good at. Optimal efficiency, not externally imposed but internally derived.

Over the top of this structure would be enough authority to keep necessary functions alive even if they were unpopular. Megatron envisioned himself as the conductor, the executive of a great and smoothly operating corporate entity, with every Transformer on Cybertron acting as one cog in the great machine that produced and consumed what it needed according to rules Megatron understood.

The idealism of Orion Pax—or Optimus Prime; whatever he was called, it changed nothing about his essential nature—would have destroyed Cybertron just as effectively as the Guild and caste paralysis was destroying it. Megatron envisioned a different Cybertron, a powerful Cybertron once again exerting its influence across the stars, spreading to recover first contact with and then control over the lost worlds . . . and to do that, strong leadership was required. Individual self-determination meant nothing if all it led to was chaos. With Megatron in the lead as Prime, Cybertronians would find the galaxy theirs for the taking.

And they would take it.

Once, that is, the irritating obstacle of the Autobots was disposed of. For long ages—longer than Megatron had anticipated when the war started—the Autobots had hung on, barely keeping enough territory together for a meaningful base of operations. Their signal victories at Kalis and to a lesser extent at Tagan Heights had taught Megatron that he was going to have to make some changes in the way the Decepticons prosecuted the war.

It was past the time when raw force was going to win the war. Megatron knew this. So now he had intensified the search for ancient artifacts or knowledge that would offer a battlefield edge. He had unleashed Soundwave's minions and he had sent select Autobot prisoners to the dungeons beneath the city of Kaon, where those who had been maimed in the gladiatorial pits now rendered the Decepticons a different kind of intelligence-gathering service.

All of it gradually brought results, and those results multiplied . . . and now at last Megatron had Soundwave's most recent report, which was evidence that a great breakthrough was at hand.

The DataNet was protected by powerful security protocols, but eventually some of Soundwave's spies and information guerrillas had gotten past them to search in the forgotten corners of the archives . . . and one of them had come back with obscure references to the Sparks of Unicron.

Go back, Megatron had said. Keep digging.

They had, and now they had brought him the news that the Sparks of Unicron, left over—so the stories went—from the expulsion of Unicron from the body of the planet Cybertron, were known as Dark Energon.

Every principle had an opposite. Energon, the source of all that gave the Transformers life and motion, had its opposite principle as well: Dark Energon, which conveyed great power . . . but at an unknown cost. The ancient texts warned against it, but Megatron had never believed those warnings to be anything more than superstitious jabber. Now, it seemed, he had reason to believe otherwise.

If this was true, Megatron thought that he might at last have found a way to crush the Autobots and the treacherous Optimus Prime once and for all.

Yet he still did not know what Dark Energon was. The archives hinted at surviving bits of Unicron himself, once dancing through near space around Cybertron, coalescing into clouds dense enough to harvest. Ancient Cybertronians had known that this material was dangerous—as Unicron himself had been dangerous—and they had sequestered it . . . inside Trypticon Station, built specifically for that purpose.

Dark Energon, according to what fragmentary sources there were, was both power source and somehow a link to the essential nature of Unicron. In the way that Primus granted his essence via the AllSpark, Unicron's destroyed physical existence found expression through the forbidden flow of Dark Energon.

That also explained why Starscream had been so reluctant to come down to the surface.

It was time, Megatron decided, to have a conversation with his Seeker lieutenant and make sure he

knew that the Decepticon movement was still firmly in Megatron's control.

"They have found it," Alpha Trion said, in the solitude of his study.

Never had Dark Energon been put to use. Never had anyone seriously considered it. That was because Alpha Trion had scrubbed through the records in the DataNet and destroyed as much as he could find of the original expedition reports, filed by the scientific teams who had gathered and sequestered the Dark Energon long, long ago.

It was the one act in his life about which Alpha Trion felt deeply guilty. Never before or since had he destroyed records in the DataNet, but on this one occasion he had felt it was necessary. He had seen only dire consequences if the existence of Dark Energon was discovered.

Perhaps he was about to be proved wrong. Optimus Prime was demonstrating himself to be a stronger and more resilient leader than even Alpha Trion had dared hope. The early doubters in the Autobot faction were now firmly behind him—with the kind of passing quarrels natural to any command structure. Optimus Prime's chosen circle of advisers might challenge his thinking or his tactics, but they never challenged his leadership. That was the only reason the war had lasted as long as it had, and Iacon had survived as long as it had.

Unless the Decepticons could harness Dark Energon without letting it destroy them. Then the return of the Primes would be the only thing that would save the Autobots—and Cybertron itself.

Optimus Prime and his cadre of trusted lieutenants—
Prowl, Bumblebee, Ironhide, Jazz—were going to need
some education about the nature of what they were up
against. Then, in Alpha Trion's opinion, they were
going to need a stroke of good fortune. Perhaps
several.

Apart from Optimus Prime's able leadership, the
best thing the Autobots had working for them was
the tendency of Megatron to overreach. If they could
encourage him to keep doing that, it was possible that
he would destroy himself. Alpha Trion remembered
how even the Primes were destroyed by some of their
number who could not stop themselves from over-
reaching. Sometimes it seemed to him that the entire
history of Cybertron was driven by individuals who
demanded more than they were able to have, and
turned their frustration into anger that drove them
mad.

Now they fought over a planet missing its AllSpark,
drained of much of its Energon, large parts of its surface laid waste . . . to the victor go the spoils, thought
Alpha Trion sadly. All that will be left is the minds
and Sparks of subjugated Cybertronians if the Decepticons have their way.

He got up to go meet the upstart leaders of the Autobot resistance. Odd, thought Alpha Trion. The
forces that once were derided as tools of the oppressive hierarchy of caste and Guild now are the Under-
gound, the guerrilla resistance, the last hope of liberty
fighting an oppressive hierarchy. War had a way of
creating paradoxes like that. It could make enemies
of brothers, murderers of lovers, heroes of the in-
significant, and cowards of the mighty.

And that, mused Alpha Trion, was just if you took the Primes as examples.

With all of Cybertron afflicted, the possibilities were endless. And most of them were bad. Those few who shone in times of war, though . . . if the history of Cybertron was any judge, leaders who proved themselves to be valiant and honest in wartime would not abandon those principles in times of peace.

Nothing was certain, however, least of all the proposition that any of them would live to see a time of peace. If Dark Energon was now in play, however it was going to come into play, then things were even less certain. For no living Cybertronian knew what effect Dark Energon would have on those who used it and on those they fought.

CHAPTER SEVENTEEN

Starscream met Megatron in Trypticon's main cargo bay. His Air Commanders flanked him, their collective posture just barely respectful enough not to be hostile. "A welcoming committee," Megatron said. "Consider me welcomed and show me what you've been hiding up here."

"I'm not sure that's a good idea," Starscream said.

"I am sure that I did not ask you what you thought," Megatron answered. He, too, had a retinue of handpicked guards. If there was to be a fight, it would be decisive. Both Starscream and Megatron knew it. Neither was sure he wanted to commit to a decisive confrontation.

"How long have you known about this?" Megatron asked.

"I still don't know exactly what it is," Starscream said. "The Air Command knew well before the war started that there was something on Trypticon Station, but we did not know what. Neither did the crew working on the station. That's why we set up an orbital command post at Moon Base One, to keep an eye on it while we made sure the Autobots didn't get control of orbital space."

Megatron nodded throughout this charade of an explanation. "And you did all of this without seeing the need to inform me," he said.

"I don't apologize for that," Starscream said. "A wrong turn early in the war might have turned things permanently in the Autobots' favor. What if you had used the Dark Energon and it crippled you, or crippled the corps of troops who fought the crucial engagements in the great battles early on? We would be dead or imprisoned."

"Or," Megatron said, barely keeping his mounting fury in check, "we might have already won without laying waste the surface of the planet to do it."

"You would have been willing to take that chance?" Starscream shook his head. "I don't think so. Now you look back and only see that it might have worked. At the time all you wanted to do was sack cities and kill Autobots. If the stories about Dark Energon are true, it would have turned your delicate gladiator sidekicks there into a scourge the likes of which Cybertron has never seen. So what if we had won the war in that way? What would be left to win?"

Megatron seized Starscream around the throat and hoisted him up into the air. "I could break the head from your shoulders, and then you wouldn't have these difficult command decisions to make," he said. "Or you could pledge to me that you are understanding the errors you have made, and swear that you will not make them again."

"There's another possibility," Starscream said.

Megatron waited. Starscream dangled at the end of his arm, no fear on his face. Never had Megatron wanted to kill another bot so badly. But he couldn't risk losing the Seekers.

"You could quit showing off for the audience and let me do what I can do to win this war," Starscream said. "This isn't a gladiator pit. No one is going to give you—or me—a thumbs up or down. You want to win the war? If you do, you're going to need me. And I'm too far in on the Decepticon side to switch now. You think you don't trust me? Imagine how the librarian feels."

"So because you're not trustworthy enough for my enemies, you're saying, you are trustworthy enough for me. Do I have that right?" Megatron asked.

Starscream couldn't nod the way Megatron was holding him, but he tried. "Yes."

"I can win this war without you, Starscream. Make no mistake about that," Megatron said, and dropped him. He landed on his feet. "But I would rather not undertake the additional complications that would require. Now, show me the Dark Energon and let us put it to use."

"The problem is that no one living knows exactly what Dark Energon might do," Starscream said.

"Then let us find out," Megatron said.

He looked around at the assembled Decepticons waiting to see what the next move would be. The main shipping bay of Trypticon Station was no place for a serious conversation, Megatron thought. And although it might be a perfect place for a public dressing-down of Starscream, he was not yet sure that course of action was the correct one.

So, for the moment, he was content to let the conversation continue under the watchful eye of the three groups present: Seekers, gladiators, and Trypticon's research crew.

"Show me where it is kept," said Megatron.

Starscream did not move. "I haven't even seen it for myself yet," he said. "I have left it up to my scientific crew, to Bitstream and Hotlink."

"This is why I am leading and you are following," Megatron said. "You let your subordinates dictate your actions."

"I ensure long-term success by not focusing too intently on satisfying short-term desires," Starscream said. "And perhaps you have noticed that the Dark Energon is here, waiting for you, when I have had access to it since the beginning of the war. Consider that, Megatron, before you start with the veiled accusations."

"Perhaps I should unveil them," Megatron said.

"Then I will, too. You consider me a potential traitor? Very well. I cannot change your suspicious nature and have no interest in trying. I have kept the Dark Energon until I was certain what it was and that we could make use of it."

"Lies," Megatron said. "You kept it until Soundwave's spies found out about it."

Starscream gave him a pitying smile. "And you think I did not know Soundwave's little Minicons were looking?"

"Enough jousting. Show it to me."

"It's in quarantine right now," Starscream said. "I leave them alone; they report to me about what they find out. It's been a long, long time since this station was investigated thoroughly. The only bots alive who know what's in there are the ones working in the Hall of Records. Maybe."

"Does that mean Orion Pax knows?" Megatron asked.

Starscream shrugged. "He might. He was there a long time, and since the siege of Iacon we know he has consulted with the Archivist Alpha Trion about strategic matters."

"You know this how?"

"Because I do, Megatron. Because you're not the only one with spies."

Megatron came closer, facing Starscream down, but Starscream yielded no ground. "We fight together, or we fight each other. Make your choice now," Megatron said.

"Do you question my commitment, Megatron?" Starscream's voice was soft. "Dark Energon has been here. I have not used it for myself, have I? I have not fueled my Seekers with it. If it is everything it is said to be, I might have seized control of the Decepticons—of Cybertron itself!—from you had I used it. Now why do you think I did not?"

Megatron said, "Because you were smart enough to be afraid of it."

"Ah," Starscream said. "The compliment that twists like a blade in the vitals. A diplomat's skill, Megatron. I would not have expected a gladiator to have it."

"I should have expected that you would," Megatron said. "And I should have expected you to be surprised that I would. You pretend Decepticon allegiance, Starscream, but you are as much a creature of caste as any Autobot pretender."

"And you are a creature of the pits. Not because of your caste, but because you see everything as if it happens under the eyes of Cybertronians hungry for either your Energon or someone else's." Starscream stood aside and executed a mock bow. "Trypticon awaits you, Megatron. Try not to destroy it—and all of us—while you take what you want."

"Now Megatron is on Trypticon Station, too," Prowl said. "What are they doing up there?"

Optimus Prime had gathered everyone together in what had become, informally, his command post: one of the reading rooms in the Hall of Records. It had a high ceiling and narrow arched windows that lent it an air of serenity much to be desired in the middle of a war. He felt he could think clearly here, and more than anything else, that would prove to be the difference between him and Megatron.

If the war was still able to be influenced at all. Alpha Trion would not say what was in the Covenant, and Optimus was not presumptuous enough to demand a look for himself. So he forged ahead in uncertainty.

"I'm afraid there's something on Trypticon Station that Megatron is going to try to turn into a weapon," he said.

"What?" Jazz asked. Bumblebee added his question signal, which was a cocked head and clicking noise.

"I don't know," Optimus Prime said. "Those records are either lost or destroyed. But there are hints that it was something the Ancients feared might destroy Cybertron if it were used in the wrong way. Alpha Trion?"

The Archivist made his way into the room. "I came down to share with you, ah . . . well, share with you the fact that I cannot share with you everything I would wish to." He reached the reading table, now repurposed as a flat space for the piling of maps, sketches, charts, reports, and the other written flotsam of command. "What do you know of Energon?"

"Time for school?" Jazz asked incredulously. "Now?"

Prowl tapped him on the arm. "Shut up, Jazz. If Alpha Trion's saying it, it's important." He looked at the Archivist and said, "Energon is . . . I don't know. It keeps us alive but I don't know what it is."

"Correct. You don't." Alpha Trion looked around at all of them. "Few Cybertronians do, and of those few, most are mistaken. Energon is in fact an emanation of Primus, the way that Cybertron itself is what remains of the physical form of Primus. It is a different form of that which makes up you and me and everything else found on this planet."

There was a pause.

"I still don't think I know what it is," said Jazz with a laugh. Prowl and Ironhide laughed, too.

"Enjoy the joke while you may," Alpha Trion said. "But consider this as well. If Energon is the emanation of Primus, what do you suppose the comparable emanation of Unicron might be? And what if some of it still exists?"

Optimus Prime was looking up through the high windows into the latticed slices of visible sky. Was that what the Decepticons were hiding on Trypticon

Station? Some kind of . . . Un-Energon? A fuel and nutrient Sparked by Unicron rather than Primus?

What would such a substance do to the user?

"If there is such a thing, and the Decepticons begin to use it," he said, "they won't be like us anymore, will they?"

Alpha Trion stopped and thought about it. "They would be sickened versions of us," he said after due consideration. "They come from the Well of AllSparks just as we did, and from the material of Primus just as we do. In the end, if this Dark Energon—for so I have seen it referred to in some obscure and ancient records—if this Dark Energon is what they are hiding, then its use will eventually destroy them. Anything derived from Unicron is ultimately fatal to life and growth. This would be no exception."

The Archivist paused then, and this time the pause lengthened as everyone around the table considered the consequences of this development. "But before it is fatal," Alpha Trion concluded, "it might well enable them to destroy us all."

There had been a pause in the war, as if both sides were allowing themselves to breathe before starting the next campaign. Optimus Prime thought he knew what was coming next. Iacon had been under siege for long enough that the Decepticons either had to finish it off or abandon the siege and fall back to their strongholds in the Badlands and in the south. In front of him he had a map of Iacon, and in his head he held an image of the vital connection between the reactor at Kalis and the energy-hungry Autobot capital.

If Dark Energon was what Alpha Trion said it was, then the invasion of Iacon would be coming sooner rather than later. Optimus Prime had the impression that the Decepticons would use this new resource as shortsightedly as they had everything else they came across. They plundered and destroyed, letting their voracious appetites for Energon deplete the sources of that life-giving fuel. More than once Optimus Prime had speculated that the war might be ended not by either side winning on the field of battle, but by neither side being able to continue because they lacked the Energon to go on.

Now the discovery of Dark Energon looked to have changed that calculus.

"What can we do?" he asked Alpha Trion.

"We can do two things," Alpha Trion said. "Either try to destroy Trypticon Station, or realize that our short-term strategy involves surviving the onslaught of Dark Energon and then counterattacking when it runs out. The universe demands balance. Nothing can grant increased strength and ferocity if it does not exact a price later."

"Great," Jazz said. "All we have to do is not get exterminated by super-Decepticons? Count me in."

"We need to change the ground of the battle," said Ironhide.

Optimus Prime was nodding. "That's what I was thinking. What we need to do is make sure they use up this Dark Energon, if they really have it, as fast as we can make them."

"I'm sick of this running," Sideswipe said. "Sick of it! When do we stand and fight?"

"When we can win. No sooner, no later." Optimus Prime looked at these, his most trusted comrades. He did not want to waste their lives, or the lives of any Autobot. "While they have Dark Energon and we don't, our priority has to be leveling the battlefield. So we strike them, make them chase us and waste their energy. Then when it is gone, we strike again, harder. Alpha Trion, will they invade Iacon because they have Dark Energon?"

"The Covenant does not say, Optimus. You know that," Alpha Trion said. "But if you are asking me for an opinion, I will tell you that I think the final invasion of Iacon is coming sooner rather than later. I do not think, however, that Megatron will mount a full-scale invasion before he has locked in a sufficient supply of Energon. Dark Energon will be exhausted soon enough that he will not be able to count on it."

"So what do we do?" Jazz asked. Bumblebee added an interrogative gesture.

Optimus Prime thought about it. "We create guerrilla teams. Each of you will head one."

"Something interesting here," Prowl said as he came in from the Grid nexus below Alpha Trion's study.

"You're heading one, too," Optimus Prime said.

"One what?"

"A guerrilla team to work the Decepticons over and force them into wasting their Dark Energon chasing us."

"Right," Prowl said.

Optimus Prime ran through a list of other personnel he would want on these teams, but before going too much further with that he wanted to hear what Prowl had brought back from the DataNet. "Now what were you talking about? Interesting what, interesting how?"

"Interesting because it's a communication from Starscream," Prowl said. "He proposes a meeting."

Looking over the communications Prowl indicated, Optimus Prime saw that Starscream was in fact suggesting that they meet. There were two possibilities here, as far as he could see. The first was that Megatron was using Starscream's reputation for unchecked ambition as a way to set up an ambush. The second was that Starscream genuinely did want to meet, which could only be because he was trying to keep open the possibility of defecting to the Autobots.

And that could only mean that he thought there was a possibility the Autobots might win this war.

Optimus Prime was not sure how this could be possible. Therefore his instinct was to believe that the suggested meeting was a trap of some sort.

"I'll go," Prowl said. Bumblebee stepped foward and indicated his desire to go with Prowl, but Optimus Prime was already shaking his head.

"No, I can't afford to lose either of you," he said. "And it's not a good idea to meet him. Prowl, send him a message. Tell him to get somewhere that has a communication channel that he can absolutely trust. If he wants to talk to me, that's how it's going to happen." Optimus Prime headed for the door. "I'll be in the Hall of Records."

Back in his old workstation, surrounded by the terminals and screens and interfaces that for so long had been his, Optimus Prime reflected for a moment on how far he had come. How far he had been forced to go, was another way to put it. The channel to Starscream was open, protected by the best security that Alpha Trion and the Records Authority Guildmasters could put together, and awaiting only the presence of Starscream himself.

Optimus Prime allowed himself to consider a possibility that seemed so outrageous that it was a waste of time to contemplate. What if Starscream wanted to switch sides? The addition of him and his Seeker contingent would help the Autobot cause immensely. Whether it would be enough to swing the balance of the war away from the Decepticons . . . that was hard to say. But it sure wouldn't hurt their chances.

An interface pinged and Optimus Prime patched himself into it. Without ceremony Starscream said, "Two things. One, if you don't know what Dark Energon is, you need to find out. Two, I need to know what I can expect from you if something should happen to Megatron."

With no time to react, Optimus Prime said, "A just peace is what I'm looking for."

There was the faintest hint of hesitation in Starscream's voice before he answered. "Understood," he said.

The connection broke off, and Optimus Prime wondered what, exactly, Starscream thought had been understood.

The die is cast, thought Starscream. There were two things left to do, two assets left to put into play. He had to do some hard and exact thinking about how best to use each. "Hotlink," he said to his tech engineer, an old Air Command mainstay. "Eliminate all records of that channel. Then destroy the server."

Then it was time for a quick trip to Kaon. On the way, Starscream did a flyby of the ruins of Altihex Casino, remembering those first days of the war, when it could still be called something else. He had guarded Sentinel Prime, making sure that the other Decepticons didn't get carried away during the course of their operation. And since then, by default as much as by design, the Air Command had been in charge of Sentinel Prime. From time to time, Megatron seemed to want to drag the old Prime off and torture him to death, or something equally unseemly. Starscream wanted no part of such a plan. His idea was to keep Sentinel Prime until he was needed as a bargaining chip, perhaps a ransom trade for a valuable Decepticon fallen into enemy hands.

On this, as on everything else, Starscream and Megatron disagreed. The compromise arrived at seemed to be that Starscream would keep Sentinel Prime locked away in Moon Base One, and Megatron wouldn't get any vindictive ideas until after the war was won.

Today Sentinel Prime was standing quietly in his cell, back to the door. He did not move or react when Starscream walked in. "You Autobots believe in redemptive action, atoning for failures of will, things like that, right?" Starscream asked.

"I am not an Autobot," said Sentinel Prime. "I am Prime. I ally myself with no movement."

"Fair enough. But if I gave you a chance to make up for being such a coward at Altihex, you'd take it."

Sentinel Prime rounded on Starscream, who took a reflexive step back despite the shackles binding Sentinel Prime's arms to the sides of his torso. "You dare?" growled Sentinel Prime.

"I do dare," Starscream said, recovering his aplomb. "You were a coward. You ran away from a fight instead of protecting the people who trusted you to lead." He stepped right up to Sentinel Prime's face. "Why do you think I decided to commit to the Decepticons?"

To his surprise, this last question made Sentinel Prime grin.

"Just how committed are you to the Decepticons, Starscream?" he asked softly. "From what I hear, that's an open question around here."

Starscream chuckled. "From what you hear? And what, exactly, do you hear in your cell?"

Sentinel Prime laughed right back in Starscream's face. "What don't I hear? You would be surprised, I think, at how much information one gleans from the way one is approached by one's inferiors. Every interaction I have with an interrogator, or a tech come to replenish my Energon, or the drone that comes through to clean . . . add those up over billions of cycles and I know exactly what is going on. Both on this Moon Base and, I suggest, inside your head."

Sentinel Prime took a step back, then continued. "A long, long time has passed since you brought me here. I am not the same being I was then. Time and solitude are great teachers."

"Not a coward anymore, then? Is that what I hear you saying?"

"Unshackle me and I will answer you," Sentinel Prime said calmly.

"I will certainly keep it in mind," Starscream said. He left Sentinel Prime there and returned to the command module at Moon Base One. There were missions to plan, Autobots to tyrannize, and one particular special project that was going to be a little more complex than he had originally thought.

It also was going to be quite a bit more rewarding.

Megatron's voice boomed from Starscream's internal audio receiver. "Where are you?"

"Moon Base One," Starscream said smoothly.

"Retrofitting and getting repairs done while you figure out what to do with all that Dark Energon."

"Interesting you should mention Dark Energon. Return to Trypticon. There are things you should see."

CHAPTER NINETEEN

There might have been several ways to pacify the staff and crew of Trypticon Station. Megatron might have announced his presence—but they already knew he was there. He might have made an example of a few of them—but the problem with that was you never knew when the example might turn into a name for a resistance to rally by. Or he might have simply left things as they were, under Starscream's control, and pushed on with the war the way it was going. He could not bring himself to do this, though. Not when the potential rewards of Dark Energon were right there for the taking, and when Starscream needed to be taught a lesson.

The only solution, then, was to treat Trypticon Station as if it were a military objective containing a valuable resource.

The Decepticon Gladiator Corps raged through the corridor and laboratories of Trypticon Station, under strict orders to preserve the station's structural integrity as well as to keep intact all of its laboratories and sealed storage areas. But those rules of engagement said nothing about the Transformer workers.

Few of them fought. Those who did were destroyed before they could assemble anything resembling an organized resistance.

Before the station completed an orbit around Cybertron, it was utterly in Megatron's hands.

This is what Starscream discovered when he jetted back from Moon Base One and landed in the command bay. Megatron stood on the command deck with Shockwave. He motioned Starscream to join them.

Starscream had already noticed that none of the personnel in place when he left Trypticon was still there when he returned. "Megatron. Where have all the crew gone?" he asked.

"I am ensuring loyalty," Megatron said. "Those were your bots, Starscream. When you made them loyal to you, you made them dangerous to the Decepticon cause. Something needed to be done."

"You don't know how to run this station. Neither does he," Starscream said, pointing at Shockwave.

"I am an experimentalist first, and theoretician second," Shockwave said. "This much is true. But as Tarn and Vos found out, I am capable of some activity in applied areas as well."

Starscream looked to Megatron for confirmation of whether the implied threat in Shockwave's response was his alone. "Our doctor here is an asset in a number of areas," Megatron said.

"Does he know anything about Dark Energon?"

"Interesting question," Shockwave said. "Would any of your staff care to begin my education about this marvelous substance? They were very reluctant to talk to me when you were not present."

It is happening, Starscream thought. Megatron and his sycophants are about to destroy everything that we have created because they have bought into the delusion that everything should be what they want it to be.

He left the command module and strode quickly in the direction of the main science lab, situated for its protection—and that of the crew—at the far end of the station, where it hung out in a bulb away from the main Trypticon structure. Guards, the typical ex-gladiators favored by Megatron for direct physical work, confronted him at checkpoints installed since he had left for his trip to Moon Base One. Starscream thrust them aside without a word. When the space was too confined and the guards obstructed his way, he beat them down and went on.

In the lab, every inanimate and nonsentient object was as it had been before. None of Starscream's staff was present, neither the original Trypticon scientific crew nor the attachés Starscream had installed from the officer corps of the Cybertronian Air Command. The new crew had the look of imports from Polyhex and Nova Cronum. These were the Decepticon science and engineering elite, who had changed sides rather than face destruction along with their prewar society. None of them had anything to say to Star-scream beyond the bare minimum required by proto-cols. "Where is my staff?" he asked a tech operating a centrifuge.

"I didn't do it," the tech said.

Starscream reached out and crushed the centrifuge with one hand. "Make me ask again," he said.

The tech still would not look him in the face, but he pointed to a sealed door labeled CLEAN ROOM.

"See how smooth things are when you answer questions?" Starscream said. He went to the door and touched the stud on its control matrix to open the viewing panel.

Inside, lining the walls, were the remnants of the scientific and engineering crew that had served aboard Trypticon Station since before the war. Some of them looked wounded. All of them looked terrified. They were restrained and their vocoders brutally torn out, dropped haphazardly among the clean-room tables and equipment.

Too soon, Starscream thought. It's too soon to put the plan into effect. Yet if Megatron is already doing this, going to such lengths . . . how much longer would it be before the entire Decepticon movement destroyed itself in an annihilation of ego and mad, grasping ambition?

"Well," Megatron said at his shoulder.

Starscream waited. When Megatron did not go on, he said, "Well, what?"

"Well, this is what happens when your superiors find that they cannot trust you, Starscream. They remove your responsibilities." Megatron opened the door. "Come inside."

Accompanied by Shockwave, they entered the clean room. "Regrettable, the amount of violence necessary to quell resistance on this station," Shockwave said.

"Who would have expected scientists to fight?" Megatron added.

Starscream saw through it. They were taunting him. There had been no resistance, and he knew it, and they knew he knew it. But he could not prove it. They were deliberately lying to him and rubbing the fact of the lie in his face.

I accept this, he thought. Because I have to at this moment. But I will not forget it.

"Now, Shockwave," Megatron said. "What you see around you is a great machine, an orbiting drone, yet perhaps there is potential for a bit of Spark within."

"And where am I supposed to get Spark? The Well produces Sparks no longer."

Megatron turned, drawing Shockwave with him. "Do not each of these have a Spark?" he asked, taking in the shackled prisoners with a sweep of his arm. "I would think there's more than enough material here for a scientist of your skill and aptitude."

The prisoners, all of them loyal Decepticons working under Starscream's orders, looked shocked. If they had not been gagged they would surely have cried out.

Starscream himself, standing at Megatron's shoulder, could not bring himself to look.

Shockwave, however, could. A light of diabolical interest shone in his face as he looked over these new materials his master had provided for his work. Strong, well-tested soldiers, in a variety of alt-forms . . . "Yes," he said. "Yes."

"Starscream, pick two of them," Megatron ordered.

"Why?"

"Unless you would rather test the Dark Energon on yourself?" Megatron prompted.

Starscream hesitated. Megatron watched. He thought briefly that this last provocation might have pushed Starscream too far, which would have been regrettable; he did not want to destroy the Seeker. All he wanted was control.

Starscream pointed two fingers. "Bring them," Megatron said. "And come with me."

The Dark Energon Facility had been retrofitted from a laboratory once used to create new isotopes of radioactive elements. It protruded from the main Trypticon hull, balancing the clean-room laboratory on the other side. Starscream had let Hotlink and his staff oversee the conversion, so when he entered the Facility with Megatron, Shockwave, and the two experimental subjects, it was the first time for all of them, unless one of the two crew members had been there before. Starscream did not know either of them.

The scientist in charge of the Dark Energon Facility was, of course, Shockwave, but since he knew nothing about Dark Energon and was not an utter fool he had delegated much of the hands-on running of the Facility to one of Starscream's scientific officers, Autoclave.

"You have been chosen for a great honor," Megatron said to the two selectees, whose names he did not know and had no interest in learning. "Not only are you going to be spared the creative ministrations of Shockwave's mutation engineering, you are going to enter the history of Cybertron as the first of the Decepticons to experience Dark Energon."

Immediately the two subjects began to struggle against their bonds and make as much noise as was possible given the gags that muffled their mouths. Megatron's guards dragged them to hanging restraints set next to one wall and fastened them there. "What we'll do is give them just a little taste at first, and record all vital signs as well as whatever responses they have to offer. Science, now, remember," he lectured the subjects, who thrashed against their new restraints. "You are in the vanguard of research that will win the war."

His tone light and his demeanor practically chipper, Shockwave went to a magnetically sealed case and withdrew a small rack of ingots, each of which glowed a rich violet. The ingots on the rack were of two sizes, one approximately what an average allotment of Energon would be and the other perhaps one-tenth as much. The rack held six of each. "Refining this from its original state must have been quite an endeavor," he said to Autoclave.

"We succeeded," Autoclave answered, making no effort to be polite or to acknowledge the shifted balance of power on Trypticon and within the Decepticon hierarchy.

Starscream watched as Shockwave registered the insult and then decided not to respond to it at the moment. "Of that we shall soon be certain," he said, and then approached the two subjects.

A guard opened the Energon input housing of each as Shockwave approached. With deft, practiced motions, Shockwave deposited one of the small ingots into the intake slot of each bot's feeder.

The effect was instantaneous. Starscream would never forget it. Both subjects spasmed as if an EMP wavefront had just passed through the lab—but then, instead of crumpling limply as they would have done in the aftermath of an EMP attack, they flexed their limbs and snapped the restraints out of the laboratory wall. Megatron's guards tackled them and tried to hold them down, but they were inflamed with the power of Dark Energon and they flung the guards aside with ease. Automatic defenses in the lab deployed, firing gyro-inhibitors and magflash canisters into the testing area. Starscream flinched away from the nauseating effects of both discharges, which leveled not only the Darkened test subjects but Megatron's guards and the two closest scientists, Autoclave and Shockwave. The test subjects lay on the floor scrabbling, trying to get their balance back; the other five bots in the area of effect were completely limp.

"You see, Starscream? They have Dark Energon. They're stronger, their will is greater, their resistances are tougher." Megatron had observed the entire process from across the testing floor, but now he lost his patience. He strode forward and seized a large ingot of Dark Energon from the rack, not bothering with the tongs. It burned coldly in his palm. He slotted open one of his intake ports and clicked the ingot into place.

It was as if he had been raised to the power of infinity. Every molecule in his body sang a high, angry, joyous song—joyous at the strength it felt and the violence it could do, and angry because it could not do that violence at that exact nanoklik. Megatron had never known weakness of body. He had survived because in body and will he was stronger than his opponents in the ring, and thus far stronger than his opponents on the battlefield. But Dark Energon made him feel as if he had been a struggling, eyeless weakling for all of his existence until the exact moment when he had first partaken of its forbidden gift. He could stand down an army of Optimus Primes, a planet of Defensors—yet he felt not the lust for murder but the desire to be victorious, to be feared, to reign supreme over all who might cross his path. Dark Energon made one conscious of the greatness of destiny, and of the glories that awaited the fulfillment of destiny . . . and of war. His hands clenched and unclenched. He wanted to fight, he wished his enemies would materialize before him so he could kill them, and then that they could be repaired so he could kill them again.

"Ah," said Megatron. "Yes. Optimus, you are in for a surprise, brother. Your last."

And already he wanted more.

He looked at the two initial experimental subjects, who were starting to get to their feet. On their faces he saw the same dawning hunger that he was feeling. "Yes," he said. "It's not enough, is it?"

Starscream, observing the way the Dark Energon infusion had altered Megatron's behavior, and that of the two subjects, shifted closer to the science team leader and started trying to help him to his feet. "Autoclave. How much more Dark Energon is there?" he asked softly.

Autoclave's voice was staticky and difficult to understand, but Starscream got the sense of it. "Not much," Autoclave said. "Enough to outfit a few strike teams."

"I can hear you both," Megatron said. He turned

his back on the Darkened subjects and added, "Can more be made?"

Leaning on Starscream, Autoclave went to a bank of computers and spawned a display of the fundamental particle structure of Energon. Next to it he put up a diagram of Dark Energon's constituent particles. "See?" he said. His voice sounded clearer; he was shaking off the effects of the lab defense machines. He'd been farthest away from the point of focus; Shockwave was only now beginning to stir, and the two gladiator bots were moving their hands and feet but nothing else.

"See what?" Starscream asked. Neither Starscream nor Megatron were scientists. They did not see.

"What it looks like to me," Autoclave said, "is that just about any amount of Dark Energon can convert any amount of Energon. Can Darken it, I mean. So if you want more Dark Energon, all you need to do is find Energon."

Which was going to be a problem. Known Energon reservoirs on Cybertron were rapidly drying up as the war consumed them faster than Cybertron's natural processes could replenish them.

He looked to Shockwave, who was still recovering from being in the firing radius of the gyro-inhibitor charges. Useless. He looked at Starscream. Untrustworthy but useful in the right circumstances. "Bring me Soundwave," he commanded. "I need answers. And Starscream?"

The Seeker paused on his way out of the lab but did not verbally acknowledge Megatron's call. Megatron decided to let it go. Sometimes it was useful to know when to end a demonstration of power. His head was clearing from the initial rush of Dark Energon. Now he felt potent but in control, violent but focused.

"Perhaps when you return, I'll let you tank up on Dark Energon. It really is extraordinary."

CHAPTER TWENTY

The first recorded encounter between an Autobot guerrilla team and a Darkened Decepticon strike force happened near Maintenance Port A46 on the surface of the Kali-Con Plain, along the route of the energy conduit between Kalis and Iacon. Optimus Prime had set up regular patrols through the maintenance tunnels in anticipation of an eventual Decepticon attack or attempt at sabotage. This team, under the leadership of Jazz, had just completed a long sub-surface inspection patrol and popped up through A46 to do surface reconnaissance before making the turn back toward Iacon.

The Darkened Decepticons hit them as soon as they came up out of the maintenance port, which was set at an angle into an overhung ridge that loomed over an abandoned village. Once it had probably had a name, but many things had been lost during the course of the war. Jazz led the six-member team up and strung them out along the ridge. Their secondary objective on the mission was to scope any ruins for possible Energon reserves. There were even special optic enhancements designed to pick up the isotopic signature of Energon that would be detectable through existing structures or containers.

Jazz had the optics and was scanning down through the ruin in the valley below. Then he heard one of the team members sound the alarm—"Breach! Breach! 'Con in the perimeter!"

All six Autobots went through a near-unconscious process of target evaluation and prioritization. When they opened fire, they blew two Decepticons into sharp-edged pieces that slid away down the hillside; but there were a lot more than two 'Cons to worry about.

Jazz got up on top of the ridge, swept the sky—no Seekers, at least none that he could see—then came back groundward to estimate the enemy strength. Right away he spotted ten, twelve, sixteen.

"Jazz team, Jazz team, hit and run. Repeat, hit and run!"

Again all six team members in concert chose targets and fired, two and three Autobots concentrating on a single Decepticon. Two more 'Cons went down but then the rest were in among them, making concentrated fire impossible. Jazz dropped his energy weapons and went straight to the vibroblade, using a two-handed approach that pared away big pieces of the 'Con gladiator who had joined him up on the ridge.

Problem was, the 'Con didn't seem to mind the missing pieces. It even laughed a little as it came after Jazz with everything it had. Right away Jazz knew he was up against something that wasn't your average 'Con ex-gladiator. Those came hard and strong, but not with much finesse, and once you started hitting them they went down. This one seemed not to notice when Jazz hit him, and he hit back faster than any gladiator Jazz had ever seen. Pretty soon Jazz found himself unsure whether he was going to get out of this one, which wasn't something he'd ever felt when fighting a gladbot before.

"Hit and run!" he called again, then went to alt-mode.

As soon as his wheels landed on the old road that followed the ridgeline, Jazz redlined out of there. Sensors told him that four of the other team members had followed. The other one was gone, no sign of him. His name had been Revo.

The line of Autobots roared down the road, Jazz dropping back to cover the retreat. Behind them, only four of the 'Cons were coming; the rest alt-formed into tracked models, which were never going to catch something with actual wheels.

Five against four, Jazz thought. "Jazz team, Jazz team," he said. "Roadblock on my count."

Four simultaneous affirmatives from the team. Jazz floored it and the five Autobots came closer and closer to a place where the road widened out to accommodate a large-vehicle turnaround near the next maintenance port back toward Iacon. A45 looked just like A46 except that the road dipped off the ridgeline just past it, with the ridge wall on one side and a drop-off on the other making that spot tailor-made for an ambush.

They hit the spot and protoformed, dropping an annihilating volley of ion cannon, laser flares, magnoskips, and plain old kinetic projectiles on the first of the four 'Con alt-forms that came off the ridgeline.

It slid, skidded, started to burn, then rolled, barrelling over the Autobots and crashing down the hillside. The next three were tightly bunched and took an incredible amount of punishment before they could protoform and engage. Jazz couldn't believe any of them were able to walk after the hail they'd come through at the ambush point.

Things after that went horribly wrong. The damaged 'Cons tore into the Autobot ranks as if they hadn't felt a shot yet . . . and the first one, the alt-form who had gone over the side in flames, vaulted back up onto the road, pieces coming off it, charred and scarred but ready to go.

All of a sudden the five-on-four odds didn't look so good anymore.

"Hit and run!" Jazz cried again. "Focus five, hit and run!"

On this cue, every Autobot in the team lit up the same 'Con. This time they put it down and kept it down until it was in pieces, but the cost was that the other three got in among them. One of these was the same 'Con that Jazz had started to chop up back toward A46. It was too late to run; if they took the time to alt-form they'd be vulnerable for a critical split second. So they fought. Jazz and his previous partner danced again, and this time Jazz pinned him to the ground with a blade through the foot and put him down permanently with a sweeping stroke that separated him into all kinds of pieces.

He looked around to check on the rest of the team, and there was no rest of the team. Two of the 'Cons were still upright. Everything else, Autobot or Decepticon, was scrap.

Jazz alt-formed and nailed both of them before they could change, too. Then he spun around and got gone as fast as he could. They didn't pursue. "Home Base," he called ahead. "Coming in hot, coming in alone. Request immediate debrief. Repeat: You're going to want to hear this. Request immediate debrief."

He ran hard and ran hot. The 'Cons couldn't catch him. No one could catch Jazz when he was at his fastest. But if they didn't do something about the Energon supply pretty soon, he wouldn't be running anywhere fast. Or running anywhere at all. "Optimus," he said to himself as the planet spun beneath him, "I sure hope you know what you're doing."

Things had been bad for the Autobots before Dark Energon, and now that it turned out to be every bit the combat enhancement that Alpha Trion had feared, things were much worse. Reports streamed in from every place where an Autobot resistance still survived. Everywhere, it seemed, the Decepticons were growing stronger and more ruthless, this new source of energy seemingly limitless and coming from a source that Optimus Prime and his intelligence network were unable to attack. Trypticon Station was too far away, and the Seeker mismatch between Decepticon and Autobot meant that a frontal assault would be suicidal.

Seemingly, however, was perhaps a key word, for Optimus Prime had noticed something about the new Decepticon tactics. They attacked in groups, deploying overwhelming strength—but they did not always try to hold the ground they gained. Optimus Prime was beginning to develop a theory that they were encountering a supply problem even worse than the Autobots had.

Which, since Autobot and Decepticon were the same form of life, could only mean that their different energy source dwindled more quickly, and demanded more frequent replenishment, than the Energon that gave life to the Autobots.

If I am right, Optimus Prime thought, I have discovered that Dark Energon has a significant downside. Now I need to figure out how to turn this circumstance to our advantage.

"How much longer are we going to run?" Jazz stormed. "We're going to run out of places to abandon if we're not careful."

"What's your better idea, Jazz?" Optimus Prime considered a map.

"Fight," Jazz said. "Simple."

Sideswipe echoed him. "Fight. Isn't there enough to fight for? The more we run, the better we get at running."

Neither of them, it seemed, was thinking about how things had turned out the last time a small band of Autobots had stood and fought Darkened Decepticons.

"The more we run," Optimus Prime said, "and the smarter we run, the better chance we have at getting Megatron to chase us too far. If we can get him apart from whatever he's using to create the Dark Energon, we have a chance. If he can keep making it, whenever he wants and as much as he wants . . ."

There was no need to finish that sentence.

"Whatever supply of Dark Energon Megatron found on Trypticon, it can't last forever," Optimus

Prime said. He indicated the work he had been doing in the archives. "According to all of this, not much Dark Energon was ever created, and not all of that was recovered and sequestered on Trypticon. If we can hold out until the Decepticons run out of it, we can turn this war around."

Standing, he faced his most trusted deputies, all of whom had clustered around the workstation. "That's why we run when it's smarter to run," Optimus Prime said. "Because the more we can make Megatron chase us, the more we can make him waste his resources. Then, when he's suddenly out of fuel—that's when we make him pay."

He fell silent then, and the rest of them knew what he was thinking. Optimus Prime could not afford to be wrong, because the final confrontation was going to take place right there in Iacon. And that battle was going to make the siege they were experiencing right now look as trivial as an argument over how many Minicons could dance on the head of a Defensor.

Megatron looked out through the wall-spanning windows on the command bridge of Trypticon Station. Below, the surface of Cybertron. So much of it was his already, and more would be with every rotation. Dark Energon had made a difference immediately. The Decepticons were sweeping across Cybertron's surface, finishing off smaller pockets of Autobot holdouts and forcing the Autobots to defend more and more of their previously secure areas. So it went. The Decepticons struck and the Autobots retreated. They were making excellent use of Cybertron's sub-surface tunnel networks, and the Decepticons could not pursue them as far as Megatron would have liked . . . because while Dark Energon was marvelously powerful, it did not last the way standard Energon did. And when it ran low, its negative qualities quickly began to overwhelm its enhancements. Several times Megatron had seen battles turn from Decepticon routs to incredible Autobot reversals because key Decepticons began to run low on Dark Energon.

The tactics would adjust. They were already adjusting. But no adjustment would matter if the Dark Energon wasn't flowing.

He spun and headed down to the Dark Energon Facility, where Shockwave had taken some time away from his main project to check on the Dark Energon Deprivation Study begun on the first two test subjects. Given that the material was in fairly short supply, Shockwave thought it was worthwhile to see what would happen when a bot grew accustomed to it and then had to return to using regular Energon.

The taste of Dark Energon was sweet, and the power it conveyed was mighty. There was not enough of it in the world to satisfy Megatron. It was the taste of power and the promise of more. It thrummed in the limbs and in the mind like certain immortality.

But the Dark Energon was running out, and when it did . . .

After the subjects had gone two orbits with no Dark Energon, Shockwave had found it necessary to muzzle them. As Megatron entered the DEF now, the two were spasming in their bonds as the desire for Dark Energon transformed itself into agony at its absence.

Megatron resolved that this would not happen to him if he had to kill every last bot on Trypticon Station and drain the Dark Energon from them himself. Although that, too, was merely postponing the inevitable. What they needed was more Energon that they could then convert to Dark Energon. The problem was twofold. One, there was a shortage of Energon that threatened to bring the war to an end regardless of whether either side wanted it over.

Two, even if there was a way to get enough Energon, there had to be a way to deliver it in mass quantities up to Trypticon Station's orbit. Otherwise he would have to risk the Dark Energon by taking it down to the surface, where anything could happen. There was no way to keep it perfectly under control once it got down to Cybertron proper.

He outlined the problem for Shockwave and Soundwave as the experimental subjects, each sprouting a thicket of monitoring cables and sensors, jerked and fought against their bonds. Infusions of Energon, it seemed, did not help much. "All I'm doing now, to be honest, is seeing how long it will take them to die, and recording what happens along the way," Shockwave said.

"Don't waste time on this if it takes away from the other project," Megatron said.

Shockwave inclined his head as he finished making a note on an interesting—to Shockwave, anyway—reading coming from one of the test subjects. "Yes," he said. "I should get back to that. I'll be in the clean-room laboratory if you need to find me."

He left, and Megatron turned to Soundwave. "Have you been looking into the transportation problem?"

"It's not really my area," Soundwave said.

"Make it your area," Megatron said.

Soundwave paused. "Energon up here in large quantities. That's what you want?" As he talked, he was thinking. Megatron could tell this because when Soundwave thought hard, the Minicons he carried got restless and became visible. Their silvery legs flicked around the edges of his trunk.

"I need an answer now," Megatron said. "Prove to

me that you haven't been wasting your time for the last million orbits. What do you know? How did the ancients move Energon? They would have needed incredible amounts to build the Space Bridges, among other things."

Soundwave stayed silent. The Minicons started to chirp in annoyance that he was not letting them go. Megatron walked up close to Soundwave, very close, and said quietly, "I do not wish to be disappointed in this, Soundwave."

"No, there is a way," Soundwave said, snapping back into the present. "I just had to find it. Teracycles ago, back before the Autobots ratcheted up the security protocols on the DataNet, my Grid burrowers recovered an interesting story. Far below the surface is a lens. It matches a lens array in the planet-facing side of Trypticon. Once there was a link between the two, but it has been destroyed, or at least interrupted, since ancient times."

"And what of this lens? What does it focus?" Megatron asked.

"It is known, or was once known, as the Geosynchronous Energon Bridge," Soundwave said. "My belief is that it is a way of reconstituting and concentrating Energon into its most rarefied form, and transmitting that form to a receiving array—where it can be restored to a more easily usable form." The spymaster could barely control his avaricious glee.

Megatron had two thoughts at once. One involved the glorious potential of an unlimited supply of Energon, piped up from the center of Cybertron to a staging area on Trypticon, where it could be transformed into Dark Energon. And Trypticon itself would be the inaccessible and invulnerable base from which the Decepticons could at last overwhelm the dwindling and exhausted Autobot forces.

And what if the link could be used the other way . . . what if Dark Energon could be force-fed directly into the material body of Cybertron itself?

Do not get ahead of the plan, Megatron counseled himself. Make certain of one thing before you begin another. "Starscream," he said. "Move the station to a geosynchronous orbit. When it is established there, I have another mission for you."

"Now that the station is under control, I was looking forward to flying missions that involved actual combat," Starscream said.

Megatron smirked. "I'm sure you were," he said. "After all, I have barely been able to keep you up here so far."

"I don't appreciate the mockery, Megatron. You know now why I stayed up here. Would you rather the Autobots had discovered Dark Energon?"

"The Autobots would never have used Dark Energon, fool," Megatron said. "You will need a better excuse."

Starscream did something then that Megatron would not have credited him with the courage to do. He stepped up to Megatron, close enough that their faces nearly touched despite Megatron being larger. "I need no excuse, Megatron," he said quietly. "Have you considered that the Autobots might have destroyed the Dark Energon? Or hidden it somewhere else? Or destroyed Trypticon Station entirely? Where would your magnificent new plans be if any of those things had come to pass?"

"Starscream," Megatron said. "An action that turns out to be correct is not the same as proof that you acted correctly. If you need no excuse, then realize that I need no reason. I lead the Decepticons and I lead them as I choose. You stay on this station at my sufferance. You continue to exist at my sufferance. Continue to earn your position and you will continue to occupy it. Become more trouble than you are worth, and I will address the situation permanently."

The challenge hung there in the air between them.

"Geosynchronous orbit," Starscream said.

Megatron nodded. "Yes."

"Won't do you much good if the Energon Bridge isn't activated and its lens isn't focused," Starscream said.

"You see, Starscream?" Megatron smiled. "More often than not, we think exactly alike."

The charge of Dark Energon was unlike anything Starscream had ever experienced. It was Energon squared, Energon with an extra dimension, Energon that made you feel as if you had never truly known what it was like to be energized before.

Fueled by its occult power, the Decepticon mission to capture the subsurface terminus of the Geosynchronous Energon Bridge was an overpowering success. Starscream and his handpicked team thundered down through the atmosphere, dodging the frantic ground-based fire of the Autobot defenses ringing the ruins of Crystal City. Few Autobots remained there; the defenses were drones, automatic routines designed to fire on any intruder lacking their most recent security clearances.

Starscream jinked and swooped through the barrage and unleashed a volley of missiles at an ion-cannon battery set into a hillside on the outskirts of Crystal City. The hillside vanished in a fireball that quickly darkened into a column of smoke that gushed from the interior of the hill, where fires would burn through the remnants of the defensive batteries until there was nothing left to burn.

He came in low and hard for a landing, reassuming his proto-form in time to hit the ground running and pound his way through the exterior wall of a cooling tower. The interior of the tower was a shaft that headed straight down into the interior of the planet—how far, Starscream wasn't sure, but far enough to circulate coolant throughout the understrata of Crystal City.

Before leaving Moon Base One, where he had staged the operation after receiving his orders from Megatron up on Trypticon, Starscream had implanted the operational records of the invasion of Crystal City in his memory. He had a nearly complete map of the subsurface districts in his head now, and he thought he knew where the Bridge would be.

A line of explosions stippled the ridgeline behind him to the north as the last Seekers made their approach runs, adding a final salvo of suppressing fire before assuming proto-shapes and joining Starscream at the tower wall. "In fast," he said. "No distractions. Everyone have the location?"

"Yes, sir," they said in unison.

"Then go!"

And they were through the hole in the tower wall, retaking their alt-shapes and accelerating straight down through the cooling shaft, Starscream at the head of the flight, crunching position and velocity in his head until he snapped off an impossible turn through the shaft wall, taking proto-form at the exact instant of impact and landing on his feet. Around him came the other Commanders, bristling with weapons and the Dark Energon–inspired urge to use them.

The lab they'd landed in was wrecked, seemingly by a battle during the initial raids on Crystal City. Preserved by isolation, the ruins of the lab looked much as they might have at that chaotic moment teracycles in the past. Starscream himself had been a part of the first Crystal City operations, but only in an overflight and bombardment capacity. This was his first time under the surface there.

He didn't like it. He didn't like being anywhere under the surface, especially not with the Dark Energon pushing him on to do something, find an enemy, engage and destroy . . .

"Coordinates accurate?" he asked his first officer Nacelle. At the answering nod, Starscream said, "Okay. Then spread out and let's find it."

It didn't take long. Their intelligence was good, their approach work had been good, and if there were any Decepticons who knew how to run a search, it was the Seekers with their deep experience in locating moving targets from great distances while coordinating among several independent units. Compared to an atmosopheric battle, finding the Geosynchronous Energon Bridge was a holiday sightseeing trip over Six Lasers.

The lens was three times the size of the biggest member of the flight team—Starscream himself. Situated in its own shaft parallel to the cooling duct that Starscream and the team had entered through, the lens looked up toward the surface and the sky beyond. What was below it, Starscream couldn't see and didn't want to know. He was not in the business of investigating the mysteries of Cybertron. He was there to follow orders and to lay the groundwork for his own advancement.

Sometimes those were conflicting goals. At that moment they worked well together.

"What's the hole in the center of the lens?" he asked. There had been nothing about it in the records. Or in any images Starscream had yet seen, and he had seen a lot of them.

According to the records he had examined during mission planning, the Geosynchronous Energon Bridge had been constructed specifically to accelerate and simplify orbital development in the near space around Cybertron. The Bridge also was used to power up the Space Bridges, which required enormous infusions of Energon at first, before tapping into subspace quantum energies for their ongoing operation.

How long it had been since the Bridge had been in operation seemed to be a matter of dispute among various sources. That didn't matter for purposes of the mission. What mattered was that the team find it, run diagnostics on it to make sure it would work, and then make it work. Then the Decepticons would have their own source of Energon, convertible to Dark Energon up on Trypticon Station, where Shockwave had also begun some kind of retrofitting on the station itself. Starscream didn't know the details, but he would be finding out.

With their own Dark Energon supply, furnished by an unjammable and indestructible link, the Decepticons would destroy the Autobots more quickly, with fewer losses, and with better prospects of having a planet worth living on. There was, as far as Starscream could see, no downside. So power it up he would.

"Hotlink," Starscream commanded. "You're on. Any ideas about that hole?"

The mechatronic engineer flipped open his toolkit. "It might just look like a hole," he said. "There is a lot of energy of all different kinds circulating through that lens. It's not just a lens. Once the Energon starts to flow, who knows what's going to happen. Could be the hole is what makes the whole thing work, and if the lens was perfectly convex . . ." He trailed off, doing some kind of complicated math in his head. "Don't know," he said, then got to work.

First he and information engineer Bitstream, who was one of Starscream's elite Air Commanders, created a secure and invisible diagnostic computer space. Then, within that space, he got to talking to the systems running the Geosynchronous Energon Bridge. "Everything seems fine," he reported shortly. "Let me run one more rehearsal of the powering-up sequence . . . right."

Looking up at Starscream, Hotlink said, "Should be ready to go."

"Then make it go," Starscream said.

Megatron was still on Trypticon, agitated and pacing but not wanting to return to Fort Scyk until he knew for certain that the Geosynchronous Energon Bridge was functioning again. Part of his agitation resulted from placing such an important mission in the hands of Starscream, who could not have been more obvious about his ultimate goals if he had stenciled I WILL BE PRIME across his torso.

The problem was, Starscream's ambition was matched—possibly even exceeded—by his ability. He was a superb flier, officer, soldier, and adviser. Megatron had learned a long time ago that no one could be trusted. He had also learned that even untrustworthy aides were useful and could be counted on in certain situations. This was one of them, since whatever Starscream wanted for the future depended on the success of his alliance with Megatron in the present.

So when Starscream checked in at exactly the time agreed on in the initial mission planning, Megatron was satisfied but not surprised.

"It is done," Starscream said.

Megatron nodded at his image. He glanced over at the scientific team, led by the waiting Catalycon, who ran a series of checks while Megatron wordlessly kept Starscream waiting. The Seeker did not rise to the bait, but that was all right. The important thing was that he know it was happening.

"It appears to be online," Catalycon reported.

"Well done, Starscream. You have succeeded. Now return to the surface. When the Dark Energon supply is replenished, you will be needed to overfly the initial assault on Iacon."

Starscream looked stunned. "Iacon?"

"Your audio system is functional, Starscream, is it not?"

"More functional than my support flights will be without their own chance to tank up on Dark Energon," Starscream shot back.

220 ALEX IRVINE

"Fear not, trusted lieutenant," Megatron said. "Follow along with what I do and there will be more Dark Energon than anyone could ever use."

Everything was falling into place. Victory over the Autobots was at hand, and Starscream was confused. Perfect.

Starscream broke off the connection. He looked around at the subsurface machinery that extended into vast spaces as far as he could see in any direction . . . yet he felt as if there were only two dimensions here. Up and down were missing, the Z-axis that set him and other Seekers apart from the surface-bound run of Cybertronian life.

He knew that this had been part of Megatron's message. The Decepticon leader sent Starscream below the surface to emphasize that he could exercise control over every aspect of his subordinates' lives.

If that was what he needed, Starscream thought—if that kept him looking the other way while Starscream put together his real plan—then a little momentary humiliation was more than worth it.

The Geosynchronous Energon Bridge thrummed quietly through the hyperfrequency lens that directed a flood of Energon toward Trypticon Station, where Shockwave's rebuilt crew helped transmute it into Dark Energon. It was a turning point in the war, and Megatron owed it all to Starscream. Not that Starscream expected Megatron ever to acknowledge that, much less make good on the debt. But that was all right as well. There would come a time when Starscream wouldn't need Megatron for anything.

He wouldn't need Optimus Prime, either. Soon, Starscream thought, he would need no one else on Cybertron. He would answer to no one. In the final fulfillment of the original ideal that had started this war, Starscream would have perfect self-determination.

Nothing else, in the end, mattered.

To that end, he had set in motion a plan. And now that the Bridge was in place and no Decepticon had to fight for energy, the time had come to execute the next phase of the plan.

Starscream had left trusted subordinates on Moon Base One when he had moved his remote command from there to Trypticon Station. Now was the time to activate them. He created a secure channel with the aid of Bitstream. Then he got in contact with Moon Base One.

"Operation Unlock, commence," he said. "Repeat: Operation Unlock, commence immediately."

He shut down the channel without waiting for confirmation. It wasn't worth the risk to keep it open. "Bitstream, erase all records of that channel," he said. If he was lucky, Megatron would not be looking for it; the gladiator's attention rarely turned to information control. He was more focused on physical means of getting his way.

The Autobots, on the other hand, would certainly notice and record the brief existence of that channel, and the fact that messages had gone back and forth through it. What they would make of the information, Starscream did not know; but if the improbable happened and the Autobots emerged victorious from the war, he intended to maximize his opportunities to cast his actions in a favorable light. With this brief exchange cataloged somewhere in the Hall of Records, he would have one more way to do exactly that.

First things first, however. He needed another charge of Dark Energon, and fast.

CHAPTER TWENTY-THREE

From Fort Scyk, Megatron monitored the reports of Starscream's mission and his relocation of Trypticon Station to a higher orbit. He had to be careful not to spend too much time off-planet and away from the seat of his power in Kaon. The more he was visible before the rank-and-file Decepticons, the more he was still the gladiator who had risen from the pits. Sentinel Prime had lost the belief of Cybertronians because he had become unreal to them. He had not spent any time with any regular bots, let alone those from the lower castes.

It had been teracycles since anyone took caste seriously—if the war ended tomorrow, Megatron could have taken credit for destroying the system— but the lesson remained. Walk among the people you would lead. Megatron lived by this precept. His second precept was that there were times when you had to kill selected members of those groups you desired to lead. So while his Darkened strike teams ran the Autobots out of their warrens, he had permitted himself the time to get reacquainted with Kaon, the Badlands, and Blaster City.

Here it had all begun. And here was where his misguided friendship with Orion Pax had broken. The final confrontation had taken place in the High Council Chamber, yes; but the break had begun, the cracks had spread, when Orion Pax had seen a little slice of the real world that the lower castes inhabited.

Megatron did not permit himself to feel regret. If the war had never happened, he would never have been more than a functionary, an agitator for the downtrodden—or he would have receded back into the subsurface world below the Badlands, a former gladiator fallen away from his days of greatness. Looking back from where he stood now, either possibility seemed worse than the death he had always evaded in the pit and on the battlefield.

Below him spread the vast army of ex-gladiators and industrial workers who had become his army. They had been there when he went into Fort Scyk to monitor the status of the dual projects up on Trypticon Station and to get reports from strike teams. The war was entering its final stages.

Megatron slotted in a fresh ingot of Dark Energon. The charge of it rocked him and he charged back up and out onto the parapet that ran between the main towers of Fort Scyk. When he burst into the crowd's field of vision, they erupted into the chant that still electrified him the way it had the first time he'd heard it: MEGATRON!

MEGATRON! MEGATRON! MEGATRON!

"Yes, Decepticons!" he called out. "Yes! Total victory is at hand! Do you stand ready for a last push to crush the Autobots and claim all of Cybertron for yourselves?"

The roar that went up shook the foundations of Fort Scyk.

"I have fought for you!" Megatron went on. "In battle I have faced down the ion batteries of Polyhex—and I still function! I have gone blade to blade with the Elite Guard of the High Council—and I still function! I have stood inside the firestorm of a fusion detonation while around me other bots blew away into molten splatters—and I still function!"

They responded to him as they always did. The ground below the southern wall of Fort Scyk became a thicket of upthrust weapons, and the surface of the Sea of Rust, on whose shores Megatron's supporters were gathered, rippled outward as if their adulation had reversed the tides.

MEGATRON!

"I STILL FUNCTION!"

MEGATRON!

"You must stand ready for a final assault on Iacon!" he thundered. "Stand ready and I will call! Our victory is at hand! A new Cybertron is at hand!"

MEGATRON!

He looked from the tower of Fort Scyk out to the west, where far beyond the steely horizon lay the city of Iacon, last bastion of the Autobots. It was his final goal, the last hurdle remaining between Megatron and the status of a true Prime. Orion Pax was not Prime material. What Prime had ever come from the Hall of Records? And Sentinel Prime . . . his time was past. He had lost Cybertron, and now few living Cybertronians remembered he had existed. When the time came for his elimination, Sentinel Prime would have no one interested in defending him. The only reason Megatron had let him live so long was for the unlikely chance he would need to parade a Prime in front of the Grid to claim legitimacy. That had always been a remote possibility, and now in the light of Dark Energon it seemed even more improbable.

MEGATRON!

There was only room for one Prime.

MEGATRON!

The sky over the Badlands looked like it always did: gray and churning. It was time to go up and through it again, to the clean emptiness of space and Trypticon Station.

By the time he had reconvened his science team on Trypticon Station, he was expecting a full report on the operational status of the Geosynchronous Energon Bridge. Shockwave had stayed up on Trypticon, now in geosynchronous orbit over the focal point of the Energon Beam's lens, while Megatron shored up his positions on the perimeter between the Decepticon-held Badlands and the northern plains area that reached out in the direction of Iacon and Nova Cronum.

"It's not enough," Catalycon said. "We can pipe the Energon up to the station every moment at full capacity and it's not going to be enough. Your army is too big and the pipeline is . . ." The scientist gestured toward the monitor. "There's not enough."

"Yes there is," Soundwave said. "Or there can be, at any rate. If what you want is enough Dark Energon for the Decepticon army, you need the Plasma Energy Chamber."

Megatron looked from Catalycon to Soundwave and back. "Why have I not heard this before?"

"We thought it was a myth," Catalycon said.

Soundwave shook his head. "*You* thought it was a myth. I told you it was real. Megatron, I knew the Plasma Energy Chamber existed. When I infiltrated Crystal City, long ago, back before the war had really started, my Minicons returned with more information than could be processed right then. One of the things they had evidence of was this Plasma Energy Chamber."

Megatron looked at Catalycon while Soundwave spoke, until the scientist was visibly terrified. "Go on," Megatron said. "Catalycon, listen closely."

"Y-yes," stammered Catalycon.

"In and below the city of Iacon," Soundwave said, "there are two Code Keys, one of Power and one of Justice. One, Justice, lies within the subsurface fortress that contains Teletraan-1. The other, Power, is elsewhere in Iacon. I have Minicons finding exactly where as we speak."

Outside, the Devastator winds began to howl. "What does one unlock with these Code Keys?" Megatron asked.

"Both are needed to control the Plasma Energy Chamber," Soundwave said. "I will let our distinguished scientist tell the rest."

Catalycon jumped at the chance to return to Megatron's good graces. "The stories—which my colleague Soundwave has done so much to confirm—suggest that the bot who controls the two Code Keys may activate the Plasma Energy Chamber. And the Plasma Energy Chamber, it is said, is the power source for the material of Cybertron itself. Whoever controls it has an unlimited supply. More than any army of Decepticons could ever find a way to use."

"Very good," Megatron said. "That sounds like what I need. Make it happen, Catalycon. And this time, listen to what smarter bots around you are saying."

CHAPTER TWENTY-FOUR

Starscream entered Iacon through the subsurface tunnel network that serviced the energy conduits from the Kalis reactor. He had seen the combat-camera records of the various hit-and-run engagements that had taken place along the course of the conduits. What the whole area needed was a solid cycle of Seeker bombardment. That would take care of the tunnels and the conduit once and for all. Megatron refused this initiative, however. He wanted to keep Iacon as intact as possible for as long as possible, since he envisioned it as his future capital just as it had been capital for the other Primes dating back to the time of the Ancients.

To Starscream it seemed as if Megatron wanted to manipulate the idiot underclass of Kaon while aspiring to the situation of the upper classes. He had begun as a revolutionary and become a hypocritical tyrant.

Which was fine. Starscream had no philosophical problem with tyranny. He planned to be a tyrant himself. The only problem was that Megatron's inconsistencies tended to send his subordinates out on highly inefficient missions—such as this one—while he ignored much more direct paths to military success.

Such as, for example, destroying the conduit and tunnels. But this was not to be, so rather than fight their way through the tunnel, Starscream and his six Air Commanders moved quickly and silently, fighting only a single brief skirmish when they encountered a sentry in wheeled alt-form, late on his rounds. The concentrated fire of the seven Seekers blew him apart into fragments of chassis before he even knew they were there. A single wheel skipped and bounced away down the tunnel in front of them.

"Move," Starscream said. "There will be records of that. We should be out of this tunnel system before anyone comes to look."

Two cycles later, they cut their way through a tunnel wall and were into the main subsurface levels of Iacon. Starscream looked at his locator. The Code Key of Power was in a locked-down and heavily guarded safe complex directly under the symbolic spires of the tower complex housing the High Council Chamber.

Megatron himself led another team into Iacon, entering through a collapsed viaduct that had once fed alt-form traffic from the city center out onto the main Iacon-Hydrax road. In a small but pleasurable irony, this was the same road he and Orion Pax had traveled when first they came to Iacon together. How times and circumstances did change.

They moved quickly and avoided engaging the few Autobot units they saw, despite the raging Dark Energon within them, which made them want to seize every opportunity for battle. For this mission, Megatron had picked only the most dedicated of his followers, the ones who had been with him from the beginning and never shown any sign of wanting to advance. They fought for him, no more and no less.

Soon after their initial penetration of the Iacon perimeter, the team found the access shaft where Soundwave's latest information told them the Plasma Energy Chamber would be. Catalycon, the most reluctant member of the team but a necessary one, also had said that the Code Key of Power was recently moved. His most recent information suggested that it was being kept near the Plasma Energy Chamber itself.

When he had heard this, Megatron had pushed up the mission timetable. He could not allow the possibility that the Autobots might locate and deploy the Plasma Energy Chamber. Such a change in the balance of Energon supply would prolong the war indefinitely.

They were very close. Megatron held the team up, scanning on all frequencies to assess potential opposition in the spaces ahead. The access tunnel they had taken this far was wide enough for two Decepticons to march abreast. Ahead a much wider space loomed; none of Megatron's sensory arrays could detect its boundaries. No energy sources or Sparks registered within.

He gestured the strike team forward, but on a slow advance, all weapons deployed, rules of engagement to not fire first but to put down any hostile unit with extreme prejudice. They entered the perimeter of the server space surrounding the great computer Teletraan-1, the heart of Cybertronian science and still its greatest product, the living mind of the planet and the well of information architecture that ultimately ran everything from Iacon's maglev system to the subsentient machinery that controlled Kaon's blast furnaces and the mining bots that spent their service lives out in the Asteroid Belt cooking out trace elements from the alloys and bits of ore.

Teletraan-1, thought Megatron. The Dark Energon desire within him flared, and for a moment he wanted to destroy it. He restrained himself. He had learned over the course of the war not to destroy things before he had some idea of whether he would need them later. This was why Iacon still stood, and why he held back now as he led the strike team into the periphery of Teletraan-1's inscrutable consciousness.

The room was barely tall enough for the larger Decepticons to stand upright in. Megatron was glad he had not brought Devastator along, or even some of the more massive Constructicons. But what the space lacked in height it made up for in the other two dimensions. As far as Megatron could see in the dim light, the room extended, featureless in floor and ceiling save for two things. One was a progression of support pillars, each as wide as Devastator's leg.

The other was, far away in the dimness, a glowing rectangular outline. "Surely," said Catalycon, "this must be it."

"We will find out," Megatron said. The Decepticons formed up and moved out onto the open floor, wary of possible ambush from any direction.

The locator on Megatron's forearm said they were getting close. Very close. Close enough that he should have been able to see the secure enclosure where such a mighty artifact would surely be kept. "Yes," Catalycon said. "That is the Plasma Energy Chamber, within."

"Upstart," someone said in the darkness. The shadows at the edge of the glowing rectangle moved.

Megatron stopped and held up a hand to stop the rest of the strike team as well. From the shadows, moving slowly but with a sense of purpose Megatron would not have been able to imagine, stepped Sentinel Prime.

Apparently this world still held a few surprises.

"So," said Sentinel Prime, standing ready in the great empty space. "You are the one who calls himself Megatron."

Megatron felt the waves of shock coming from the gladiators who had accompanied him. Sentinel Prime, alive and escaped? And—most difficult to believe—ready to fight?

Starscream, thought Megatron. He has done this. He will pay for it.

First, however, it was time to put an end to Sentinel Prime. After all, the Covenant called for only one Prime at any given time, did it not?

"Before you accuse your subordinates, know that they are blameless," Sentinel Prime said. "I bear the blame for letting your Decepticon movement survive beyond the malcontent Badlands districts where it was born. All Cybertronians would have been better off had it been snuffed out there."

Sentinel Prime moved to the center of the room, positioning himself between Megatron and the entrance portal to the interior of Teletraan-1, where Catalycon said the Plasma Energy Chamber would be locked away. "My errors cannot be undone," he said, "but they can perhaps be atoned for. Your war ends here. Surrender and Cybertron will return to peace with you alive. Fight on and Cybertron will return to peace with you dead."

"You have forgotten one possibility," Megatron said. "When I defeat you, the war will go on and I will be alive. But once I have captured the Plasma Energy Chamber, the Autobots will not survive for long. So perhaps you are partly right on that score."

"Do you remember, far back before this war began, when you were still one gladiator boss among many in the murder pits?" Sentinel Prime asked. Megatron gave no answer, and Sentinel Prime went on. "Because I had heard of bots dying in these pits, I sent two of my officers to investigate. Their names were Bumper and Fastback. Do you remember them?"

Still Megatron said nothing.

"You killed them both," Sentinel Prime said. "To protect your organization, which you later started calling a revolution. But you were a killer from the beginning, Megatron. No matter what you call yourself now, you are still just a killer."

"What if I did kill them?" Megatron asked. "What are two lives balanced against the misery of millions caused by your castes?"

"Do you tell yourself that every time? Do you imagine that is what you will tell yourself when, at the last, Optimus Prime has you at the end of his sword?"

"Optimus Prime is a librarian!" Megatron snarled. "The High Council signed the death warrants of every institution in the Cybertron of old when they named him Prime. He was a stooge of Alpha Trion, and now he is a stooge of whatever Council members still live."

Megatron drew his great sword, feeling it manifest from the fiber of his body. "And now," he said, "I will speak to you no more, Sentinel Prime. For there is something inside Teletraan-1 that I need to have, and you are in my way. Stand aside or die."

Sentinel Prime's Energon Sword blazed forth in the dim space. "I am still Sentinel Prime, upstart," he said. "I fought battles for the future of Cybertron before you were ever compiled, before your proto-form first crawled out of the Well of AllSparks."

"And I will fight battles after you are gone," Megatron said. "Thus the past becomes the future."

The first strike of Sentinel Prime's blade knocked Megatron back, unbalancing him. He crashed into a support pillar and barely evaded a second blow as he brought his own sword to bear and raked it in a vicious arc through the air where Sentinel Prime's head had been a nanoklik before. On his backswing he felt the blade nick Sentinel Prime's shoulder just before a stiff-armed smash to Megatron's face knocked him over backward.

He leaped to his feet and circled with his opponent. "More fight in you now than there was at Altihex Casino," Megatron said. "You think you can make up for all of your precious little Autobot fools who have died protecting an idea not even you believed in?"

Swords clashed, Megatron deflecting a searching thrust and Sentinel Prime in turn flicking away Megatron's riposte.

"The way I seek to atone is to make a better future than the past I have allowed to happen," Sentinel Prime said.

Megatron nodded and offered Sentinel Prime a

mock salute. "Well said. I will have that engraved over the scrap heap where your body lands."

Again they clashed together. Somewhere behind him, Megatron heard two of his retinue make a bet— not over who would win, but over how long it would take and whether Sentinel Prime would land a telling blow first.

Ah, Dark Energon. No one could touch him while it circulated through his systems. He answered every stroke of Sentinel Prime's sword. When the sword blade touched him, the pain was invigorating; the Dark Energon took it and made it into strength. Yet when Megatron's blade bit into Sentinel Prime's frame, the ancient leader had only his will to rely on, and the Energon he had always used.

Gradually Megatron wore him down. First a blow to his leg that scraped down from hip to knee, creating a shower of curling bits of metal. Then they grappled, and Megatron was younger, faster, and fueled by Dark Energon. He rained blows on Sentinel Prime's head, striking sparks there as well, beating the former leader of Cybertron until—with the last of his will—Sentinel Prime threw Megatron off and got to his feet. Once more he deployed his sword.

"You may kill me, Megatron," Sentinel Prime said. "I sense that you have the essence of Unicron within you, and it gives you a strength that is hard to resist."

" 'Impossible,' you mean," Megatron said. He felt strong, ready, as if he were just getting started.

Sentinel Prime assumed a ready position. "But beware the cost. The universe offers nothing for free. Neither does Unicron."

Megatron raised his sword in a salute, no mockery

this time. It had been a worthy fight. But now the time had come to end it.

Once again they clashed, the collisions of their blades striking flares from each other and Energon discharges—light and Dark—arcing from their bodies to creep along the support pillars or bleed away into the floor. Lights blinked on around the glowing rectangle of the doorway. Was Teletraan-1 awakening to their presence? Megatron's team looked around, shifted their weapons. To them, Teletraan-1 was practically a myth, and the Dark Energon had baffled their thought processes. It made them outstanding soldiers but it did not fit them out to think subtly. They banded together, their wagers forgotten, wondering what else Cybertron might create when Megatron destroyed their former Prime.

Sentinel Prime's sword pierced the point of Megatron's shoulder. Megatron threw back his head and roared, the sound of agony modulating to a Darkened glee. He reached up, with the same arm that was wounded, and clamped his hand over Sentinel Prime's and over the guard and hilt of his sword. "To wound me," Megatron said, "you must get close enough that I can wound you as well."

And he brought his blade over and down, severing Sentinel Prime's arm.

The howl that escaped Sentinel Prime was a lament for all that he had failed to do, and all that he now knew he never would do. Megatron threw the arm away, the motion also dislodging the sword from his shoulder. He struck again, opening a rent in Sentinel Prime's other arm and again splitting the side of the doomed leader's head. Sentinel Prime staggered. Megatron swung from the side, the blow biting deep into the side of Sentinel Prime's trunk. Megatron yanked the blade free and Sentinel Prime sank to his knees. He lifted his remaining arm to ward off the next blow, and Megatron struck it off at the elbow.

"Once you were a great leader," Megatron said. "But you grew weak. Just as Cybertron grew weak. I am here to make it strong again."

He raised his sword high overhead, Dark Energon flickering out of it to spark against the ceiling. Then he brought it down in a final stroke that cleft the armor over Sentinel Prime's torso from the base of his throat to the gleaming belt on which he wore the sigil of that noble myth Vector Prime. Sentinel Prime toppled onto his side. A tremor shook its way outward through his limbs; then the former leader was still. A dying gleam of his Spark still showed, so faintly that it could barely be seen even in the dimness, in his optics.

Megatron cast his blade aside. "Catalycon," he called out. "Where is the Code Key of Justice?"

"You are closer than you realize, Leader," the scientist answered. "Look within the body of Sentinel Prime himself."

Starscream had found the Code Key of Power exactly where it was supposed to be, molded into the substructure of Iacon's Hall of Justice. He appreciated the joke and wondered if the Code Key of Justice was hidden away within some edifice or fixture named for power. The guards charged with protecting the Code Key of Power did not know what they were protecting and did not fight very hard for it. The moment

Starscream and his team killed the first two of them, the others fled. They were new Autobots, some of the last to come from the Well of AllSparks before the ejection of the Well. Probably they had spent their entire time within Iacon itself, being too inexperienced for Optimus Prime to trust them on missions against superior Decepticon troops.

And probably they had come to think of the Decepticons as nearly mythical, as mythical as the names and deeds of the Primes—so that when Starscream and his force appeared from the subsurface darkness, it might as well have been the guards' nightmares come to life. Darkened Starscream found humor in this, the idea that he was a walking nightmare. When he flew, he would be a dream of falling.

Now, with the Code Key of Power in his possession, he and his Air Commanders were about to change the course of the war. Sentinel Prime would already have made himself known. The next stages of the plan laid themselves out neatly before Starscream. They ended with him holding both of the Code Keys, controlling the Plasma Energy Chamber, and becoming the unquestioned and absolute leader of Cybertron.

The rendezvous point lay just ahead. Starscream visually checked off the six members of the Air Command, all senior officers, all hardened veterans and loyal believers in Cybertron.

Which did not necessarily mean loyal believers in Megatron's vision for the planet of their creation.

This was going to be the moment, Starscream thought. The Decepticon forces had grown stale and unmotivated, their energy sapped by the endless war even as the advent of Dark Energon had created a new subclass of Decepticon supersoldier. Already Starscream mistrusted Dark Energon, though. It seemed to have effects beyond the battlefield. With strength it also gave eternal hunger for more Dark Energon. Starscream looked into the faces of those Decepticons who had tasted it, and what he saw was not belief in the Decepticon cause but desire for Dark Energon, whoever could provide it.

A planet of sapped and stupefied addicts was not a planet worth fighting and dying for. Starscream resolved not to use Dark Energon again. The time had come to change the way Decepticons fought—and change, to be effective, had to begin at the top.

He watched Megatron's inevitable victory over Sentinel Prime, moving quietly closer without Megatron's team noticing. Gladiators to the core, they were unable to take their eyes off a single combat. Starscream signaled his team to spread out, staking out a perimeter around them in the event that the next and final phase of his plan did not proceed exactly the way he envisioned it.

A ringing impact drew Starscream's attention away from the illuminated doorway, on the other side of which was the Plasma Energy Chamber and the key to ending this war. Sentinel Prime's arm clanked to the floor. His sword, pitted and dull, skidded and spun away into the shadows.

Starscream came closer.

Sentinel Prime lay mortally wounded. An age was ending.

And Starscream's plan was moments away from coming to fruition.

Megatron stood over the dying Sentinel Prime in

triumph. Then, as Starscream entered the periphery of the room, Megatron turned to his science lackey Catalycon. They exchanged words, and Starscream thought—there? Could that be true?

If he could get his hands on both Code Keys, then he would not have to fight Megatron. He edged closer to Sentinel Prime, seeing . . . oh, yes . . . the searing glow of the Code Key of Justice. Too good to be true! There it was, behind a translucent interior layer of shielding through which the Code Key's glow was filtered into a diffuse brilliance almost like an emanation of Spark. He could possess both Code Keys before his final confrontation with Megatron. This was an unexpected stroke of fortune, one that surely must tilt the odds decisively in Starscream's favor; he had assumed that he would have to fight and dispose of Megatron before taking possession of the second Code Key.

One of the rewards of good planning was that accidents tended to work in your favor. Starscream had seen it before, and he was seeing it again now.

Megatron's back was turned. Starscream's team was in place.

It was time to make the final, irrevocable move. The next Prime would not be Megatron. It would be Starscream. And his age would begin the moment his fingers came into contact with the Code Key that gleamed within the ruins of Sentinel Prime's body.

He reached out. It was almost close enough to touch.

"Megatron, look out!"

The Decepticon who called to his leader was known as Blackout. As he shouted, he threw his body between Starscream and the Code Key of Justice, which gleamed in the torn-out hollow of Sentinel Prime's torso.

"Nooo!" Roaring in fury, Starscream flung him out of the way with a blow that would have killed many Transformers, but Blackout had suffered in the pits of Kaon, and no single blow could do him in. He fell, though, and struggled to get up for a moment before collapsing to the floor.

Starscream could not believe the twist of fate that was undermining the perfection of his plan. Sentinel Prime housed the Code Key of Justice?! And Starscream had released Sentinel Prime to make a stand against Megatron, thereby *delivering* to Megatron the other half of the combination that would unlock the Plasma Energy Chamber?

Sentinel Prime, his consciousness fading, looked Starscream in the eye. Even in the extreme of his agonies, he had enough presence of mind to give his captor and liberator an ironic smile.

Impossible, Starscream was thinking as Megatron rounded on him and without a moment's thought blasted him away from the body of Sentinel Prime with an ion-cannon bolt. The impact of Starscream's body against one of the immense support pillars that were spaced across the vast interior sent a booming echo through the floor, felt by every sentient being present in the room. "Where you cannot fly, you are at a disadvantage, Starscream," Megatron said. "You have never yet figured that out."

Another blast flung Starscream farther away from Sentinel Prime before the Seeker could get to his feet. "And you are at a disadvantage against me because I am stronger than you," Megatron added. "My will is stronger. And I know you for the ambitious plotter that you are."

He assumed alt-shape, roaring across the open floor on heavy treads that tore into the steel plates. Starscream saw him coming and changed his shape as well! Incredible, Megatron thought. There's no room—

But Starscream knew exactly what he was doing. In his alt-shape for a split second, he fired his thrusters to dodge Megatron's unstoppable charge. Then, suspended in midair, Starscream reassumed his proto-shape and rained down a volley of missiles. Everything around Megatron disappeared in the intense flare of tactical photon warheads. He felt the floor shake with the impact of the detonations, felt ringing agony through every system. Even before the explosions had subsided, Megatron was reshaping himself again, rearing up on two legs to catch Starscream as the Seeker fell.

The two of them fell in a blur of savage blows and grappling moves. Again the floor shook as they landed, and Megatron delivered a series of pile-driver blows to Starscream, crushing him into the floor so hard that when he parried the last and rolled away to counterattack, he left behind a visible depression.

Megatron relished this, the final hand-to-hand confrontation, untainted by missiles or beams. The meeting of bot to bot, as it had been in the pits. This was when he was most alive. He even preferred to abandon hand weapons. The true test of a bot's might and a bot's will came when he met another with nothing but bare hands.

Again he and Starscream came together, Starscream punishing Megatron with lightning-fast spinning kicks and blows that seemed to come from nowhere. That was the Seeker in him, dodging and rolling and never quite where you thought he would be.

Weathering the storm, Megatron awaited his opportunity. Starscream came after him again and again, flurries of blows, but Megatron knew—yes. The moment came when Starscream grew just that little bit overconfident. He opened himself up, let his balance go just the tiniest bit to add a bit more force to a roundhouse punch, and before he even knew it was happening, Megatron was inside the arc of the swing, Starscream's arm flicked out of the way and Megatron's greater mass first lifted Starscream and then drove him down again.

Then it was over. Megatron hit Starscream, and hit

him again, and again and again and again until Starscream stopped resisting.

Rearing to his feet, Megatron looked around him. The Seeker contingent stood watching silently on one side of the vast space, near the aperture where they and Starscream had first entered. To the right, loosely clustered around the silent body of Sentinel Prime, Megatron's own inner circle of gladiators stood. All was silent.

He bent down over Starscream. "I still function," Megatron said.

He hauled the battered Seeker conspirator to his feet and spoke again, louder now, for the benefit of all assembled—and perhaps for the benefit of Optimus Prime, who might well have access to these events because of Alpha Trion's superb management of the Grid.

"You would make a useful example, were I to kill you," Megatron said. "Yet I believe I will keep you alive because you will make a better soldier than example. Would you care to continue your beating, or can we agree that you serve me and this coup plotting is a thing of the past?"

Starscream returned only a venomous stare. Megatron let him. "Excellent," he said. He turned his back on Starscream, knowing the moment for an assault had passed. It was time now to continue the theater of leadership, which meant—now that the villains had been identified and punished—pinning medals on the heroes. Megatron walked over to the Decepticon who had blocked Starscream's move for the Code Key of Justice.

"What do you call yourself, Decepticon?"

"Blackout," answered the bot. He was clearly a product of the Badlands. His exterior was scored with the marks of energy release, some much older than the main battles of the Civil War.

"You have a great future, Blackout," Megatron said, clasping hands with him. He looked around the room, making sure that everyone present had seen him bestow his favor on this Decepticon foot soldier. "I give you a task. Take the body of Sentinel Prime to Kaon. May it lay there, down in the pits that he so despised. When I have finished destroying the Autobots, I will return triumphant to Kaon and I will find some use for Sentinel Prime's remains. Perhaps in my first act as Prime, I will call for a vote on its method of disposal."

"Yes, Megatron," Blackout said.

"Yet first we must recover what Sentinel Prime sought to protect," Megatron cautioned. Without looking back at Starscream, he reached out a hand, palm up. "The Code Key of Power, if you please, Starscream."

Starscream handed it over without a word. Megatron felt its weight like the certainty of victory. "And now," he went on, "it is time to have the rest of what we came for."

In a blaze of released Energon, Megatron tore away part of the dying Sentinel Prime's inner torso shielding, the last layer of defense protecting Sentinel Prime's vitals and whatever else might be contained within the torn wreckage of his chassis. Inside—as the victorious Decepticons and even Starscream edged closer and saw—lay the Code Key of Justice. It shone and gleamed like the ideal of Justice given form. For a moment, seeing it brought Megatron back to the first heady days when his ideas about freedom and self-determination were just ideas, traded back and forth in the gladiator barracks while the pit surgeons worked clumsily to patch up the day's wounds.

Now ultimate freedom was within his grasp. Once the Plasma Energy Chamber was his, there would no longer be a way for the Autobots and Optimus Prime to resist. The Decepticons would have total sway over Cybertron, and the true era of greatness would begin.

Megatron reached out and laid his hands on the Code Key of Justice. He held it up to his followers, and a nanoklik later held up the Code Key of Power.

Then he approached the doubly locked code plate containing the access levers that would grant him the use of the Plasma Energy Chamber.

It was the last thing he needed to do to end the war and take control of Cybertron, in the name of freedom and in the name of Decepticons. Forever.

He inserted the keys and turned them.

The code plate came to life and glowed, searching the Keys and matching their signatures against its countersigns. It unlocked. Behind it a door unlocked, and a bright cylindrical chamber was revealed, at the center of which stood a smaller cylinder on a pedestal. It blazed with a light too bright to look at; every Decepticon within view polarized his optics.

The Plasma Energy Chamber. A concentrated hyperplasma of Energon, drawn via a transdimensional gateway from the endless supply of Energon that enlivened the planet Cybertron itself. To possess the Plasma Energy Chamber would be like having the Core of Cybertron under his direct control. It was within arm's reach.

Megatron walked into the chamber, bathing himself in the radiance of the Plasma Energy Chamber and in the anticipation of finally—after teracycles of war and frustration with the impossible resilience of Optimus Prime and the Autobots—finally realizing his dream.

He reached out to take the Plasma Energy Chamber. But before he could touch it, several things happened at once.

In the Hall of Records, Optimus Prime was preparing for a counterstrike against the Decepticon invasion.

He knew that Megatron was below the Council towers, and he knew that Starscream had infiltrated the city by means of the Fusion Link to Kalis. With him were Jazz, Ironhide, and Sideswipe. Their four-member team was ready and about to deploy when Alpha Trion appeared from his study, calling down from a catwalk over the former reading room that Optimus had repurposed as a staging area for small-team guerrilla missions.

"Optimus Prime," Alpha Trion said. "Teletraan-1 has deployed an emergency measure. The Plasma Energy Chamber is in danger of falling into Decepticon hands."

"And what has Teletraan-1 done to protect it?" Optimus asked.

Alpha Trion looked amazed at the words he was about to speak. "It has reactivated Omega Supreme," he said. "That is not a name I ever thought to speak again."

The walls fell away from around Megatron. In the sudden immensity of the space around him, he saw cells and gears, gyros and hydraulic joints, appear and begin to activate themselves, rising up from the plates of the floor and extending down from the ceiling. Something built and took shape from the very structure of the city itself, and as it did the huge chamber cracked and groaned under the extraordinary stress. The pillars began to shift. Some of them cracked in the middle or snapped off near floor or ceiling. Slowly, but with gathering momentum, the entire area began to collapse into itself.

Before him, he saw the Plasma Energy Chamber

begin to descend. He reached for it, but a suddenly upthrust cage of unbreakable alloy appeared and his fist crashed into it with no effect other than a large bang. The floor shifted, pitching him backward, and as he skidded on the tilting plates, Megatron realized was was happening.

The entire room—for all he could tell, the entire level—was an alt-form unlike any he had ever seen. And it was reassuming an original form not seen in more cycles than any Cybertronian could count.

With both hands he seized the cage surrounding the Plasma Energy Chamber as it drew level with the floor. But the process under way was stronger even than Megatron; inexorably the cage sank down into the floor, tearing itself free from him one finger at a time. When he looked up again, the ceiling was collapsing.

Optimus Prime came to a halt in the street outside the High Council Tower, near the ruins of the Traffic and Security Administration complex destroyed in the last Decepticon bombardment. He looked on in astonishment as the tower began what appeared to be a controlled collapse, falling in on itself without touching the surrounding structures.

And as it fell, something else was growing from within it.

"Omega Supreme," said Alpha Trion from behind him. Optimus Prime turned to see his mentor coming up behind the four Autobots who remained from the movement's early leadership. Together the four of them watched Omega Supreme reborn.

*   *   *

Omega Supreme had been the chartered Guardian of Cybertron's most important artifacts since the disappearance of the Primes, and his status was nearly as legendary as theirs. Most citizens of Iacon who watched his reappearance in Cybertronian history felt as if they were watching a story come to life. Optimus Prime certainly felt that way. The alt-form of the Guardian was a rocket, long and heavy, its thrusters clearly designed to assume directional functions once free of Cybertron's gravity well and the panels along the length of its fuselage clearly concealing weapons and sensor systems that would be deployed in space. In launch mode, the rocket was a great needle balanced atop a fire that was too bright to look at directly, even with polarized optics. The only Cybertronians who could have seen the rocket's exhaust without damage were the industrial bots who spent their lives in the blast furnaces and arc-welding shops of Tagan Heights and the Badlands.

Few of them were there to see Omega Supreme return to the living history of Cybertron. The specific protocol invoked by Teletraan-1 told Omega Supreme to assume his alt-form and automatically incorporate the Plasma Energy Chamber. Where he was taking it, no observer knew. "Could be one of the Moon Bases," Alpha Trion said. "I hope it is not Trypticon—although I would not be surprised if Omega Supreme could destroy the Trypticon Decepticons by himself, Dark Energon or no. This planet has only rarely seen a fighter as mighty and dedicated as Omega Supreme."

*   *   *

The immense physical presence of Omega Supreme was more than the mind could assimilate. How could he exist? Did this mean the other myths were true as well?

The perimeter room, already damaged by the fights that had killed Sentinel Prime—or nearly—and humbled Starscream—perhaps—was about to pancake straight down. The Decepticons held themselves tight to support pillars as the parts of the ceiling farthest from the pillars slammed down around them, sending out rolling walls of dust and concussion. Omega Supreme's assumption of his alt-form was nearly complete. It would have been long ago, thought Megatron, had he not been built into the foundation of the High Council Tower and the wall of Teletraan-1.

Six thrusters, their exhaust nozzles wider than Megatron's arm span, took form and locked into place. Steam began to drift from their interiors as Omega Supreme's power systems brought themselves online.

"The Plasma Energy Chamber is inside!" Megatron screamed at his followers. "Destroy Omega Supreme!"

Energy discharges stitched across the thrusters and the lower part of Omega Supreme's fuselage. They left scorch marks but had no other visible effect. "Again!" boomed Megatron, adding his own fire to the salvos.

No effect.

A rumble spread through the collapsing basements of the High Council Tower. Debris from upper floors rained down around them as the remains of the building fell away from Omega Supreme. And a second rumble, yet more menacing than the first, brought with it the first dim glow from within the thruster cones.

"Megatron," Catalycon said. "The exhaust! We'll never—"

"We retreat for now, then. But only for now." Megatron yelled out a signal and his retinue began to fall back, zigzagging their way from pillar to pillar as the final collapse of the High Council Tower approached. Megatron recognized bits of the balconies where he had pled his case in the Council Chamber. Long ago, that had been. Before he had known what betrayals Orion Pax had planned.

A falling statue of one of the Primes crushed Catalycon where he stood. The gladiators and Seekers looked to their commanders. Starscream was looking up, and Megatron knew immediately what he was thinking. He and the Seekers could get out if there was an opening above. Megatron and the other gladiators would have to climb, or burrow their way back to where the tunnels remained intact.

The rumble from the thruster cones intensified, and pilot flames appeared high up within their housings. "Starscream," Megatron said. "If you fly out of here thinking that you leave me to my death, know one thing."

"What's that?"

"If I am not dead, you will be. But," Megatron said, "if you fly out of here on a mission I choose for you, that would be a different situation, and might entitle you to mercy."

"And Dark Energon, yes?" Starscream had resisted

becoming Darkened, but Megatron could see it in him. He had the desire, the same as the rest.

"If your mission succeeds, we will have all the Dark Energon any of us could ever want." Megatron was speaking louder now, over the rising rumble of the thrusters and the settling booms that came from the wreckage of the High Council Tower. Above them he could see open sky.

"Do not fail, Starscream. Bring Omega Supreme down or die trying."

And the world disappeared in fire and light.

From the street beyond the Plaza of the Primes, Optimus Prime watched as the thrusters of the mighty rocket ignited, the blast and heat wash knocking the watching Autobots back on their heels and obliterating all remaining trace of the High Council Tower. "Not a good time to be down subsurface," Jazz observed.

"That's true," agreed the laconic Ironhide.

Optimus Prime knew what they were thinking and hoping: that Megatron and Starscream had somehow been trapped by the immense shifts below the surface, and that they had been unable to get clear of Omega Supreme's alt-form exhaust radius.

"I wouldn't count on it," he said.

"Who's counting? A bot can dream," Jazz said, watching as the huge rocket of Omega Supreme slowly lifted off into the blackness of the sky.

A transmission reached them: "Autobots. This is Omega Supreme. Your circumstances are dire. You would have done well to awaken me before things reached this point."

"We did not know—" began Optimus Prime, and then seven contrails, running in perfect formation, rose from the wreckage surrounding the crater where once had stood the High Council Tower.

Starscream and his Air Commanders had survived.

The Seekers loyal to the Autobot cause were all running patrols, either to protect the fusion-power conduit along the Kali-Con Road or far to the east, where the danger of mass incursions from Decepticon foot soldiers—or their vehicular alt-forms—was a constant danger.

The sole exception was Jetfire, the Autobots' sole defector from the Seekers, who was deep in a lab devising ways for some Autobots to engineer their alt-forms' flight capability. It might well have been a dead end scientifically, but Optimus Prime believed that the Autobot chances in the war would improve dramatically if they could at least harry the Decepticon strength in the air. Automated defense missile batteries were useful sometimes, but to make a real difference the Autobots needed intelligent warriors in the air to match up with Starscream's well-trained and battle-hardened squadrons.

They did not have those warriors right now, as Starscream closed in on the rocket form of Omega Supreme and the critical cargo he carried.

"Roll out!" Optimus Prime ordered his lieutenants. "We're not going out on counter-infiltration patrol today. Megatron is either still in Iacon or on his way. Let's get him."

The natural rotation of Cybertron would have carried Omega Supreme's launch point away to the east as he rose straight up out of Cybertron's gravity well, had he not detected the pursuit of Starscream and undertaken evasive action. Deploying wings since he had achieved enough altitude that the thickness of the atmosphere wouldn't tear them apart, Omega Supreme arced away back to the west, remaining over Autobot-held territory while still trying to fulfill Teletraan-1's imperative that he reach space and go on to the designated location for the Plasma Energy Chamber.

Where that was, he did not know yet. The protocol for that was to be unlocked when he reached orbit and had shaken off the Decepticon pursuit.

Having lain dormant for most of the war, Omega Supreme had to assimilate much of the contemporary history of Cybertron through a high-level Grid connection. The facts shocked him:

```
Eighty-five percent of the surface of Cybertron
under Decepticon control
Only three members of the High Council at the time
the rebellion began still alive—and all three, in-
cluding Ratbat, gone over to the Decepticons
The AllSpark ejected from the Well
Sentinel Prime dying
```

It was a miracle, concluded Omega Supreme, that the Autobots still fought on. And that miracle could be laid squarely at the feet of Optimus Prime. Amazing that a data clerk could take control of history and raise himself to take on one of the more dire challenges that Cybertronian civilization had ever faced.

Internal challenges were always the most dangerous. This was always true, and for Omega Supreme it was particularly true, as he had seven Seekers hot on his trail.

Grimly he went on, accelerating in a spiral toward the zero-gravity haven that—unless Teletraan-1 had plans he did not know about—awaited him on the other side of Trypticon Station.

Optimus Prime was gifted with extraordinarily acute optics. He zoomed in on the aerial battle taking place over Iacon just as the seven Seekers split into three flights of two and attacked from left, right, and below. Volleys of missiles spat from the wings of all seven Seekers, and a nanoklik later explosions flared along Omega Supreme's flanks.

Then the Guardian returned fire—or no, Optimus Prime realized he had fired first, but his armaments were different. Omega Supreme's normal missile batteries could not be deployed in the atmosphere while he was flying at full speed; instead he had a string of missile pods located near his thruster cones. They opened and ejected round missiles, which, once they were clear of his slipstream, reconfigured themselves to fly and target the nearest enemy. Optimus Prime had read about this system in the archives long ago, when he was merely a clerk.

Now he saw it in use, as one of Starscream's Seekers suddenly seemed to be surrounded by a cloud of tiny sparks. These were the drop-missiles' engines flaring into life.

A moment later the Seeker disappeared in a blackening fireball. Pieces of it, none bigger than Optimus Prime's head, tumbled in a long, shallow arc from the impact point back toward the surface of Cybertron.

Not a nanoklik after that, the second member of that flight spun out of control as one of its wings blew apart into shrapnel that flew back and shredded its tail. Helplessly it began to spiral away into the rugged distance.

Optimus Prime did not see it hit the surface, because simultaneously with Omega Supreme's fatal hit on the second Seeker came a bright flare from the rocket's own exhaust. Optimus zoomed in and saw that two of the nozzles were blown away. Already the effect was visible; Omega Supreme's perfect upward spiral suddenly flattened out, grew ragged.

The five remaining Seekers, Starscream among them, cut in and concentrated their fire on the damaged spot. Their missiles struck home even as another of Starscream's officers exploded a nanoklik later, falling out of the coalescing fireball armless and with legs flailing because it had reverted to proto-form in the panic of its devastating injury. Omega Supreme's long form yawed off its axis and then, as its thrust failed further, began to tumble.

"No," Jazz said next to Optimus Prime.

All of them watched. "How can they destroy the Guardian?" Ironhide said, in a display of emotion unlike any Optimus Prime had seen from him.

Omega Supreme's fall to the surface seemed to take forever, as the four Seekers harried him all the way down, stinging his armored exterior with continued volleys of missiles and ion-cannon bolts.

"Mission change again," Optimus Prime said.

"What now?" Prowl asked.

"Move out for the impact site," said Optimus Prime. "If the Plasma Energy Chamber survives the impact, you can believe that Megatron will be coming after it."

As he finished speaking, Omega Supreme hit the surface. Starscream and the other three Seekers pulled out in sharp climbs from the mushrooming explosion that rose from the impact site. The pillar of fire hung in the air, seemingly fed by additional explosions from the impact. Optimus Prime imagined all of Omega Supreme's missiles exploding, tearing his alt-form apart—or dismembering his proto-form, if Omega Supreme had somehow managed to reassume it at the moment of impact.

Optimus Prime mobilized, taking alt-form with the rest of his squad and redlining toward the impact site, but he could not imagine how this mission might end in success. He would recover the Plasma Energy Chamber, perhaps, and perhaps could even sequester it somewhere again, but the loss of Omega Supreme was disastrous for the dwindling hopes of the Autobot cause.

They arrived at the crater, skidding to a halt and re-assuming proto-form as soon as their momentum wouldn't pitch them into the smoking depths of the crater itself.

Across the rim, partially obscured by that smoke,

loomed the figure of Megatron, in alt-form, his tracked hulk bristling with weaponry and surrounded by the wheeled turrets of his closest gladiator minions. They reassumed their proto-forms nonchalantly as Starscream and the other three Seekers roared overhead.

"We've come for the Plasma Energy Chamber," Megatron said. "But we have found so much more."

"You're about to find a little more than you bargained for," Sideswipe growled.

Megatron grinned, the violet light of Dark Energon playing about his eyes. "Wonderful," he said.

There was no chance, Optimus Prime thought. He did not want to waste the lives of those Autobots who were dearest to him, and who meant the most to the potential survival of the Autobot cause. He was about to order a retreat. Three of the powerful Seekers had fallen that day, as well as who knew how many of Megatron's other soldiers down in the subsurface collapse. Even that total could not balance off the loss of Omega Supreme, but the Autobot situation was dire enough that they could count this a success on the mere grounds that they had not lost any of the bots they had begun the day with. Yesterday they had not known Omega Supreme was available. Therefore his loss was not so terrible.

And the Plasma Energy Chamber could not have survived, could it?

"Are you thinking what I'm thinking?" Jazz asked quietly.

Optimus Prime looked at his oldest friend. Bumblebee, too, awaited whatever order he would give.

"I might be," he said.

"Outstanding," Jazz said with a wink. He turned and without another word blew the turret off one of Megatron's gladiator alt-forms.

No! Optimus Prime was about to say—but then he realized, yes. What else could they do? They could go down fighting, because if the Plasma Energy Chamber had survived only for the Autobots to lose it, all was lost.

He fired, too, lighting up a line of shell explosions across the opposite rim of the crater. From the smoke came a fusillade of return fire, and around the crater Optimus Prime could see the proto-forming gladiators, Darkened and in full charge. The Dark Energon made them feel invincible, and sometimes Optimus Prime thought they nearly were. It was certainly harder to put them down when they were Darkened than at other times.

They would fight. If this was to be the final confrontation of the war, then so be it. Optimus Prime would meet Megatron and best him, or he would die in the attempt.

"Librarian!" came Megatron's voice from the smoke. "Let us decide things once and for all!"

Optimus Prime reared back and threw a fallen piece of Seeker spinning across in the direction of the voice. He heard the impact and the surprised and angry shout of Megatron.

"Coming for you, brother," Megatron said, low and menacing.

"You know where to find me, brother," answered Optimus Prime. "One shall stand, one shall fall."

He was ready, with his three closest Autobot confidants, to take on these dozen or more Darkened De-

cepticons with their Seeker support. They would fight
as they knew how to fight.

And then, once again, everything changed as the
gargantuan proto-form of Omega Supreme stood
ponderously up out of the crater.

Optimus Prime could not remember a sight that inspired him more. Through all the long ages of the
war, all the defeats and the signal successes, all the
death and the ruination of Cybertron—here, this res-
urrection of Omega Supreme had him believing anything was possible. "Fight, Autobots!" he thundered.
"For Cybertron, fight!"

The battle was joined.

Omega Supreme destroyed two Decepticon gladiators before they had fully comprehended the fact that he was not destroyed. Wounded? Yes, his proto-form bore the marks of Starscream's missiles and the rest of the Seeker's armaments. But he could stand, and he could fight. He picked up two gladiators, each only two-thirds his size, and hammered them together until pieces started to come off them. Then he dropped them into the depths of the crater his impact had made, and he joined his fellow Autobots in their battle.

Megatron drove the wavering gladiators forward. "Remember," he said to each and every Decepticon, "every death means more Dark Energon for you! And victory over the librarian means Dark Energon for all, as much as you can consume! Now kill for me, Decepticons! End this war and capture Cybertron for yourselves!"

This speech, thundering out in the smoke and the chaos of the battle, rallied the deranged Decepticons even as the attacks from the Autobots tore through them. Megatron was right: Every time a Decepticon died, the Dark Energon from its body flowed out and then infused its nearest comrades—as if Dark Energon were somehow conscious, and sought to unify itself into one great pool that could power anything imaginable. The battle, so recently turning in the Autobots' favor, became a stalemate again, small groups of Autobots and Decepticons fighting in a deadlock at two points along the crater's rim.

Ironhide and a Decepticon came together, and the force of their collision broke the weakened edge of the crater, catapulting them into its depths. Optimus Prime watched them fall until he could not see; then he fought forward, breaking the leg from a gladiator bot and leaping into the crater after Ironhide just as two other Decepticons leaped after their comrade.

The five of them crashed together in a melee that ranged across the burning slag at the bottom of the crater. Optimus, merciless in the cold fury of battle, caught one of the gladiators as it sprang toward Ironhide, who had slipped on the treacherous footing. He bore the Decepticon to the ground, crushing it under his weight. It struck at his face with the energy spike that sprouted from its forearm, but Optimus Prime leaned inside the arc of the blow. He caught the Decepticon's head in both hands as its energy spike grated along the back of his neck, burning and sending a nauseating charge through his body—until he reared back and snapped the Decepticon's head from its body.

The energy spike fell away. Optimus Prime looked up to see that Ironhide had already finished off the other two Decepticons. "Let's go," Optimus Prime said.

They scaled the crater wall and reemerged into the battle.

And it was then, as Omega Supreme smashed through the massed rank of Darkened gladiators, that Megatron outflanked him and smashed him down to one knee with a hammer blow that the Guardian never saw coming. The Darkened gladiators fell upon him in a mass. Optimus Prime joined the battle, pulling one of them away, but so many of the gladiators had died that the Dark Energon concentrated in each of the surviving ones made them shockingly powerful. Optimus Prime and Jazz together barely dispatched the gladiator, with Jazz taking out one of its legs and then the two of them blowing it apart with ion-cannon blasts. Ironhide waded into the mass of gladiators as well, suffering terrible damage and inflicting even worse—yet it was almost as if every gladiator they dispatched made the others so much more powerful that the transference of Dark Energon created defeat from victory.

Omega Supreme crashed to the ground at the edge of the crater, setting off a small cascade of bits of landscape and destroyed Decepticons. Three of Megatron's gladiators survived. Ironhide and Sideswipe caught one of them in a perfect crossfire, Ironhide's cannons striking fatally through its head after Sideswipe straightened the 'Con up with a strike to the small of its back. Optimus Prime, Jazz, and Prowl struck simultaneously at the second, destroying it in the act of tearing loose a cable from the back of Omega Supreme's good leg. The third struck out with a hooked chain, shredding the side of Ironhide's face.

With a roar of pain startling because Ironhide was renowned for his stoicism and toughness, the bruising Autobot spun away and fell into the crater. The last Decepticon gladiator, brimming with the Dark Energon infusions of its dead fellows, sprang at all five of the remaining Autobots. Bumblebee caught it in midair, tumbling over backward as it lashed the chain over his back. Jazz and Prowl closed in, with Sideswipe hanging back looking for the right shot.

Optimus Prime turned back to Megatron in time to see Omega Supreme reach out and crush the skull of the last surviving gladiator even as the other four Autobots attacked it. A swirl of Dark Energon appeared to spill from the dying Decepticon's head, only to twist back up and round Omega Supreme's arm on the way to Megatron, who inhaled it with a gasp. "Ahh," he said. "You, Guardian, will never know the pleasure."

He drove his sword into Omega Supreme's back. Omega Supreme opened his mouth but made no sound. He swung an arm back, knocking Megatron to the edge of the crater. Optimus Prime took a step toward the falling Guardian, but Megatron acted first—extending an arm, he blew the edge of the crater out from under Optimus Prime's feet, sending him downward once again, rolling with a small debris slide until he crashed into the obstacle of Ironhide. The Autobot veteran arrested Optimus Prime's slide. "Go, go get him," Ironhide said. "Can't see."

Optimus saw the damage the chain had done to Ironhide's face. He looked back up to see the rest of his allies staring in shock at the sight none of them had ever imagined seeing.

Omega Supreme lay unmoving, facedown, one arm dangling over the unstable edge of the crater. He was alive, but barely; the glimmer of his Spark was very faint. Megatron stood poised over the Guardian, blade against the back of his neck. "Shall I kill him?" He taunted the Autobots. "I came for something else, but if you press me I will kill him and then take what I want."

From overhead came the sounds of Seekers, and a moment later Starscream and his three surviving officers landed, proto-forming as they touched down. "Always arriving right at the end, Starscream," Megatron said.

"I didn't see you facing down the missiles up there," Starscream answered. "You wanted the Guardian. You have him."

"Yes, I do. Lend a hand here," Megatron said. He and the three Seekers turned Omega Supreme over on his back, the Autobots looking on but unable to intervene. "Wait until you see what I plan, brother. I do not need to take Iacon if I can wait for Iacon to take itself. And I do not need to kill Omega Supreme because once I have what I came for, the killing part of the war will swiftly come to a close." Megatron reached into the body of Omega Supreme and tore free the Plasma Energy Chamber. Omega Supreme spasmed and tried to rise but could not. He fell back, lying on his side, his life's fluids leaking from the holes torn and blasted through his armored exterior.

Megatron said, "First Sentinel Prime and now you, Guardian. You die so easily it is difficult for me to take any pride in the killing. You Autobots should learn that when you hide important things within your bodies, bad things are going to happen."

He tucked the Plasma Energy Chamber into both hands. "Optimus Prime, what do you have hidden within your body? Soon I will have my chance to find out, brother!" Megatron proclaimed, holding it up.

But Optimus ignored the taunt. "Sentinel Prime?" he said.

"Oh, yes," Megatron said. "He is missing something I tore free of his body as well. Probably he is dead now, if not from losing the Code Key then from the collapse that accompanied the Guardian's awakening. I lost a number of fine soldiers in that collapse. But if you get to Omega Supreme immediately . . ." He shrugged. "Sometimes the unexpected does happen."

Optimus Prime understood. He was being told that Omega Supreme might live if the battle ended now. And to make the decision a little easier, Megatron had fed him a tidbit about Sentinel Prime. Optimus had known Megatron for a long, long time. His former friend turned dire adversary was a skilled liar, but Optimus Prime knew the signs. He did not think Megatron was lying about this. He had come for the Plasma Energy Chamber, and he had it.

If the battle was over, and Omega Supreme survived, then the Autobots would have won the day, Optimus reasoned. The Decepticons had taken heavy losses. He could accept that, regardless of what Megatron wanted with the Plasma Energy Chamber. The Autobots would have the Plasma Energy Chamber back. Alpha Trion's searches in the ancient corners of the DataNet were beginning to bear fruit. A few more Seekers were beginning to defect to the Autobot cause. The times were dark, but Megatron was drunk with his success and with the pervasive effects of the Dark Energon. What would he and the rest of the Decepticons do when it ran out? How long before they would be tearing one another apart—especially with Starscream always ready to sow discord wherever he was?

Megatron thought he was toying with the Autobots, but in his towering megalomania he had lost track of the idea that someone—or something, some phenomenon—could be toying with him.

Optimus Prime pointed a blackened finger at Megatron. "Brother, you will find that Dark Energon is not the boon you believe it to be. And you will end up wishing you had never come to Iacon in search of the Plasma Energy Chamber. Prowl, find Ratchet! With me, Jazz! The rest of you, guard Iacon!" Optimus Prime said. He leaped back to the bottom of the crater and from there rushed through the sheared opening into the tunnels that would lead back into the center of Iacon.

Behind him, Megatron alt-formed and accelerated away to the west. Of all the Autobots, only Bumblebee did not follow Optimus Prime. Moving at an angle away from Megatron's path, he stormed off into the wastes, assuming his alt-form and disappearing in a wash of rust particles that hung in the air behind him. He knew where Megatron was going.

CHAPTER THIRTY

In the ruins of Crystal City, down in the depths, where the lens of the Geosynchronous Energon Bridge shone with its starlike brilliance, Megatron stood with the Plasma Energy Chamber. He was alone, and did not speak. Opening one of his intakes, he removed a vibrant ingot of Dark Energon and held it in one hand, observing it as if he had never seen anything in the world that could give him such delight. In his other hand, he held the Plasma Energy Chamber balanced on his upturned palm. He approached the lens and held the Plasma Energy Chamber up so he could be certain that its shape and diameter matched the depression in the center of the upward-facing surface of the lens. He appeared satisfied, and slowly—demonstrating, for Megatron, an unusual hesitation—he sank the ingot of Dark Energon into the top of the cylinder of the Plasma Energy Chamber.

For a moment, nothing happened. Then the Plasma Energy Chamber grew brighter, and brighter still. Its brilliance reduced Megatron and the remains of the installation around him to faint outlines, and then obscured Megatron entirely . . .

And then it began, slowly and horribly, to be tinged with the sickly, hungry violet of Dark Energon.

The glow, still intense, dimmed. Megatron averted his gaze, even he unable to look directly at the now-polluted Plasma Energy Chamber. He reached out and found the lens with one hand, then brought his hands together until by touch he had placed the Plasma Energy Chamber into the depression.

The lens turned violet at once. Below it, violet tainted the channel that led from the lens down into the depths of the Bridge as the bolus of Dark Energon bled slowly down into the very core of Cybertron. Megatron watched, baring his teeth in triumph, his arms outstretched over the violet radiance. He had inverted the original purpose of the Plasma Energy Chamber, turning it to his own purposes—and now victory was that much closer. Now the Decepticons would never starve for Dark Energon. Now the Autobots would have to scavenge and scrape for whatever Energon they might find amid the ruins of Cybertron's war-torn cities.

Sooner or later, the weary, Energon-deprived population of the planet would turn to Dark Energon because even those who did not wish to would have no choice. Megatron realized that he had just made it possible for the Decepticons to win the war without firing another shot.

Not that he would do it that way. Where was the fun in fighting a war if you weren't going to fight? And when he crushed Optimus Prime—when he finally had the librarian under the heel of his boot—

Megatron wanted to have fought for that moment.
That was the gladiator in him. It would never die,
whether he took over Cybertron or . . . he looked up
the shaft in the direction of the limitless space beyond. What other worlds were there to conquer, beyond even the worlds Cybertron had known before
her long senescence?

Megatron would find them, he resolved as he
looked up the shaft and watched the violet spread.

From several subsurface levels above, having just
ducked out of Megatron's view up the shaft where the
lens focused its beam toward the distant receiver on
Trypticon Station, Bumblebee watched. *No,* Bumblebee tried to say, but there was nothing he could do.
The Plasma Energy Chamber, transformed and dese-
crated, had been transformed into a reservoir of Dark
Energon that Megatron used to infect the very core of
Cybertron itself. The change in the planet was a feeling in Bumblebee's physical form, as if something had
been untuned ever so slightly, the substance of the
world thrown into a new balance that was hostile to
everything that had lived there before.

Cybertron would now make Dark Energon. The
essence of Unicron had returned to alter and debase
what Unicron himself could not destroy.

Never had Bumblebee wanted anything more than
he wanted to fight and die at that moment. But what
would it gain? Optimus Prime had drilled that principle into all of his lieutenants. What does a fight gain?
If you are to die, what do we gain by your death?
Honor is honorable, but dying for the sake of honor
when you could live to fight and defeat an enemy was

a waste. Optimus Prime's formulation of it was simple: "Never let courage be the enemy of reason."

Bumblebee almost did. But in the end, reason prevailed.

He had to report back to Iacon and tell Optimus Prime and Alpha Trion what he had seen.

In the shattered subsurface levels of Iacon, Optimus Prime searched for Sentinel Prime in vain. With him, Jazz turned down byways that terminated in cave-ins or unstable tilting floors leading to bottomless dropoffs. Neither of them knew how far down the damage went, or in truth how far down the tunnels of Iacon reached. They were moving toward the outer edges of the immense complex devoted to the function of Teletraan-1, and then they circulated around that edge, knowing that the Plasma Energy Chamber had been hidden somewhere in that area.

"How do you think he got out?" Jazz asked along the way. "He's been hidden away for how long, and then suddenly he appears right when Megatron's about to get the Code Keys and find the Plasma Energy Chamber? I'm suspicious."

"You know what would make you more suspicious? If I told you that Starscream did it."

"Starscream?" Jazz looked skeptical.

"I think he's been looking for a chance to take things over on the Decepticon side," Optimus Prime said. "He contacted us a while back and gave the impression that the war might end if he could . . . you know . . ."

"Kill Megatron?"

Optimus Prime was nodding. "Yes. Kill or get him

out of the way. I don't know if it would have worked, but I think that's where Sentinel Prime came from. I think that Starscream let him go. But now we need to find out where he's gone, if he's still alive."

"Optimus," Jazz said after a pause, during which they started to see evidence of scorching and noticed the collapsed wreckage was in smaller pieces. "Maybe he's just dead, and there's no point in going to look for him."

"If I find that out, you'll be right," Optimus said.

"But while you're finding it out, what are you missing up in the Hall of Records? What kind of head start are you giving Megatron? You need to think about the living."

Stopping and pivoting to face Jazz, Optimus said, "You think I'm not worried about the living? How much would it help us if Sentinel Prime were alive, and could be repaired, and fight alongside us?"

Jazz stepped right up and stood his ground. "I don't know. You ready to not be Prime anymore? You ready to go back to being Orion Pax?"

They stared each other down, both bots holding themselves back from the next intemperate comment that would escalate things to the point where hard feelings lasted beyond the moment. "We're close," Optimus said at the end of the difficult pause. "Too close to not find out now."

Jazz didn't say anything else. He walked on, and they kept looking. Shortly after, they started to have their questions answered.

It wasn't that difficult to tell when they had arrived at the site of Sentinel Prime's return. "All you have to do is look for the place where everything got melted,"

Jazz said. "Then when you can't tell what anything is? That's the place with the thing that you're looking for."

Optimus Prime didn't say anything. Jazz had to talk, and he had to complain. That was all right. It balanced off Optimus's own tendency to take everything too seriously. Plus, Jazz was right. All either one of them could see was a cooling pool of slag directly under Omega Supreme's launch, and partially melted and scorched ruins radiating out from that area. Part of Teletraan-1 looked to be damaged; Optimus would have to call in a repair crew once they had made sure that no Decepticon ambush still lurked in the area.

As soon as they got a few good steps away from the launch site, the signs of battle were everywhere, visible even in the aftermath of the collapse. Here were marks of detonation, there were bits of a Decepticon who had met a violent end, or a smeared pool of vital fluid.

"I don't see any Prime around here except you," Jazz said.

Optimus didn't, either. "Jazz," he said, "I can tell when Megatron is lying. He wasn't lying."

"Maybe you're not as good at reading him as you thought."

Both of them kept up the search for some time before Optimus Prime spoke again. "No," he said with confidence. "He believed what he said to me. That means that someone survived down here, and got away." He looked around. "But where, is the question . . ."

His portable Grid node chimed. Optimus ran the communication through a security protocol; it came from inside the Hall of Records. He allowed it, and Prowl's voice spoke from the speaker set next to Optimus's jaw. "I'm going to tell you something that you already know, but you don't know I know," Prowl said.

"Then tell me instead of telling me you're going to tell me," said Optimus Prime.

"I don't know where you would find him down there," Prowl said. "But there are two things you need to know up here."

"Tell me."

"One, Bumblebee came back. Megatron has polluted the Plasma Energy Chamber. The Core of Cybertron is now making Dark Energon. The other is that—we're not sure how this happened—but Sentinel Prime got a short message out over the Grid."

Optimus Prime looked around at the ruins and the bodies. "No wonder," he said.

"No wonder what?"

"No wonder I didn't find him here with all of these dead Decepticons," Optimus Prime said. "Where is he?"

"We're still trying to trace the path of the message," Prowl said. "There have been a lot of disturbances on the Grid. But we think it—"

The signal cut out. Optimus Prime tried to open a channel again, three times, but got nothing. "Jazz," he said, "we need to get back up to the Hall of Records right now."

It felt like the end.

By the time Optimus Prime and Jazz had gotten back to the surface and taken some nourishment in the command post, Bumblebee's report had struck a note of doom through the Hall of Records. It was difficult to maintain any sense of optimism in the main reading room, where the windows still looked out across the ruins of the High Council Tower toward the pall of smoke that hung over the site of the battle for Omega Supreme and the Plasma Energy Chamber.

"Are you sure?" Optimus Prime asked.

"Are you asking me or Bumblebee? Because he can barely talk," Prowl snapped back.

"Prowl. I don't think anyone here needs sarcasm right now," Optimus Prime said quietly. "I'll ask again. Are you sure that you heard from Sentinel Prime?"

"Yes," Prowl said.

When he didn't elaborate, Optimus Prime prodded him. "What makes you sure?"

"The signal traces to the last relay from the Badlands, the low-orbit satellite that serves everything from Slaughter City to Hydrax. Except for the space-port. That was on its own part of the Grid, but it's been cut off since way back. Beginning of the war, al-most." Prowl started to sink into his reports and intelligence-gathering, which was what he always did when personal relationships got difficult to negotiate.

"Is that your only data point?" Alpha Trion asked. "What else?"

"The frequency is commonly used by the under-ground gladiator circles, usually for internal commu-nications that they don't want picked up by the regular Grid. That makes me think it originated from Kaon or Blaster City," Prowl said. "And when I started to backtrack the signal, the trace was elimi-nated by an antitracking protocol that dates from— anyone want to guess?"

"Beginning of the war, maybe? Written by gladiator gangsters to keep people from tracking their matches?" Jazz prompted.

Prowl inclined his head in Jazz's direction. "That's it," he said. "We used to run into this all the time when I was on the Hydrax-Badlands circuit." Prowl had been a civilian police officer, working as a liaison between the militias of various city-states and the High Council Guard, which was nominally in control of civilian law.

"So Sentinel Prime is in Kaon," Sideswipe said.

No one had to answer.

"What now?" Prowl asked quietly.

Optimus Prime did not know. But he thought that the first step would be to withdraw all of the groups of Autobot guerrillas from the outer limits of their territory. It was time to make a last stand at Iacon, and they would need every Autobot to do it.

He did not remember bringing the idea up directly, but it entered the conversation. It was debated back and forth, with increasing intensity, until an unexpected voice broke the conversation apart and reassembled it along lines that they were all ashamed they hadn't followed in the first place.

Bumblebee was struggling with the hastily configured repair to his vocoder, and his speech was broken and barely audible. But knowing Ratchet's fix was at best temporary, he forced himself to join the debate.

"A last stand? Well, we can't let Sentinel Prime just die," he said. "What kind of Autobots would we be?"

The simple—some of those present, in moments of weakness, might even have called it naïve—sentiment shut everyone in the room up. The silence went on long enough that young Bumblebee started to look deeply uncomfortable. Then Prowl said, "He's right."

"Sentinel Prime was never an Autobot. He didn't care about the movement back at the beginning," Jazz said.

Ironhide stepped up, his face still shiny with fresh welds where Ratchet had put him back together. "He came around," Ironhide said. "Not everyone gets the message right away."

"Yeah," Cliffjumper said.

Jazz wasn't convinced. "But how long did it take him? How do we know the whole thing isn't a setup by Megatron? Or by Starscream, even? That Seeker's got more schemes in him than Ironhide's got scars."

Ratchet poked his head into the middle of the argument long enough to bring the first bit of good news

they'd had in some time. "Omega Supreme is alive,"
he said. "I put him mostly back together. He'll live.
And knowing him, he'll force his way back onto the
battlefield."

The Guardian lived. They could all take a little sol-
ace from that. And when Ultra Magnus reported in to
say that he and his band of commandos—loosely
known as the Wreckers—had intercepted and destroyed a Decepticon armored convoy on the Iacon-
Hydrax road, everyone relaxed a little. The situation
was still dire; there was still not enough Energon and
far too much Dark Energon; the Decepticons out-
numbered and outgunned the Autobots, controlling
most of Cybertron and its resources, not to mention
its space.

Yet as long as there lived Autobots to carry on the
fight, all was not lost.

"Will he be able to fight anytime soon?" Optimus
Prime asked.

Ratchet looked down at the floor. "That depends
on what you mean by soon. I'm going to say no.
More or less, I put him back together after he was
blown apart in midair, crashed from a nearly orbital
height, took a whole lot of shots from a whole lot of
bots, and then had his trunk rummaged through for
the Plasma Energy Chamber. If you think he should
be fighting soon after I patched him up from all that,
maybe you need a different medic."

And with that, Ratchet left. No one was sure what
to say. They had never seen Optimus Prime be so
offhandedly thoughtless before. Now he was conscious of it, too, and wasn't sure how to handle it. He
owed Ratchet an apology. That would have to wait,

TRANSFORMERS: EXODUS   283

though. Before he had time to soothe hurt feelings, he had a war to fight and a planet to save. "Bumblebee is right," Optimus Prime said. "We need to go get Sentinel Prime. Alpha Trion, that means we need to know where he is."

"I already told you where he is," Prowl said.

Optimus reached out and put a hand on Prowl's shoulder. "I know. It's good work. But let's be certain, and as soon as we're certain, we'll go."

Alpha Trion went back into his study to do whatever it was he did in there that he wouldn't let the rest of the Autobots see, and Optimus Prime returned to the large reading table on which he still kept the charts and reports he needed. All of the data on those charts also existed in his head, but Optimus Prime liked to see things in front of him, in the real world.

"Bumblebee," he said, "tell me what you saw in Crystal City."

After he had taken a few cycles to process what it meant, Optimus Prime stepped up to his Autobot subordinate and clapped him on the shoulder. "Thank you for the report, Bumblebee. That was a bold action, and it was rewarded. It is good that we know this even though the knowledge brings no pleasure." Looking around the room, Optimus Prime thought again—how many times had he thought this?—that he was gifted with superb followers. No leader could survive without them.

"Now we go to Kaon," he said. Looking back at Bumblebee, he added, "And when we return, we must do something about Trypticon Station. Unless we have already waited too long."

CHAPTER THIRTY-TWO

Alpha Trion had a last resort. It had been in place since just after the final Breaking of the Primes, and Alpha Trion himself had checked on it periodically in the endless cycles that had passed since, to make sure it was all still functional. He knew that he had to tell Optimus Prime. He also knew that once he set this plan in motion, circumstances and Optimus Prime's own sense of responsibility to the Autobots under his command would make it nearly inevitable.

Yet what other option was there? The Plasma Energy Chamber was polluted and turned into a conduit for the corruption of the Core of Cybertron itself. This was a crisis unprecedented in the history of Cybertron—and Alpha Trion had seen that history from the beginning. What other choice could he make?

It was time, he decided, to face the real possibility that Cybertron might never be the same.

He ran his fingers over the cover of the Covenant, and then flipped it open. It fell to the page for the coming orbital cycles. Alpha Trion could not read it all—he never could where the future was concerned, and he considered himself fortunate to be able to read it at all—but from what he could see, he was making the right choice.

It remained to be seen whether Optimus Prime would feel the same.

Optimus came in as Alpha Trion was reading the last comprehensible bits of the near future out of the Covenant. "I must go to Kaon," Optimus Prime said to Alpha Trion. "Sentinel Prime still lives. How can I leave him there, I who have appropriated his title?"

"It was put upon you by the High Council." Alpha Trion corrected him.

Optimus was silent for a moment. "But I did not refuse it."

"The way I remember it, you tried to," Alpha Trion said with a chuckle. "Which made those of us in favor of naming you Prime all the more certain that we had made the correct decision."

"Wait—" Optimus understood what Alpha Trion was saying. "You?"

Alpha Trion shook his head. "Not just me. But someone had to start the conversation. I had watched you for a long time, Optimus Prime. I had seen the way you tried to handle Megatron, and the way you considered every idea from every angle. Yours was the kind of leadership Cybertron needed."

"I'm not sure of that. Where has it gotten us?"

"Where would we be if you had not taken the lead?" Alpha Trion countered.

Optimus Prime had no answer.

"Before you go to Kaon," Alpha Trion went on, "there are a few things you need to know."

"Why can they not wait until I return from Kaon?"

Alpha Trion's face was bleak. "Because, Optimus Prime, you might not return. And because even if you do, the war might still be lost. Listen to what I have to say, and then we will see whether you think it should have waited on your speculative return."

The team selected to infiltrate Kaon Prison—for that was where careful analysis of the Grid said Sentinel Prime was being held—consisted of Jazz, Prowl, and Optimus Prime himself. A backup team of Sideswipe, Bumblebee, and Jetfire waited to aid in the extraction of the first team, and also to let them know if the Decepticons detected their entry. It was easier than might have been expected to enter Decepticon-held territory, for the simple reason that few Cybertronians who were not already Decepticons would want to go there. The Decepticons did not fear infiltration because they assumed they had the Autobots terrified— if not of Megatron, then of the creeping influence of Dark Energon, which the infiltration team could see everywhere. The six of them came easily to the edge of Kaon, along the road from Slaughter City. They had not yet had to fight, primarily because they traveled in alt-mode and made sure they looked like they were on ordinary business. Optimus Prime even towed a trailer full of nonsentient machine parts all the way from the edge of Decepticon territory to the edge of Kaon itself. There he signed it off to a bored manager at a refurbishing plant for war veterans being retrofitted for industrial work.

And there the team divided. The backup trio skirted the perimeter of Kaon until they found a good place to set up, in a former High Council regional office now long gone to disrepair.

Optimus Prime, with Prowl and Jazz, headed for the center of the city, where they would find the black pyramid and then descend into the farthest reaches of subsurface Kaon. For that was where they would find Sentinel Prime, in the notorious Kaon Prison.

The exterior of the pyramid was lightly guarded. Prowl worked his way around to the side of the sentry while Jazz strolled up to the opposite side and said, "Say, 'Con, where can I get some of that Dark Energon?"

The sentry looked at him as if he hadn't understood a word. Then Prowl caught him from the other side, severing the vital conduits through his neck in absolute silence. Jazz caught the body and the two of them dragged it off to the side while Optimus Prime worked the door open. Inside, the pyramid was dank and dripping with the oozy presence of Dark Energon. It was as if the substance had begun to grow there; Optimus Prime could feel its seductive presence working at the edges of his mind. "Don't touch anything you don't have to," he said quietly as they moved forward.

"Don't you worry about that," Jazz said.

Optimus Prime remembered the way down to the gladiator pits, which was where the prison now was—at least according to the best intelligence they had. It was all they had to go on, so they went on it. The levels between the surface and the prison, where once aspiring gladiators had trained endlessly in hopes of their first selection, were now largely empty, their equipment rusting into ruin. It was a vision of a future Cybertron, felt Optimus Prime. If Megatron won the war, all of the planet would look like this, seeping with Dark Energon, its citizens gone or enslaved. Only the Autobots could prevent that.

"This place is awful," Prowl said.

"Sure is," Jazz said. "If Sentinel Prime weren't in here, I'd say we should blow the whole thing up."

"Well, he is," Optimus Prime said. Prowl and Jazz shut up.

Far down past the level where Optimus had seen his first gladiator match, they found the prison. It was a huge open space, cold and slimy with condensations of Dark Energon. Openings in the walls led away to unknown places. "Underworld," Jazz said.

"That's what I was thinking." Prowl kept toward the center of the room.

It was possible that the Decepticons had made some kind of deal with the denizens of the Underworld. Optimus Prime wouldn't have put it past Megatron— or, more particularly, Shockwave, to whom the Underworlders would have been just another supply of interesting spare parts to reassemble. Whatever the nature of that relationship, the prison space did carry a whiff of the Underworld.

The prisoners were all dead, and by the looks of it had been so for a long time. Shackled to the walls with no way to access Energon, they had languished slowly until finally their Sparks went out to rejoin the AllSpark in the infinity of space. The sole exception was Sentinel Prime, who lay chained to a pillar in the center of the room. Optimus Prime started toward him and was ambushed by a pair of Darkened Decepticon Guardians who charged from the tunnels and struck him down with energy whips. His optics fuzzed out and a raging agony spread down his spine and out through his limbs as he hit the floor. He rolled, anticipating another blow and instinctively bringing his ion cannons to bear.

As his vision cleared, he saw that Jazz was down and Prowl was squared off against both guards, skipping nimbly across the floor to prevent them flanking him while he fired off a steady stream of deadly throwing stars and energy daggers. One of the guards was visibly slower than the other, and Optimus Prime could see why; three stars, bunched closely together, were stuck in the joint of his right hip. Dark Energon, mixed with lubricants and other vital fluids, leaked from the wound.

Optimus Prime took aim and blasted that guard exactly on the existing wound. The guard screamed out and went down, the leg hanging on only by a few cables. Blindly he swung around and snapped out his whip in Optimus's direction, but the guard was slow and Optimus was feeling the electric charge of battle fury. He caught the whip in one hand and used it to drag the maimed guard over.

The guard said something in a language Optimus Prime didn't recognize. Had Dark Energon scrambled his language center? Were the guards down here taught only the Underworld dialects?

Optimus Prime had no time to be a linguist. He finished off the guard and joined Prowl's assault on the other. Where Prowl used knives and stars, Optimus Prime went the more direct route. He knocked the guard down with a heavy salvo of ion-cannon blasts and kept hitting him as Prowl moved in for the kill.

They looked around the chamber, checking for any more guards. Everything was silent. "Check on Jazz," Optimus Prime ordered. He wanted to do it himself; Jazz was his oldest friend and Optimus Prime could not imagine life without him.

But he was Prime, and he had responsibilities.

"Sentinel Prime," he said, kneeling at the side of his predecessor.

Sentinel Prime's torso still gaped open where Megatron must have found the Code Key of Justice. Along his back and legs, fused and scorched metal told the story of how close he had been to Omega Supreme's launch. Other, fresher wounds told another story: of his savage treatment since he had arrived at Kaon Prison.

"Do not call me that," Sentinel Prime said.

"It is who you are," said Optimus Prime.

"No longer. You are the true Prime," said the dying Sentinel Prime. "The High Council was wrong about many things, but in that action—whatever their reasons for taking it—they have proved correct."

"I never meant to usurp what was yours," Optimus Prime said.

"That was never my thought," returned Sentinel Prime. "The title of Prime must inevitably pass away. I held it for longer than I should have. May you hold it and be truer to it than I was."

"You were true in the end," Optimus Prime said. "That is what will be remembered."

Sentinel Prime closed his eyes and lay silent. For a moment Optimus Prime thought he had died. Then, with his eyes still closed, Sentinel Prime said, "There is something you must do."

"Tell me."

"You must enter the Core," Sentinel Prime said. "I hear it speaking to me now, in a voice that grows fainter every cycle. Megatron, the fool, has infected it with Dark Energon. If something is not done, Cybertron itself will die." He let out a long moan. "And so will all of us . . ."

Those were the last words of Sentinel Prime.

Optimus Prime stayed still for a moment, out of respect for the Spark of Sentinel Prime. Then he reached out and broke the chain holding Sentinel Prime's body to the pillar. He lifted his predecessor's body and said to Prowl, "How is Jazz?"

"Oh, I'll be all right." Optimus Prime turned to see Jazz sitting up. "One of those whips caught me right on the back of the neck. I could hear everything you were doing, but I couldn't move." Jazz stretched his arms out and wiggled his fingers, then rolled his head back and forth. "Think I'm all better now."

"Then let's get out of here," Optimus Prime said.

They laid Sentinel Prime to rest in the Crypt of the Primes in Iacon, where he joined the lineage that stretched back as far as there was history on Cybertron. The ceremony was simple, as befit the circumstances. There was no time for the elaborate ritual that accompanied the entombing of previous Primes, or other important Transformers who found their resting places in the adjoining crypts. Around the Crypt bristled thickets of anti-air batteries and mobilized Autobot rapid-reaction units. Optimus Prime half expected Megatron to disrupt the ceremony in some way, perhaps to complicate Optimus Prime's claim to the lineage and the title.

Over the freshly welded crypt, Alpha Trion intoned the traditional liturgy of the Passing of the Primes. In the last part of this, he officially handed on the title to Optimus Prime, making official in the history of Cybertron what had before been only de facto.

"Don't forget your friends now that you're fancy." Jazz needled him as they processed from the Crypt back to the nearby Hall of Records.

Optimus Prime's head was full of the liturgy, which

had him thinking of the Passing of the Primes, their initial leaving from Cybertron. "How many of them do you think are still alive?" he asked Jazz. "The Thirteen, I mean."

"None."

"What do you mean, none?"

"I mean, the Thirteen are a myth, O.P.," Jazz said. He alone among Autobots had seized the freedom to address Optimus Prime so informally, but he also had enough discretion to do it only when they were alone. "They never existed. They're principles to guide us, you know? They don't have to be real for us to learn from them."

Optimus Prime shook his head. "I don't believe that."

"You don't have to," Jazz said. "True things stay true whether you believe them or not."

Back in the Hall of Records, they worked through a collective debriefing about the mission to infiltrate Kaon and exfiltrate the body of Sentinel Prime. "Something was not right in there," Optimus said. "Where was the resistance? Where were all the Decepticons?"

"Perhaps Megatron is finding out that Dark Energon is a mixed blessing," Alpha Trion said.

"That could be it," acknowledged Optimus Prime.

"Or they could all be rallying in one big army that we don't know about, and it's going to come down on us all at once," Jazz said.

Everyone looked at him.

"It's a possibility," Jazz insisted.

Optimus Prime nodded. "It is. That's what I'm worried about. What if he didn't care that we recovered

Sentinel Prime? What if he figures he's got the war already won because of the Dark Energon?"

Alpha Trion held Optimus Prime's gaze. "Then we must do what we talked about."

"Are you sure?"

"You will be sure once you go to the Core and see whether Sentinel Prime was correct," Alpha Trion said.

"Then we had better go. Bumblebee, Jetfire, you're with me this time. Jazz, Prowl, you need to rest. And Sideswipe, I need you to make sure that Jazz and Prowl stay here."

To a chorus of grumbles, Optimus Prime left the Hall of Records. He had made almost all of his subordinates angry. Either that meant he was a good leader because he was not playing favorites, or he was a terrible leader because he did not understand their needs. Time would tell. First he had to see what the Core looked like.

Cliffjumper and Ultra Magnus, along with his commando team, escorted Optimus, Bumblebee, and Jetfire to the southern terminus of the Well of AllSparks. There, deep in the canyon that had housed the Well, was the portal that led most directly to the Core . . . and was most likely to get Optimus to the Core without running him into roving bands of Underworlders. They would not care about the surface, or about his objective, and he did not want to fight Cybertronians who were not sworn to the Decepticon cause.

"We will stay here," Ultra Magnus said. "In case you need some cover when you're on your way out."

"If we need cover on the way out, things are probably going to be a lot worse up here already," Optimus Prime said.

Ultra Magnus shrugged. He was not a bot who demonstrated much in the way of fear. "We'll take care of it, Optimus Prime," he said. As if by saying it, he could ensure its truth.

Into the Well of AllSparks went Optimus Prime, with Bumblebee and Jetfire, descending steadily by means of the maintenance catwalks installed in the prehistory of Cybertron, by bots long dead, to service machines that had not functioned in teracycles. At various periods in its history, the Well had been the focus of superstitions beyond number. For long eras, bots were born from it and wandered into the surrounding emptiness without knowing where to go, because the mysteries of the Well were terrifying to contemplate. In more enlightened times, settlements and agencies had sprung up in the levels of the Well closest to the surface, to take in new Transformers and teach them the ways of Cybertronian civilization. Now those were gone, since the AllSpark itself was gone—and the Well was dark, its depths scattered with the debris and flotsam of endless cycles of war and neglect.

Through this, Optimus Prime and his team descended until they came to the hidden door—known only to Alpha Trion and to the Primes—that led into the deepest interior of Cybertron, that led to the Core itself.

This door, and the tunnel complexes beyond it, had been described to Optimus Prime as shining and alive with the very heartbeat of Cybertron. But what he saw when he opened the door and shone a light over its threshold was something very different indeed. The tunnel stretched before him in a curving, sweeping descent. It was dark, where it should have been alive with the powerful internal radiance of the Core. And where the lights of Optimus Prime fell on the floor and walls of the tunnel, they could see the beginnings of violet stains.

"There isn't much time," Optimus Prime said. "Let's go."

The farther down they went, the more obvious were the effects of Dark Energon. The pernicious violet suffused the surviving lights, seemed to slither along the conduits that fed power from deeper in the planet to the higher levels of the Well, seemed even to hang in the air and beguile the Autobots' optics, making them see things that were not there—which then made them wonder if they were not seeing some things that were . . .

"What would happen if we tried it?" Jetfire asked.

Optimus Prime and Bumblebee took steps away from him and kept him between them. They were ready if he made a move. Bumblebee's various armaments sprouted and armed. Optimus did not arm, but he held out a hand toward Jetfire. "You can't think that," he said.

"I can't? Who are you to tell me what I can't think?" Jetfire took a step toward Optimus Prime. "Isn't that what we're fighting for, the right to think what we want, and do what we want? So why do you get to tell me I can't think that?"

"Because if you think that right now, it's because the Dark Energon is getting to you, Jetfire. And if the

Dark Energon gets to you right now, you'll have to die."

There was silence in the corridor. Eventually Optimus Prime broke it.

"And if you die, Jetfire—if we have to kill you because otherwise you'll fall victim to the Dark Energon and try to kill us—then that makes it that much harder to survive whatever waits for us down there." Optimus Prime pointed away down the tunnel. "So you think whatever you want once we get back to the surface. But right now we—all of us—are acting not for ourselves, but for all the other Autobots and all the Cybertronians who need us to succeed. We don't get to doubt. *We need you.* Is that clear?"

Jetfire was too proud to apologize, and too proud to look away from Optimus Prime, but he acknowledged his leader's words. "Yes. Clear."

"Then let's go."

They kept on. Before they had gone too much farther, they came to the first of the places where Dark Energon had rotted the structure of the tunnel so badly that it was not safe to walk across. "Now you need me," Jetfire said. "Hang on."

Deftly he assumed alt-form for a split second, the change never quite complete as he fired his alt-form engines, essentially performing a rocket-assisted leap across the rotten part of the floor, with Optimus Prime and Bumblebee hanging on to his arms as they became almost-wings and then arms again . . . as he landed on the other side of the rotted, rusting, Darkened part of the floor.

It was a trap. They realized it too late.

What looked like a solid part of the floor was in

fact the collapsed part and they went through it as if they had tried to step on a cloud. They fell through a great empty space in the heart of Cybertron, where its substance had been eaten away by the entropic side effects of Dark Energon. Jetfire assumed his alt-form at once, reflexively, before either of the other two could catch hold of him again. He maneuvered below them and braked, slowly, taking their weight with an audible change in the pitch of his engines. But he held, exerting all of his strength. Optimus Prime and Bumblebee faced each other across the back of his fuselage, each barely hanging on. "Now we need him," Optimus Prime said. Bumblebee grimaced.

Far, far below them, there was a light. It was violet, but at its core, was that a spark—or a Spark—of pure white?

The flight there seemed endless, but that was because of the way Dark Energon was beginning to deform even the Autobots' perceptions of time and space. Many times they thought they had gotten close to the light, only to find that it was farther away, or in another direction, or had disappeared altogether. Laboriously they worked their way through this Darkened labyrinth of illusions until at last, exhausted and confused, they stood before the Core of Cybertron—and sorrowed at what they saw.

The Plasma Energy Chamber had sunk down the long channel from the lens to the Core itself, and there it had burrowed in, sprouting Corruption Spikes that held the Plasma Energy Chamber inside the Core and prevented the Core from ejecting it, or healing itself. Like a broken-off arrowhead in a wound, the polluted Plasma Energy Chamber had spread its infection throughout the body of Cybertron itself. If it were not removed, Cybertron would die.

"Sentinel Prime was right," Jetfire said.

"It's even worse than he described it," Optimus Prime said. "We'll have to—"

Before he could complete the sentence, or propose a plan, Bumblebee lost his composure. He could stand it no longer, this abomination at the Core of the planet he loved so deeply. In perfect silence, Bumblebee assaulted the Corruption Spikes, braving the sickening radiation they emitted to shatter them one by one, freeing the poisoned Plasma Energy Chamber from the Core. At first he went after them with his hand cannons, but when Jetfire and Optimus Prime screamed at him not to damage the Core he put them away and started breaking the Spikes off with his bare hands. As each one broke, Dark Energon seeped out of the fracture to dribble down to the floor, where it pooled and ran into cracks. The Core itself flickered, dimming and then regaining streaks of its normal brilliance that coruscated across its surface for a moment before subsiding. Bumblebee shattered a juncture where three of the Corruption Spikes had grown together. He flung the fragments aside and started kicking at where the remnant Spikes grew from the floor. Slowly, he made progress, but Dark Energon splattered all across his chassis and Optimus Prime feared for the consequences to him when he had finished.

When the last Corruption Spike was broken off and its stump stomped and shattered down to floor level,

and the Dark Energon dripping from the Spike fragments had seeped away, the three Autobots approached the Core. Optimus Prime reached out a
hand and touched its surface. He could feel the energy surging within, but also he could tell that something was wrong. Even with the Corruption Spikes
gone, the Core did not return to its original brightness. They waited, watching as the last traces of Dark
Energon's violet taint receded from the Core and the
paths that led from it toward the surface. Even the
great channel that led to the Geosynchronous Energon Bridge and the lens gradually purified itself of
Dark Energon.

Still the radiance of the Core was uneven and weak.
It achieved something like its full brilliance only in
those places where Optimus Prime touched it. "I
don't know what to do," he said.

Bumblebee, watching, shrugged. His vocoder had
gone out again. He looked around as if searching for
some clue a previous Prime might have left—but the
chamber of the Core was featureless and steel gray,
save for the blackness of the pits where the Corruption Spikes had been uprooted. The Spikes themselves
had deliquesced and disappeared. "Take out the
Plasma Energy Chamber," Jetfire said.

Optimus Prime did, holding it out away from him
as the Dark Energon tainting its substance wriggled
and writhed out of it in tendrils that tapped against
the shielding on his arms. He set the Plasma Energy
Chamber down away from the Core and turned back
to face it.

It was a little brighter now. And in a voice that only
Optimus Prime could hear, it began to speak.

Optimus Prime. You have fought valiantly, but you come too late.

"No," said Optimus Prime. "There must be something more I can do."

Perhaps there is, and perhaps there is not. But there is yet one thing you may gain from your journey here.

A different brightness flared within the core, then took shape. Optimus Prime had the sensation that the Core was opening, peeling back an infinite number of layers each of which was thinner than a single atom and revealing to him what mysteries lay concealed within. The shape slowly resolved itself into an object, and the object slowly gave up the details of its appearance, surrounded by the wavering radiance of the sickly Core. It seemed spherical, its exterior multifaceted and scored with ancient runic script whose meaning Optimus Prime could not decipher.

First you were given the title Prime by the High Council, Optimus—but that title is not theirs to grant. Alpha Trion pled your case as well, but even one so ancient and respected as he cannot determine the succession of Primes. Not when Sentinel Prime still lived. Though Sentinel Prime had long since failed the role appointed him, the title was still his, and it was not until he passed it along to you that it was entirely yours.

Now you shall have one other thing of which Sentinel Prime, for far too long, proved unworthy.

Behold the Matrix of Leadership.

It manifested fully out of the Core's glow, the jewel from the hilt of Prima's sword, the symbol and talisman of each successive Prime since the dawn of Cybertron's history.

Take it, Optimus Prime. Be worthy of it, and be worthy of the title of Prime.

Optimus Prime reached out and the Matrix of Leadership settled into the palms of his hands. The feeling of it changed something within him, as if he had only in that moment become conscious of the totality of his existence, the strength and power that lay within him, the responsibility he had to his fellow Cybertronians.

Take the Matrix of Leadership into you, Optimus Prime. Let it guide you as it has guided the Primes who came before you. May it defend you as it defended Prima until his time had come to yield it. May it keep you on the righteous path and guide you when you are uncertain. May it strengthen you both in body and in spirit. May it be the light within you, that you may be the light of the Transformers who would follow you.

"I am not worthy of this," Optimus Prime said, just as he had when the High Council, so many ages in the past, had first bestowed the title on him and touched

off the war that now—only now, perhaps now—
might be coming to an end.

*You are. But it is up to you to remain worthy of it.
This is the essence of Primus, the animating principle
of all Cybertron and everything that has ever lived on
Cybertron.*

He felt his body absorbing the Matrix of Leadership as he brought it to his chest. It infused him with
its sense of . . . not invincibility, but certainty. Power
without the desire to use that power over others.

*Now you are truly Prime. And now you must lead
your Autobots on the most perilous journey yet undertaken by any Cybertronian.*

Optimus Prime listened. He was dimly conscious
that Jetfire was talking to him, but the voice of the
Core was far more important. He shut out the physical world and listened only to the Core.

*The Dark Energon is gone, the Corruption Spikes
are broken, the Plasma Energy Chamber—which was
an infection that spread through the body of
Cybertron—is purged. In this you have done well.
But the Core, this Core, is terribly damaged. Eons
will pass before it can generate enough Energon to
sustain Transformer civilization again. And eons will
pass before the material, the crust and structure of
Cybertron, is again able to sustain the cities and industry of Cybertronians. The Dark Energon sickness
was deep, and the healing must, too, be deep.*

*So you must leave, Optimus Prime. You must lead
your Autobots out into the vastnesses of space. Use
the Space Bridge if you can, but even if not . . . still
you must go. Build a ship that can carry every Autobot and go. For if you do not go, you will die, and the*

Autobot movement will die with you, and all that will be left of Cybertronian civilization is the few Decepticons who might survive the endless ages in the ruins until the Core has healed itself and Cybertron can live fully once again.

Wherever you go, wherever the Autobots follow, you must return, Optimus Prime. You must return when the planet has had time to heal. Bring back the Matrix of Leadership. You will know when. When you bring it back, you will be able to restore Cybertron to its former greatness . . . but that cannot happen yet. The Core is too sickened, the structure of the planet too infected by the remnants of Dark Energon and the polluting effects of the essence of Unicron.

There will come a day when the Core and the Matrix, working in concert through the person of you, Optimus Prime, will be able to restore Cybertron. And not just restore—you will lead Cybertron into a new age of unimagined wonders. This is your destiny. The Matrix of Leadership has awaited you. Guard its power within you, for one day it will be the light that leads us out of our darkest hour.

But that day is not come yet.

That day is far in the future.

Now you must go.

The path back to the surface was clear. The Geosynchronous Energon Bridge had gone dark, and its channel stretched straight and true from the Core to the remains of Crystal City. When the Core fell silent, Optimus Prime led Bumblebee and Jetfire to the base of that shaft. They started climbing in silence, and had come perhaps a third of the distance back toward the surface when Jetfire said, "What happened in there?"

"The Matrix of Leadership," Optimus Prime said simply. "Cybertron granted it to me."

"What did you mean when you asked where," Jetfire said.

Optimus Prime was silent.

"Where what?" Jetfire asked.

"You saw the state the Core was in, didn't you?" Jetfire and Bumblebee both nodded. Optimus Prime paused, knowing that the next thing he said would mean life or death for more bots than he knew. "If Cybertron is sick, then we must leave Cybertron until it can heal. That is what the Core charged me to do. Lead the Autobots away from Cybertron until . . ." He trailed off. The truth was, Optimus Prime did not know how long they would have to be away from Cybertron, or what awaited them out in space, or what would happen if they survived long enough to return.

"But we have nowhere to go," Jetfire said. "Do we just run for it? Fly into space and hope there's Energon out there somewhere? This is a death sentence."

"That is what the Core told me," Optimus Prime said. *Build a ship* . . . "Project Generation One."

"What's that?"

Optimus Prime shook his head. He refused to say anything else until they had completed the climb back to the surface of Crystal City. It was dark, and above them the pinpoint light of Trypticon Station hung still, its orbit keeping it forever hanging over the lens of the Geosynchronous Energon Bridge even after the Bridge had stopped transferring Energon.

Optimus Prime wondered how much Energon was stored on the station, and how much of it had been re-created as Dark Energon. How would Megatron get it back down to the surface of Cybertron for his masses of Decepticons?

Or would he keep it all for himself and his inner circle during the times of turbulence and scarcity that the Core said were on the way?

"Jetfire," Optimus Prime said. "Mind giving us a lift back to Iacon?"

Hanging on to Jetfire's wing, Optimus Prime looked down over the shattered landscape of Cybertron. Now all of Cybertron was Optimus Prime's responsibility. He had to care for it and lead it forward the best way he knew how. And it was dying. Much of it was already dead.

No Seeker patrols tried to intercept them. No Decepticon ground forces tried to shoot them down. It appeared for all the world as if Megatron was pulling his forces back and simply starving the Autobots out, waiting for the supply of Energon to dwindle enough that they would be weak when he made his final advance. The landscape below was empty. Nothing lived there. An Energon spring, which for as long as Optimus Prime could remember had provided sustenance for a large part of the population around Kalis, was utterly dry. Surrounding it were the signs of a battle, and the blasted frames of the dead.

The Matrix of Leadership, absorbed into the very fiber of Optimus Prime's body and being, showed him in a flash the history of all others who had held it, all the way back to Prima himself. He understood fully the scope of his responsibility, and the pain that came with it. He understood that the Core did not speak lightly, and that his responsibility was to the long arc of history, not just to the friends who would speak to him today. By the time they reached Iacon, Optimus Prime knew that leaving was the only possibility.

Not all of the Autobots felt the same way, however. Jetfire remained the most vociferous proponent of staying to fight it out. "If we have to die," he said to the assembled Autobot command trust in the Hall of Records reading room, "let us die on our home planet, fighting for it. Not running out into space after we waste who knows how much time and life building a giant ship when we could be fighting! We'll never make it back, and we will die knowing we fled and failed. Not me."

"You are not understanding this," Alpha Trion said. "During the time of Cybertron's healing, the planet will not be able to support more than a fraction of the life that exists here now. Autobot, Decepticon, unaligned . . . all will die unless they leave. And for the Autobots, the choice will be to die for lack of resources, die at the hands of Decepticons—or succumb to Dark Energon, while it lasts, and then die when it is gone."

"Death, death, death, or death," Jazz said. "If you're asking me, I'm going to go for the death that has a ride in a spaceship first. Let's build this Ark."

"Jetfire," Optimus Prime said.

"Prime," the former Seeker acknowledged.

"We need time to complete Project Generation One. And I think the only way we're going to get it is to create the biggest diversion Cybertron has ever seen. So I need you to do an inventory on every space-worthy craft we can find. Are there enough to get every Autobot off Cybertron? If not, how many of them can we get?"

"If you can't get everyone, how do you decide who stays and who goes?" Prowl asked.

Optimus Prime shook his head as he looked up and out the windows toward the crater of Omega Supreme's crash. "I don't know," he said. "And it doesn't matter. All that matters is that Megatron believe it for long enough to finish the Ark."

"We're all going to die for this Ark," Prowl said. "While you're wasting time and Energon building it, Megatron is building the army that's going to come from the east and destroy Iacon."

"That's my decision," said Optimus Prime. "I have made it. If you don't want to go along with it, you know what the other choices are."

And later he asked Alpha Trion, "It's begun. Will it work?"

"If you don't do it, all of the Autobots will die, and Cybertron itself will die," Alpha Trion said.

"I am doing it. Project Generation One is begun. Not all of the Autobots believe in it, though," Optimus Prime said.

"Not all Cybertronians have ever believed in anything," Alpha Trion said. "Unanimity is not a characteristic of our race." The Archivist looked worn. He was refusing his full portion of Energon, arguing that it needed to go to those Autobots who might be called upon to fight.

"Alpha Trion, you must use the Energon you're allotted," Optimus Prime said. "I'll make it an order if you insist."

"And I'll refuse it, and if you throw me in prison I won't be able to do what you want," Alpha Trion said. "You don't have time to work over engineering plans. I do."

There was no arguing that.

"Now leave me alone so I can plan," Alpha Trion said, and Optimus Prime did.

CHAPTER THIRTY-FIVE

Across Autobot-controlled territory, every spaceworthy ship was collected, inspected, and redeployed to a makeshift launch facility quickly constructed on the broad plain between Iacon and the polar ruin of Six Lasers Over Cybertron. Aerialbots, the few Seekers loyal to the Autobot cause, patrolled over the facility, but no Decepticons came closer than a single Seeker that ghosted along the horizon for a moment until Jetfire rocketed out to challenge it. Then it was gone again, over the pole in the direction of the Hydrax Plateau.

"You know Megatron won't let this go on forever." Alpha Trion counseled Optimus Prime the first time Optimus headed for the facility to see what the Autobots were going to have for the great feint that would cover their exodus to the stars.

Optimus counted the ships and ran a mental tally against the number of Autobots he needed to evacuate. He didn't like the mismatch between the two numbers. It was great enough that he thought Megatron could not possibly be fooled.

"I'm surprised he has let it go on this long," he said.

"The other possibility to consider is that he hasn't let it," Alpha Trion said. "Perhaps he has problems of his own."

"He'd have to have serious problems to not send over a flight of Seekers to strafe our launch facility," Optimus Prime said. "It's almost worth sending a little reconnaissance mission out to see what things are really like on the other side of the pole."

"Wasted lives," Alpha Trion commented.

Jazz, who was standing at Optimus Prime's other shoulder, said, "You need someone to go, I'll go."

"No, I don't think so," Optimus Prime said. "Where we need some recon is up in lower space. I wouldn't be surprised if Megatron is watching us and waiting for a chance to wipe us out all at once."

"What do we do if that's the case?" mused Alpha Trion.

"Fight our way through," Jazz said. "There's no other way."

Another flight of small ships—a motley collection of tankers and a single Energon-ingot freighter—cruised in over the launchpad. "No," said Optimus Prime. "I don't think there is. At least we have to make Megatron think that way."

What he was about to ask of the Autobots weighed heavily on his mind.

"Are we ready?" Megatron asked. "There is one correct answer to that question."

Shockwave waved him forward into the space that had until recently been the Dark Energon Facility. Now it was a nerve center, an incredibly dense array of fibrous processing material woven around an imprisoned cluster of Sparks that circulated in their invisible prison. "Yes," he said.

Without a word, Megatron turned and left the lab. Former lab, he corrected himself. Very well, he thought. Dark Energon was turning out to be a difficult resource to manage; it was harder and harder to enforce discipline among rank-and-file Decepticons when distribution of Dark Energon was controlled and clearly not egalitarian. So Megatron had separated his forces into units according to how much Dark Energon he anticipated having. Those he could afford to feed the Dark Energon would be his shock troops. Those he could not . . . they would have to scrap over the dwindling supplies of regular Energon like the lowly Autobots, or those doomed Cybertronians who had refused to take sides.

The sudden cutoff of Dark Energon—and the destruction, apparently, of the Geosynchronous Energon Bridge—had prolonged the timeline Megatron had for the end of the war, but not fundamentally changed it. He still had the Trypticon project moving forward, and the librarian was never going to be able to surmount the fundamental lack of Energon available on the surface.

He did wish he knew what had happened to cut off the Bridge, though. He would not have thought it possible that any Autobot could have gotten close enough to the Core to interrupt the flow, given the intensity of Dark Energon between the rim of the Well of AllSparks and the interior levels where the Core was said to reside.

Something was different recently; he could tell that much. The Autobots were hunkered down deep in their territory, abandoning their forays into the contested areas of the planet for Energon and scavenged mechanical parts. At first Megatron had thought that this was because their Energon deprivation was starting to sap them of initiative and resolve, but then he noticed the large-scale movement of ships to their makeshift field north of Iacon. Then everything became clear.

They were giving up and trying to get off the planet. They realized that they could fight against the Decepticons no longer.

That was just fine, Megatron thought. In fact, that was just perfect.

"We will rendezvous at the Space Bridge," Optimus concluded.

"The Space Bridge? It doesn't work," Jazz protested.

Alpha Trion stepped into the conversation before it degenerated into a useless back-and-forth. "We don't know whether it works or not," he said. "There's no indication in the Covenant or in any of the records that it is actually broken, or even explicitly nonfunctional. It has not been used in . . . well, teracycles. But I am older than that Space Bridge, and I still function."

There was a ripple of nervous laughter at both the joke and the fact . . . Had they ever seen this before, wondered several of the Autobots in attendance? Had anyone ever seen Alpha Trion make a joke?

None of them could remember.

And anyway, it would only be funny if the Space Bridge worked.

Jetfire came up with a small, nimble former asteroid

scout ship—*Eight Track*—to use as a mobile command post and flagship. "Perfect," Optimus Prime said. He watched as Jetfire tried to pretend the praise didn't mean anything to him. Part of leadership, thought Optimus Prime, was realizing how important leaders could be and realizing that everything you did might be much more important to someone else than it was to you.

"Now let's roll out," he ordered, and the general order went out.

Optimus Prime found to his suprise—and sorrow—that Alpha Trion had no intention of coming with the Autobots. "How can you not?" he asked. "The Autobots would not have survived this long without you."

"There will be no extra room on the Ark. And perhaps you need to learn to survive without me," Alpha Trion said.

"Perhaps," Optimus Prime allowed. "But there's no reason to rush the time when that becomes necessary, is there?"

Alpha Trion gestured around his study. "I cannot leave this. My work here is not done. It can never be done. The Core requires you to come back after the planet has had time to heal itself, correct?"

"But it also warned me that everyone needed to get off-planet for the duration of that healing," Optimus Prime said.

"The Core and I . . ." Alpha Trion thought for some time before going on. "There is a relationship there. I do not believe that Cybertron will kill me after all the time I have spent inhabiting its surface."

"Megatron will."

"He'll have to find me. Vector Sigma is very well protected, Optimus. I do not think even Megatron will dare its defenses after what happened when he got too close to Teletraan-1." Alpha Trion approached Optimus Prime and guided him to the study door. "You have Autobots to rally and keep alive," he said. "I need to finish outfitting your Ark and see what else might be worth saving before the Decepticons run out of Dark Energon and tear the planet apart."

"Will Vector Sigma be able to protect you?" What Optimus Prime really wanted to ask was whether Vector Sigma existed at all. But if Alpha Trion believed in it, Optimus thought, he was ready to believe in it, too.

"It will. Now go. I have an Ark to prepare, and you have a fleet to manage."

The evacuation of Iacon and the surrounding areas took much less time than Optimus Prime had anticipated. Part of the reason for this was that his Autobot subordinates managed the evacuation superbly—and part of the reason was that there were far fewer Autobots left than even the archpessimist Jetfire could have guessed.

"Is this all of them?" he asked sadly. "Can this be all?" He turned to Optimus Prime. "This is what you're risking to finish your Ark. Is it worth it?"

"It will be," Optimus Prime said simply.

The flotilla of a few dozen ships carried all of the Autobots. Optimus Prime didn't have the heart to quote the exact number to Jetfire. He looked up to the skies, still expecting an assault at any moment. But there was no sign of a real attack, though satellite reports from the few remaining Grid points to the east suggested that a large army of Decepticons was mobilizing to march on Iacon.

Optimus Prime was glad he would not be there to see it when they sacked the city.

The *Eight Track* took off last of all the fleet. It was a nimble vessel, and performed even better than might have been expected under the sure hand of Jetfire. The fleet reached the lower reaches of Cybertronian space utterly without incident. "Everyone have the location and bearing of the Space Bridge?" Optimus Prime called out over the fleet frequency. "It looks much like the wrecked Bridges, remember. Don't go by what you see. Trust the coordinates from the DataNet and your instruments."

Moving in a prolate spheroid cluster, the ragged fleet achieved space and the artificial gravity systems kicked in—on most of the ships, anyway. Some of them had not been tested for orbital use in teracycles, and although they all flew within their design parameters, a number of their secondary systems experienced failures.

"Any sign of pursuit? All ships check in, report any Decepticon contact."

One after another, every ship checked in. Some reported individual Seeker flybys, but there were no engagements. "He knows he's won," Sideswipe said. "He's letting us go because we're quitting." The disgust in Sideswipe's voice was hard to handle.

"It's not quitting, Sideswipe," Optimus Prime said. "We can't win if the planet is about to tear itself apart. We're getting out of the way so Cybertron can heal. That was never going to happen with the war going on."

"It feels like we quit," Sideswipe insisted.

Optimus Prime nodded. "I know it does. I know." But, he was thinking, if Megatron overcommitted his space-based resources, there were possibly enough Autobots to counterstrike and clear the skies for the Ark. And even if they didn't get out on this try, they had gained time to finish the Ark. These were dark times. The Ark was the only light Optimus Prime could see to lead them out. He couldn't tell Sideswipe this, though. Not every Autobot knew of the Ark, and of those who did, not every one of them approved. Jetfire and Prowl especially considered it a waste of resources better dedicated to fighting Decepticons.

Ahead of them, the Space Bridge registered on their instrument panel. The other defunct Bridges strung away from it in a loose chain around the equator of Cybertron. "So this is how we go back to the stars," Optimus Prime said.

Jazz shrugged. "Any way it works, it works."

Which came to seem ironic, given what happened next. Megatron was not done with them quite yet, and escape was never going to be that easy.

From Trypticon Station, a violet beam lanced out. Where it came into contact with the subsentient transport vessel, veins of Dark Energon curled across its exterior. There was a pause, a few nanokliks during which witnesses on nearby ships thought that perhaps something in the weapon had gone wrong. Then the VK991 disintegrated in a blast that overwhelmed the video arrays of every ship in the area—not to mention the optics of the unfortunate Transformers who happened to be watching through nonpolarized windows.

"What happened!?" Sideswipe yelled.

Jetfire rammed the *Eight Track* into reverse, backing away from the main body of vessels headed for the Space Bridge. "Spread out!" he shouted into the commlink. "Spread out, circle the planet, approach the Space Bridge from the other side!"

"It won't work," Prowl said. He pointed at the chart of Cybertronian orbital space on the command terminal. "See? Trypticon's got a clear field of fire over any approach to the Space Bridge."

Another violet beam pinned another transport,

which blew apart just as fragments from the first explosion began to ping against the *Eight Track*'s hull. "I knew it," Jetfire said. "There's no way Megatron was going to let us go. Your Ark is a waste of time, Optimus. Time and Energon and Autobot lives. Have you figured that out yet?"

Then Megatron appeared on the screen of every Grid-linked computer on Cybertron. "Autobots," he said. "The war is over. It is time for us to discuss the terms of your surrender."

The frame expanded, revealing the vast army of Kaonian and Badland-bred gladiators and industrial bots turned soldiers. They stood behind Megatron, weapons bared and raised over their heads, keeping absolutely still and maintaining perfect silence. The combined show of power and discipline was terrifying.

"You appear to think that you can simply leave this war when its progress is no longer to your liking," Megatron went on. "I am afraid that I—and Trypticon Station—cannot permit this. How will you teach future generations of Transformers the value of perseverance when you fling yourselves into space at the first sign of difficulty?"

A third Dark Energon–powered beam destroyed a third Autobot vessel. Megatron glanced off the frame and then went on. "How many more vessels do you think Trypticon can pick off before you reach beyond its range?" he asked. "And where do you think its range ends? For all you know, it might be able to blast your ships to atoms all the way out to the Space Bridge."

"How does he know we're going to the Space Bridge?" Jazz wondered.

"Maybe he doesn't," Optimus Prime said. "Look at the way he's talking. He knows we're seeing this, but he doesn't know where we are." He looked at the rest of them on the command deck. "It's Alpha Trion. He's baffling the feedback, but Megatron doesn't want us to know that."

"He doesn't know we're on this ship," Prowl said. "And he's not on Trypticon Station."

"You, brother—Orion Pax, who now calls himself Optimus Prime—you lead your Autobots away. Who is the one who does not believe in the individual now? Most of Cybertron wants the Decepticon way. They want my way, brother." Behind him, the army stayed frozen, but they said one word, powerfully and in unison:

MEGATRON!

"Can you muster such an army, brother? If you can, meet me in Iacon. I will be there soon. And so will you . . . unless you would rather join your comrades in a vacuum grave." Megatron offered a cruel smile as Trypticon Station destroyed a fourth ship, this one very close to the *Eight Track*.

"We can't keep letting Trypticon have easy shots," Prowl said.

Jetfire's hands were tight on the control yoke. "The alternative is to let Megatron have them down on-planet," he said.

Optimus Prime nodded. "Autobot ships," he said over the commlink on the command frequency. He trusted that Alpha Trion would also have secured that frequency, if he could do so much to interfere with the

Grid's feedback to Megatron's point of origin. "Return to the surface immediately. Do not—repeat, do not—try to run the Trypticon blockade. Do not engage hostile Decepticon units on your way back to the surface. Return to your launch sites and await further instructions."

The fleet, if it could be called that, heeled around and fell back into the gravity well of Cybertron, making its way down to the surface while avoiding the dangerous airspace of the Tagan-Hydrax-Kaon area. In less than a hundred cycles, all of the ships had made safe landings on the polar plain between Iacon and the ruins of Six Lasers Over Cybertron . . . except the *Eight Track*, which skimmed along the Asteroid Belt, ducking in and out of the debris field to baffle Trypticon Station's detection arrays.

They stayed there until they saw that Megatron was not making any immediate attack on the landed ships, or on Iacon. "He just wants to keep us down there," Optimus Prime said. "He knows that as long as we're on the surface, he can grind us down."

"The only way he loses is if we get to the Space Bridge," Prowl said. "So that's objective number one. It has to be."

"Then what we do is hit the station right now, before anyone there knows we're coming," Jazz said.

Optimus Prime was looking at a magnified image of the station. There would be no way past Trypticon Station for the Ark, either, for which he was risking this great feint. Every cycle they spent in space was another cycle during which Alpha Trion led the finishing work on the construction of the Ark, at great costs in Energon that fighting units badly needed.

"Here," he said, pointing at a blank expanse of the station's hull, on the far side from the windowed bridge area and the rotating radar fixtures. "Blind spot," he said. "Or if it isn't, I don't see the sensor that covers it."

It was then that a personal communication for Optimus Prime appeared on the command terminal, on the frequency that he and Megatron had used for their initial clandestine communications, so long ago. "Brother," he said.

Optimus Prime toggled his response to audio-only. "Odd that you still call me that, Megatron. Your actions have been anything but brotherly."

"Family relationships are the most difficult," Megatron said smugly. "Brother, you know you cannot win. When I said the time had come to discuss terms, I meant it. You have lost. All you need to decide now is how many of your Autobots you want to die."

"No, it is a question of how many Autobots would rather die than live in your Cybertron," Optimus Prime said. "Brother."

"That's where you prove that you still don't understand what was at stake from the beginning. It was never about what any individual wanted, librarian. It was about making them feel like they were important. The Guildmasters and caste hierarchy did not do that. I did. That's why I have won. Now, do you want to fight on? I will kill the rest of you if I must. But that does not leave much for me to rule once you have yielded to me the Matrix of Leadership."

Optimus Prime did not say anything. How did

Megatron know he had been granted the Matrix of Leadership?

"Everything I want to know about on Cybertron, I find out," Megatron said. "That's what you're wondering, brother, isn't it?"

Optimus Prime gestured to Jetfire to push out of the Asteroid Belt toward the blind side of Trypticon Station. He moved off the bridge and toggled the communication to full video; for what he was about to say, he wanted Megatron to see his face. "There are a great many things I wonder, brother," he said. "One of them is how you came so far from when we first knew each other. You fought the castes, and now you kill your own soldiers with Dark Energon so they will fight a little harder for a little longer. They are your gladiators, Megatron. And somewhere, one of them sees you the way you once saw the High Council."

A familiar expression of contempt replaced momentary confusion on Megatron's face as he mastered his initial reaction. "That Decepticon who views me the way I once viewed the High Council?" he said. "He is already dead, though he doesn't know it yet."

"And you, perhaps, have lost the long war, though you can only see the first battles that you have won," Optimus Prime said, then cut the connection.

He stood for a moment in the small alcove between the bridge, airlock, and cargo bay, regaining control over his emotions. Then he walked out onto the bridge and looked out ahead of the *Eight Track*, where the blank space on Trypticon Station grew steadily to fill the ship's forward field of vision. "We're ready?"

"We're ready," Sideswipe said. "Ready to go."

CHAPTER THIRTY-SEVEN

Magnetized cables shot out and tethered the *Eight Track* to the side of Trypticon Station. As soon as the connection was verified, Jetfire reeled the ship in and vacuum-sealed the ingress tube that sprang out from the outer airlock. Every Autobot waited in gyro-cracking tension as the ingress tube slowly pressurized. If they did it too fast, it would make noise that would echo on the other side of the hull. If too slow, they ran the risk of someone on board noticing that the ship's center of gravity, and possibly the angular momentum of its rotation, had changed ever so slightly.

None of those things happened. Jetfire popped the interior lock on it and stood aside. "As long as no one moves this ship," he said, "you can drill a hole right in through here with no loss of atmosphere in the station."

"Seems like the station could stand to lose its atmosphere," Jazz said.

Ironhide agreed. "Maybe after we destroy the Bridge receiver, we can just blow the whole thing up? How about that, Optimus?"

"I'm not against it," said Optimus Prime. Jetfire finished cutting the hole through Trypticon's outer hull. "Ironhide, you and me first," Optimus Prime ordered.

Jetfire kicked the section of hull loose and Optimus Prime, Ironhide at his side, charged through, weapons at the ready. They hit the opposite wall, covering the ring corridor until it curved out of sight in either direction. The rest of the team—Jazz, Bumblebee, Prowl, and Sideswipe—came through, also locked and loaded. They met no immediate resistance.

Moving with the ease and economy that came with long experience fighting together, they cleared a series of storerooms and small laboratories. Moving on, they found the crossing passage that connected the concentric ring passages to the Energon reservoirs—now Darkened—and the weapons systems support machinery in the center of the station.

Just outside the weapons-support area, two drones materialized from the walls of the corridor and laid a withering fire down the length of the hall. The Autobots dove for cover behind doorways and protruding bulkheads as the mechas advanced. They were, fundamentally, gun batteries with legs and semi-sentient targeting mechanisms. The hail of energy-cannon fire kept them all pinned down, and prevented them from noticing right away that in the first salvo, Prowl had taken a brutal series of shots. He lay barely conscious in a doorway that opened into an interior hall, a maintenance tunnel from the looks of it.

"Get in the hall!" Sideswipe and Optimus Prime shouted at him over the sound of the energy bolts exploding against the walls and floor. Prowl tried to drag himself into the shelter of the hall, fluid pooling below his legs.

As the mechas advanced, Bumblebee stepped out of a ventilation alcove next to one of them. He braced the muzzles of both his arm cannons against its processor box and fired. In a flash of light and a spiraling web of electrical discharge, the mecha dropped, a last blast of fire echoing from the eight barrels of its battery.

The other mecha swiveled and unloaded in Bumblebee's direction as he feinted to the left and then rolled right, tracked by the barrels of the surviving mecha's guns. Optimus Prime knocked it off balance with an ion-cannon blast and Sideswipe followed up, getting close enough to finish off the mecha with a series of blows to the same processor assembly that Bumblebee had targeted on the other one.

In the silence that followed, the Autobot team looked up and down the corridor and ahead through the transparent plasteel that separated the hall from the weapons housings. "Those weren't Decepticons," Ironhide said. Bumblebee was kneeling next to Prowl, deploying battlefield first aid he had learned from Ratchet in the few battles they had fought together.

"No," Optimus Prime said. As they watched, the forms of the mechas began to disassemble and merge with the structure of the corridor. Within a few nanokliks, there was no sign that those mechas had ever existed.

"Trypticon Station is alive," Jazz said, looking around in plain amazement.

"Shockwave," Optimus Prime said, with undisguised loathing. "He has done this."

After that the mechas came thick and fast, turning the station's interior corridors into shooting ranges. Optimus Prime's team, with Prowl limping and not much of a combat asset, barely held its own. The very walls and floors of the station became weapons and traps. It was a nightmarish engagement for a team used to straightforward battle with Decepticons. Fighting an enemy that could assume alt- or proto-forms was one thing; fighting an enemy that could manifest from any part of any wall, and knew where you were at all times, was completely different.

"We're not going to make it out of here unless we—" Jazz started to say as they were pinned down in a cramped laboratory with spectrographic equipment morphing into laser fixtures all around them. They fought off this latest onslaught in a blazing cross-hatch of ion discharge and laser burst . . . and in the brief respite they had before they knew the next of Trypticon's attacks, Optimus Prime finished Jazz's sentence.

"Unless we hit the station where it lives," he said. They spawned a schematic of where they had been, overlaid on the historical structure of the station, overlaid in turn on the observed structure as they had approached it in the *Eight Track*.

The only place where there could be a sufficiently sophisticated Spark-fueled mind, capable of overseeing all the actions of a structure the size of Trypticon Station, was in a bulb-shaped protrusion that wasn't in the original layout. It stuck out from the portion of Trypticon's exterior near the spot where the *Eight Track* had planted its ingress tube.

"Figures we came all this way just to have to go back where we came from," said Ironhide.

"Let's do it," Sideswipe said. "The more we wait, the more Trypticon can do."

Optimus Prime held them up for a nanoklik. "We're going to need to stay tight here. Everyone together, Prowl in the middle of the group. We move at his pace, we take out anything we see. When we get to the lab, there's no telling what we'll find. So here are the rules of engagement: Whatever's in the lab, shoot it. Clear?"

"Clear," Jazz said.

"Don't slow down for me," Prowl said.

"Then keep up," Jazz said.

Together they formed up and moved out, working their way to the corridor that ran around what would be the station's equator if it were a planetary body. The inside of this corridor was a series of machine shops and living quarters; the exterior was all small laboratories, airlocks, and vacuum-indifferent shipping chambers, from which canisters had once been launched to fall to the surface of Cybertron with durable goods that would survive the impact. Once Trypticon had been a small, precision manufacturer of complex alloy materials.

Now that skill had been redirected by its new intelligence into the creation of ever deadlier semi-sentient defense systems.

In the hall, the walls erupted with the extruded forms of dozens of Minicons, each armed with tiny vibroblades that could cripple a bot's legs, dropping it to the floor where the Minicons would swarm. But working together, Optimus Prime's team managed to destroy most of them before they closed in. There followed a brief and savage engagement. The Minicons died easily, but every Autobot in the unit bore wounds in the aftermath. Ironhide and Jazz were the worst off, with their legs badly slashed and other wounds up and down their arms. "End this, Optimus Prime," Ironhide said.

Ahead lay the door frame they believed led to the housing of Trypticon's intelligence. On the door itself was the legend DARK ENERGON FACILITY.

Bumblebee was through the door first. Immediately he was silhouetted by laser and ion discharges, low-frequency to damage circuitry and systems without endangering the integrity of Trypticon's hull. Ironhide and Jazz came through next, with Optimus Prime close behind and Sideswipe pushing right after.

The interior of the lab was dark and suffused with what must have been a large part of the remaining Dark Energon piped up from the surface via the Geosynchronous Energon Bridge. In the midst of a synaptic array, crackling with energies on every frequency from infrared to ultraviolet, sat a magnetically bonded sphere within which not one but several Sparks danced. Seeing it was like watching the inner workings of an atom; the Sparks moved in symphonic choreography, never quite where you expected them to be but always in a way that was somehow pleasing, somehow made you think that you had been given access to a secret that few sentient beings were privileged to witness.

"Shoot it," Optimus Prime said.

The lab exploded around them.

* * *

They got back through the ingress tube—"Egress tube now," joked Jazz on his way through—as Trypticon Station, its mass a hundred times that of the *Eight Track,* fired off its emergency thrusters according to a recall protocol installed billions of cycles before Shockwave re-created the station with the intelligence of its imprisoned Sparks. All of the Autobots who were piling back into the *Eight Track* and shouting for Jetfire to jettison the ingress tube had just seen a sight unlike any they had ever seen before. The closest was Optimus Prime, who felt that the sight of the disintegrating Spark array in the former Dark Energon Facility was akin to some of the hallucinatory sights he had seen during the last stages of his sojourn to find the Core and free it of the Dark Energon taint. Jetfire might have agreed with him if he had seen the inside of the Trypticon lab, and Bumblebee might have agreed if he could have spoken; but as things were, Optimus Prime was the only one thinking of the interior of Cybertron in its Dark Energon–fueled agony.

Inside the lab, the Spark array had exploded and seemingly every fiber of the synaptic array had gone up in flames with it. The Sparks themselves had stayed in their tight formation, their orbit like the electron shell surrounding the mystery of consciousness as their sudden liberation caused shockwaves throughout the structure of Trypticon Station. Mechs formed and disappeared; entire sections of the station reconfigured themselves, venting their atmospheres or chemically altering themselves so that where there had been vacuum there were single rooms with atmospheres of pure xenon or chlorine or oxygen.

Optimus Prime's team had seen very little of this, since they had been running for their lives in the direction of the *Eight Track,* but Jetfire had seen it all since he had tapped the *Eight Track*'s sensors into the main internal surveillance network on board Trypticon Station. Thus the station's schizophrenia and spasmodic behavior was well recorded for all of the team to see . . . as they fell back into the atmosphere of Cybertron, tethered to it by the forces of angular momentum, which prevented the ingress tube from releasing. "I don't care what you have to do to get it off," Jetfire shouted over and over, "just get it off!"

"It won't release!" Ironhide answered. Physically the strongest of them all, he had hauled on the tube-release lever with all of that strength, and applied it to the secondary mechanism as well. But even Ironhide's strength could not overcome the laws of physics, and the problem grew even more severe as they entered the atmosphere. The entire ship began to shudder because Trypticon Station began to shudder, friction creating turbulence and turbulence shearing off bits of the station's exterior.

The ingress tube was made of admirably strong materials. It would not break, it seemed—or perhaps it would only break on impact with the surface of Cybertron, which approached with dizzying speed. "Yes or no: Can you get us away from this wreck before it hits?" Jazz asked Jetfire.

Trypticon started to tumble faster, and Jazz never did get his answer.

Trypticon Station's impact, on the edge of the Mithric Sea, caused a visible shock wave that propagated across Cybertron's surface like an earthquake. The ruins of Crystal City shattered into even smaller pieces. The Titanium Turnpike heaved and twisted into what looked like a roller coaster. Landslides occurred across the heaving spines of the Manganese Mountains, and the shock was felt as far away as Iacon and, in the other direction, Stanix and Kaon. The visible fireball rose blazing to the limits of Cybertron's atmosphere before it dissipated into a layer of smoke that began to enclose the Northern Hemisphere of the planet, walling it off from orbital observation.

On the ground, observers initially thought that Optimus Prime and the rest of the crew of the *Eight Track* had been destroyed with Trypticon. Then it became clear that one largish piece of debris shed by the station just before impact, when the stresses from its journey through the atmosphere were at their highest, was not just a piece of debris. It moved against gravity. Could it be? The assembled Autobots barely dared to believe it.

The *Eight Track* veered away from the rain of trailing debris from Trypticon's long fall through the atmosphere. When it landed at the edge of the launch facility, a detail from the last-ditch preparations in the Hall of Records was there to meet it. "I can't believe you made it!" he shouted over and over.

"We sure did," Jazz said. "But I can't believe it, either. Jetfire, you never did answer my question."

"Look around," Jetfire said.

Optimus Prime felt the surface of Cybertron beneath his feet. It was home, it would always be home . . . but if he and the other Autobots stayed, they would die. What could he do?

"And it's ready!" Sideswipe cried out. "Alpha Trion says the Ark is ready to go!"

A thrill of possibility went through Optimus Prime. It was time to tell everyone about the Core's plan, which he had prepared at such terrible cost. "You're sure?" he asked.

"Alpha Trion himself confirmed it. He has images." Sideswipe showed Optimus Prime the outline of an immense ship, city-sized, within the walls of the Well of AllSparks. Put together from the great machinery that had housed the AllSpark before Optimus had sent it into space, the Ark hulked inside the canyon wall, where Seeker patrols and satellite observations would not recognize it for the ship that it was. Virtually every drone under Autobot control had put in some time on the Ark over these past orbits, and material had been cannibalized from the wreckage of Omega Supreme's activation as well.

It was one of those times—those frequent times—when Optimus Prime would have given orbits of his life for a moment just to think. But bots depended on him to make good decisions, and fast decisions, and more often than not every decision he made had to be both. He jacked open the Autobot frequency and counted on Alpha Trion to keep the transmission from Megatron, even if only for a few cycles. Every moment was precious. "If there's any traffic in space, any of our traffic," he said, "freeze it. No one is to approach the Space Bridge. If it's only going to work once, we need to make sure that we can get everyone through. It's time to go!" Optimus Prime commanded. He opened the broadest Autobot frequency he had and told the entire planet of Cybertron, "Go, Autobots! All of you who are not already on board a ship, rendezvous at the Ark! Coordinates are with you, Autobots. There isn't much time. Quickly!"

He broke off the connection and ran to catch the *Eight Track* for the short suborbital hop to the Well of AllSparks. It took off, jammed with its regular crew and a number of extra personnel from the Hall of Records and Iacon's civil-defense militia who had disembarked from ships of the original fleet. They had just reached their cruising speed when Jetfire, at the controls, said, "Uh-oh."

Optimus Prime looked up. "Uh-oh what?"

"Look." Jetfire pointed toward a screen on the cockpit console, where an orbital camera was looking down at the impact site where Trypticon Station had crashed down.

Trypticon Station, in a bipedal form larger than any walking bot Optimus Prime had ever seen, was rising again. It rose to five times the size of Devastator, an immense shape that loomed like a walking city over the exploded landscape around the station's impact. Violet light shone from its Darkened optics and weapons arrays deployed from its shoulders and hands. Before it had fully completed the assumption of its alt-form, the bipedal Trypticon was already walking, from the Mithric shores toward the yawning chasm of the Well of AllSparks.

Megatron was too far away to catch them before they got to the Ark. But Trypticon was not.

"How are we going to fight that?" Prowl wondered.

Jetfire said, "I will go. I and Springer"—he indicated a flight-capable commando from Ultra Magnus's unit—"can at least slow him down while the rest of you get away."

"It's a noble offer," said Optimus Prime. "But I think we can do it another way."

"I know a way," said another voice. Before he turned around, Optimus Prime knew it was Ultra Magnus. "Some Autobots must remain," Ultra Magnus said. "If all of us leave, how will we know that there is anything to return to?"

Optimus Prime had no answer for this. "I cannot ask you to do this," he said.

"You didn't," said Ultra Magnus. "I offered. And my bots are with me. Whatever they build, we will destroy." Ultra Magnus gestured to the team assembled around him. "Meet the Wreckers, Optimus Prime. We will fight for you until you return."

Ratchet had appeared in the middle of Ultra Magnus's pledge. "And Omega Supreme will fight with you, Wreckers."

"The Guardian lives?" Ultra Magnus looked first amazed, then pleased in a way no Decepticon would have wanted to see. "Our fight will be that much easier, then."

Optimus Prime nodded in satisfaction. "Well done, Ratchet. You work wonders with the resources we have."

"In a contest between resources and ingenuity," Ratchet said, "never underestimate ingenuity."

The planning for the final act went quickly. If they could not count on Megatron not to fight, they would have to engage him quickly, distract him, and then get the Ark to orbit before he could mobilize his space-based or space-capable forces to attack it. Jetfire pointed out here that the Ark was large enough that nothing in the known arsenal of Decepticon or Autobot could destroy it. Optimus Prime resisted this idea, then realized that the reason he was resisting it was that—for the first time—the Autobots had the upper hand with a weapon that the Decepticons could not answer.

Could it be?

"Look at you, O.P.," Jazz said. "For once we have an advantage, and you're about to throw it away because you're afraid it's not real."

"I don't think so," said Optimus Prime. "Get everyone to the Ark. Now. Everyone in alt-mode who is built to carry. We go through the subsurface where we can, but we're going to have to be on the surface at some times, which means we're going to have to fight Trypticon."

"That's what we're for," said Ultra Magnus.

Optimus Prime shook his head, reconsidering his earlier acceptance of Ultra Magnus's offer. "It can't be just you."

Ultra Magnus stood, and his commando Wreckers stood with him. "It sure can," he said. "All due respect, Optimus Prime, there's not another Autobot who can fight like me, and there sure isn't another Autobot team that can fight like this one. You send us out and tell us when to make the move, we'll make sure that Trypticon never comes near you while you're getting the Ark loaded up. That's a promise."

Optimus Prime put both hands on Ultra Magnus's shoulders. "We do not deserve your courage," he said.

"My courage is mine to offer," Ultra Magnus said. "And I offer it to Cybertron, and to the Autobots."

"I'm going, too," Jetfire said, stepping from Optimus's side over to Ultra Magnus's. Over the protests of Prowl and Ironhide, he went on. "The Wreckers are going to need a Seeker," Jetfire said. "Someone's got to cover things while you're off-planet. Don't worry. We'll be here when you get back. Ultra Magnus—I'm going to recon the Trypticon situation. Be back in a short cycle."

He assumed his alt-form without another word and blasted away, low in the sky over the Well of AllSparks.

"Well?" Ultra Magnus said to Optimus Prime. "Aren't you going to go after him?"

Optimus Prime shook his head. "No. We're fighting

for self-determination. And he has made a courageous choice. I think we should respect it by getting as many Autobots safely to the stars as we can."

They stepped back from each other. "I will give you the signal," Optimus Prime said. Ultra Magnus, followed by his Wreckers, left the Hall of Records. Optimus Prime wondered if he would ever see them again.

"Did we not have this conversation before?" Alpha Trion asked. He made no effort to disguise his irritation.

"Alpha Trion, I beg you. Come with us. Your wisdom will stand us in good stead over the course of our voyaging. You remember when Cybertronians reached out into the universe once before. None of us do." Optimus Prime stayed in the doorway of Alpha Trion's study. As always, the book lay open on his desk, and Trion's Quill lay next to it. At times Optimus Prime felt as if every move he had ever made was inscribed in Alpha Trion's book.

"How long would you have me look over your shoulder, Optimus Prime?" Alpha Trion asked. "If you would lead the Autobots, you must learn that in the end, a true leader is that bot who knows that the decisions he makes are his and his alone."

Optimus Prime had nothing to say. He was in part ashamed, but in part he was angry.

"Go, Optimus Prime," Alpha Trion said. "And take Teletraan-1 with you. I have already sent it to the Ark. Vector Sigma will protect me while Cybertron repairs itself. This has always been my plan. I will rebuild those parts of the DataNet that have been destroyed, and I will survive. That is all anyone can ask in the times that are coming."

Optimus Prime was overcome. How could he leave his adviser, his mentor, his most trusted counselor Alpha Trion?

"Whatever it is you are contemplating, Optimus Prime, know that I refuse it," Alpha Trion said. "I have stated my intentions. Respect your elders."

"I will," said Optimus Prime, though it hurt as nothing he had ever said.

And then it came to him, but whether just intuition or a deeper knowledge flowing from the Matrix, Optimus did not know. But with certainty, he knew that he was standing before one of the Thirteen, the original Transformers from whom the entire race had sprung. And he was leaving him behind. He took his leave, sorrowing at his loss but now certain that Alpha Trion knew what he was doing.

Then, with reports coming in of Decepticon armies swarming in from the east and over the pole to the north, it was time to lead the Autobots to the Ark.

Optimus Prime arrived at the southern end of the Well of AllSparks in the company of his closest Autobots: Jazz, Bumblebee, Prowl, and Ironhide. Seeing them there made him think of the others—how many dozens, or hundreds, whose names he had known and who now were dead. And how many others would not make it to the Ark, would not join this stream of Autobots working their way down the side of the canyon to the open doors that led to the Ark's interior?

Too many. Far too many. But this was the only decision a leader could make.

He turned to Sideswipe, who was on standby at the base of the main entry to the bridge sector of the Ark. "Sideswipe. We're going to need a pilot."

Once every Autobot within sight, after multiple horizon-to-horizon sweeps, had been taken on board, the outer bay doors of the Ark were closed and Optimus Prime gave the order for it to lift off. He thought of saying farewell to Alpha Trion, who would even now be escaping through the subsurface warrens of Iacon just ahead of the invading Decepticon army. And he thought of saying farewell to those brave, brave Wreckers—including Jetfire—who had held up the marauding juggernaut of Trypticon, at great cost to themselves . . .

The Ark rose from the wall of the Well of AllSparks, destroying the access shaft that had led Optimus Prime down to his destiny of receiving the Matrix of Leadership. The canyon wall of the Well toppled into its depths, covering the wound left when the AllSpark itself had been ejected from Cybertron eons before, in the early stages of the war when Optimus Prime was first coming into his own as a leader. The Ark rose still more, and Optimus Prime could see the curvature of Cybertron's surface, the shape of this wounded world that was the only home he had ever known.

And as it rose, the army of Decepticons poured out of the east and began the final sack and plunder of the great city of Iacon. In the skies above them, Seekers overflew the city, their lethal rockets falling by the hundreds on the defensive batteries that ringed the city. The final destruction of everything that reminded Megatron of the caste-bound system he hated was under way.

Yet Megatron himself rode skyward, in single-minded pursuit of the Ark, his vessel the reconfigured Trypticon. With him were Starscream, Lugnut, Soundwave—the elite of the Decepticons. Even as his Decepticon armies overran Iacon, Megatron triggered Trypticon's third form, the great, Nemesis-class battleship capable of carrying an army and destroying anything else that had ever flown. The multiform Trypticon was the greatest triumph of Shockwave's science . . . Shockwave, who, as Megatron and Starscream chased after the Autobots, looked out over a Cybertron that was unexpectedly—and, to his deranged mind, marvelously—his and his alone.

Cybertron would never be the same.

CHAPTER THIRTY-NINE

Trypticon rose from the surface, finishing the change to its Nemesis mode as it freed itself from Cybertron's gravity well and exited the planet's atmosphere. On it rode Megatron, Soundwave, Starscream, and their closest cadre of Decepticon commanders. Megatron raised Shockwave, whom he had ordered to oversee the final push into Iacon. Now that he understood Optimus Prime's real objective—how could he have missed it?—he needed to change Shockwave's commission.

"Shockwave, I leave Cybertron to you until I return. And I will return, make no mistake. Do not think of this as a promotion. Rather, I need someone to keep my position warm for me while I go and take care of the Autobots once and for all. I can count on you?"

"You will find Cybertron exactly as you left it," Shockwave promised.

"I hope not," Megatron said. "What are you going to do with all of your time? You are going to rebuild. Take the Autobots who survive. Do not kill any more of them than you have to. The rest, indulge your scientific curiosity. See how the Transformer might be improved, what might be learned from composing new forms. Then put them to work. Through work they will learn what it must have been like to be in one of the lower castes, and they will understand that the Autobot cause was a doomed one. When I come back, Shockwave, I want to find a Cybertron on which there is not a single Autobot left. That is your task. Do not fail me."

On board the Ark, as it passed across the ephemeral and ever-shifting boundary between atmosphere and space, Optimus Prime's old personal frequency—Orion Pax's, really—sparked to life again. "So you managed to bring down Trypticon Station even after Shockwave's innovations," Megatron said. "Congratulations, brother."

"Now I am brother again, Megatron?" Optimus Prime found that the farther he got from Cybertron, the less he wanted to hold to the old ways of communication he had kept there.

"We will always be brothers. We are bound together," Megatron said. "You cannot escape me, brother. I will hound you across the stars if I must, until every star in the galaxy has burned itself into a cinder. I will hunt you, and I will find you, and when I find you"—he held up a clenched fist into the frame—"I will, as I promised, see what the Core might have sequestered inside the body of the so-called Prime."

"Hunt me then, brother—if your hunt means that

Cybertron will escape your madness." Optimus Prime looked out into the space beyond the Asteroid Belt and the two Moon Bases; there was the chain of Space Bridges. Some were little more than clusters of debris, remnants of ancient accident or sabotage; others still had the look of the gateways they were; and one, the one that Alpha Trion had confirmed, still had the faint glow of Energon life.

Next to that image, a stern-facing sensor array showed the outline of the Nemesis, gaining swiftly. Megatron, thought Optimus Prime, you betray your true colors. Now that Cybertron could have been yours—a sickened Cybertron, in constant upheaval, perilous to any and all life on its surface, but still yours—you throw it aside to pursue a grudge.

"Faster," he said, and the Ark understood. Power thrummed through it as it accelerated. Megatron's ship still gained, but more slowly.

Optimus Prime looked over at his pilot. "Sideswipe, will that ship catch us before we arrive at the Space Bridge?"

After a brief calculation, Sideswipe answered with the one answer that maximized the complexity of the situation. "It's too close to call," he said.

"Faster," Optimus Prime said again—and again he heard the pitch of the hyperdrive engines increase, and again he hoped it would be enough.

It was, or it was not. Eons would pass before Optimus Prime knew. What he could know was what he could observe, which was—after he had found the time to reflect, and consult the Ark's records, and puzzle out some of the more mysterious readings from its various sensors—something like this:

The Space Bridge, unused for more cycles than anyone knew how to count, functioned—for a moment. Its radiance enveloped the Ark. Inside, standing on the great ship's bridge, Optimus Prime considered all that had been lost.

Then, as the pursuing Nemesis came into contact with the Space Bridge, before it had fully processed the Ark, the Bridge collapsed and disintegrated within a unit of time so small that no Cybertronian could have known what to call it or how to measure it. One moment they were on the Space Bridge, the next a great number of things had already happened without them having actually experienced any of them in what they could have conceived of as real time.

The disintegration of the Space Bridge released enough energy—and Energon—to momentarily and locally tear the fabric of space-time. Through that tear fell the Ark, and the Nemesis, emerging . . . somewhere. The tear then knit itself back together as the energy discharge dissipated, and the Ark of the Autobots floated in space, amid unfamiliar stars.

That was Optimus Prime's conjecture as he stood at the bridge of the Ark looking out into an emptier space than he was accustomed to seeing. Megatron's Nemesis was nowhere in sight. And nowhere on any of the Ark's sensor arrays, which could detect ship-sized objects halfway to the nearest star.

"Where are we?" Jazz asked.

Prowl was squinting at the display. "I have no idea," he said. "These stars aren't on any chart that was in the Hall of Records." A sensor lit up on the control panel, and Prowl froze.

So did Optimus Prime. "Is that what . . . ?"

"Yes. It is."

"The AllSpark," breathed Optimus Prime. "It is near."

"Not near, exactly," Prowl said. "But close enough that the Ark could detect it."

"Then let us go find it," said Optimus Prime.

The Ark carrying the surviving Autobots adjusted its course and thrust away, the unfamiliar stars of an unfamiliar spiral-arm galaxy spreading away from them on all sides. "When can we get home again?" Bumblebee asked, his vocoder temporarily working again. "Does the Ark know the way?"

"I know the way," Optimus Prime said. He tapped his chest and felt the tap resonate in the Matrix of Leadership, which together with his Spark animated him and made him who he was. He was the leader of the Autobots, the bearer of the Matrix that would light the Cybertronians' darkest hour.

They were in a place no Transformer had ever been, fleeing a despotic enemy from a homeworld that was about to convulse and partially destroy itself before it could begin a process of healing that would be as long as the life spans of some hot stars. Yet they would persevere, because they were Autobots. They had seen worse, and survived. They would survive this as well, with the AllSpark out there as their beacon and the promise, sometime in the distant future, that they would be able to return to Cybertron and claim it for their own once more.

"*Let Megatron chase us across the stars,*" thought Optimus Prime.

"*We will wage our battle to destroy the evil forces of the Decepticons wherever it may take us.*

"*And one day, we will go home.*"